AFTER ...
Audrey's Story

LESLIE JOHNSON

PUBLISHED BY:

Leslie Johnson

Ebook ISBN 978-1-0693588-5-1
Paperback ISBN 978-1-0693588-4-4

AFTER … Audrey's Story

This book is a work of fiction. Names, characters, organizations and events portrayed in this novel are either products of the author's imagination or are used fictitiously. References to real people, events, establishments, organizations or locations are intended only to provide a sense of authenticity and are used fictitiously. Any resemblance to actual events, places and organizations or persons, living or dead, is entirely coincidental.

DEDICATION

This book is dedicated to my sister Margo Oliver. When I get to where you are, let's get some horses and ride the range singing at the top of our lungs like we used to. I miss you.

ACKNOWLEDGEMENTS

The publishing of AFTER … Audrey's Story is a miracle. I was about halfway through the story when my computer crashed, and I had not backed up the latest version. A computer expert managed to salvage it, but it was written on Scrivener. I had the Scrivener CD but my new computer did not have a CD-ROM and I didn't want to pay for the program again as I hadn't found it to be particularly helpful.

It took a few months to find someone who had Scrivener, and he converted my story to Word for me. Thank you, Charlie Kirkby, for coming to my aid.

There was a lot of turmoil in my life at that time: I was starting a new job, I was selling my house: I was looking for a new home, so it was even more months before I had the chance to even look at this book.

Because I am a pantser (I write by the seat of my pants) and not a plotter (someone who has an outline for the entire manuscript), I didn't have any recollection of where I wanted the story to go. I was also struggling with inspiration, and writing had taken a back seat to all the other noises in my life.

A few more years went by as I worked on the rewrites of my first two novels and Audrey's story sat on the cloud waiting to be finished. I was finally able to give her that attention after I retired from my job.

Audrey didn't get the same exposure to my writing group as the other two novels. Some of it was read, but mostly I kept her to myself. Still, I would like to thank the members of The River Bottom Writers for encouraging me to keep going, especially when I wanted to stop. You are my peers and I owe you a lot more than a thank you.

And lastly, I would like to thank my editor, Jonas Saul, for reading and editing my words to strengthen them and make them more powerful. He helped me bring my childhood dream to fruition. He has been encouraging and helpful with his insight into the writing process and his feedback. Thank you, thank you, thank you.

CHAPTER ONE

Listening to one of my treasured gospel songs, I danced around the kitchen, preparing supper for my family. Life was good. God was good. I sang along at the top of my lungs as I bent down to scoop a few potatoes from the bin in the pantry. Placing them in my apron, I danced back across the floor to the sink, feeling the music filling my soul. I almost felt like I was in heaven. Music was so uplifting, and praising the Lord was good for my soul.

Later, with the potatoes boiling on the stove, I used the mixer to make icing for the cake I'd baked earlier. We always had dessert in our house. Sometimes, it was simply cookies and ice cream, but more often, I had something more substantial. Sour cream chocolate cake with vanilla icing was on the menu tonight. It was one of my daughter Nora's favorite desserts.

Andy came through the door as I spooned the corn into a bowl. He washed up in the mudroom, dropping his coveralls into the washing machine before entering the kitchen. "Hello, honey." He said as he brushed my cheek with his lips. "Have a good day?"

"It was a great day." I smiled as he took his place at the head of the table. Nora set the last glass down and slipped into her chair. I sat across from her, placing the corn in the middle of the table. Nora reached across to me, and the three of us joined hands, bowing our heads in prayer.

I squeezed Nora's hand and began. "Father, we thank you for your bounty. We are a blessed family with so much to be grateful for. Your love abounds, and we bow before your greatness. Thank you for watching over us and keeping us safe from harm. I ask that you continue to guide and protect Brenda and her friend Andrea. Keep them in your bosom, oh Lord, as they walk the fine line that leads to you. I am not fully aware of their situation, but I know you see it all and are in control. Thank you, Father. Your greatness knows no bounds. I also ask for Your blessings for the upcoming Harvest Party and guidance on activities that will show honor to You. Bless this food to our body's use, and our hands unto Thy service. In Jesus' name, we pray. Amen."

Two amens echoed mine. We released our hands and began passing the bowls to one another. When we'd all filled our plates, we dug in.

"This is good, hon." Andy smiled as he finished a bite of his liver. I beamed, glad for the compliment, even if it was the same one every night.

The conversation turned toward the Harvest Party. Nora and her youth group were going to be a big help. I had recruited them to man the booths and assist with handing out the prizes at the end of the night. Of course, the prizes were cheap toys from the dollar store—coloring books, crayons, and other things. I didn't want to break the bank, and it was important that every child go home with something.

On Wednesday morning, several of us would make treat bags for all the children using the candy that the participating families would donate. We had sixty kids coming, so we planned for seventy bags, just in case.

The doorbell rang as I put the cake and the dessert plates on the table. I shrugged my eyebrows at Andy. "Are you expecting anyone?"

"Nope." He shook his head.

"Me neither," Nora added.

Andy got up. I placed a hand on his shoulder. "I'm up. I'll go."

I opened the front door and switched on the outside light simultaneously. Two constables stood on the doorstep. The somber expression on their faces turned my stomach over. I swallowed hard.

Andy appeared, and I reached for his hand, moving away from the officers.

"Mr. and Mrs. Taylor?"

We nodded. "I'm Constable Peterson, and this is Constable La Fleur. May we come in?"

"Oh, I'm sorry, sure. Yes." Andy stepped back.

I moved back, knocking into Nora, who was standing silently behind me. We stumbled over each other. One police officer reached to stabilize us. Then he moved us quietly across the hallway and into the living room. In the comfortable space, the three of us sitting on the couch—one constable on the edge of the chair and the other hovering in the doorway, we waited. Holding our breath, we waited to hear why they had come to our house.

My mind went to Logan. He was at a rodeo college in Riverton, Wyoming. Had he had an accident? Why was the officer taking so long to say anything? I was getting ready to shout at him when he spoke.

"Do you have a daughter named Brenda?"

I could see Andy nod out of the corner of my eye. Brenda? What could she have done that would warrant a visit from the police? She was not a bad girl. Sure, she didn't go to church like she should, but deep down, she had a good heart. Had she had a car accident? Oh,

God. Please be with her. She needs to know your love. Why are we sitting here? Shouldn't we be on our way to the hospital or something?

"I'm sorry to inform you that your daughter is dead."

"What? How? What are you saying?" Andy yelled—his face blotchy.

"In the late hours of last night or the early hours this morning, someone murdered your daughter, Brenda, in her home in Crawford."

"Murdered?" I whispered. "Who?"

His chocolate eyes melted with sorrow. "Our investigation is ongoing."

"I don't get it. She was just here for the weekend. She only went home yesterday. This is impossible." My mind raced, trying to make sense of his absurd words.

"What about Andrea?" Nora asked, tears flowing down her pale cheeks.

The constable looked at her. He shook his head.

"Oh my God!" Andy whispered, wiping his mouth.

I thought I was going to be ill. Then I knew I was going to be sick. Rushing from the couch, down the hallway into the bathroom, I lost my supper. After washing my face, I returned to the living room to find the police had gone. Andy was staring out the window. Nora was curled up on the couch, crying. I slipped down next to her and wrapped my arms around her. We cried together, rocking back and forth until I was dry on the inside.

CHAPTER TWO

Andy hadn't moved from the window. He stood there staring into the night, his hands in his pockets, lost in his private world. He physically shook off those thoughts, turned to us, and asked if we wanted tea. We nodded, and he moved to the kitchen to put the kettle on. He made a pot of black tea, strong and sweet, just like he preferred it. He poured hot tea for all three of us, no one speaking as we lifted our cups and sipped. Thoughts were swirling through my mind.

I couldn't believe what had happened. God couldn't—no, He wouldn't do this to me. I had spent my life serving Him. I was a good and faithful servant. It was simply not possible that Brenda could be dead. It was a mistake, a lie, and as I allowed these thoughts to take wing, I felt better. I would call her, and she would answer.

Andy finished his tea and mumbled something about calling the pastor. I didn't give it much thought. We didn't need a pastor, did we?

Fifteen minutes later, the doorbell rang again. It startled me so much that I shrieked and jumped to my feet.

"Calm down, Audrey. It's just the pastor."

"The pastor? What pastor?"

"Pastor Newberry." He moved toward the door.

"Pastor Newberry?" I asked as he pulled the door open.

The large man rushed into the house. His authoritative nature pushed out all the air, and panic stole through my body. I wanted to tell him to leave, to get out and let me breathe. However, I stood with a stiff smile because my mother had taught me to be welcoming when people visited.

He smiled benevolently and took my hands into his enormous paws. He shook them together and professed God's love. I couldn't follow. It was all a blur. My face must have registered my confusion. He stopped. "Oh dear, Audrey. I can see that you are in shock."

He ushered me toward the couch and pushed me down. A burst of anger flared in my chest. What was he trying to prove?

"I hate to be rude, Pastor, but I assure you we do not need you now. I appreciate your sentiments, but I don't think the police were right."

Andy looked at me like I'd lost my mind. "What do you mean, Audrey? They wouldn't come to tell us she was gone if they weren't sure."

"Well, why didn't they ask us to come and identify the body or anything? I mean, hand me the phone. I'll call Brenda, and she'll tell you herself that this was a mistake."

No one moved. "Fine then, I'll get the phone myself."

I marched across the room, looking defiantly at my husband. I picked up the receiver and dialed the number. The phone went straight to voicemail. "See!" I exclaimed triumphantly. "The call went straight to voicemail. That means she's on another call." I turned back to the phone. "Brenda, it's your mother. Please call me when you get this message. It's important. Thank you." I hung up the phone.

"Audrey, that doesn't mean anything."

"Well, yes, that's true. But that doesn't prove she's dead. If she were dead, I'd know it. A mother knows these things."

"Audrey, please. See reason." Andy implored.

"No! You see reason. You want to believe she's dead? Shame on you. God would not do this to me. He loves me. He is a loving father, and I cannot believe that MY GOD would permit something so horrific to happen to someone who serves Him faithfully."

Pastor Newberry shook his head. "Bad things happen to good people, Audrey. It is not God's will for us to suffer, but this isn't Heaven. In a sinful world, these events occur. He has given us free will, and sometimes, when we make choices or face the consequences of someone else's choices, bad things result. God does not have control over these matters."

"What do you mean?" I'm shocked that the pastor would speak so blasphemously. "God is good, God is great. God is in control. Didn't you just preach on that this past Sunday?"

"Yes, but …"

"But nothing. I refuse to believe she's dead. Now, I would appreciate it if you would leave us."

Pastor Newberry stood and moved to the door. He stopped beside Andy and spoke a few words I couldn't hear, but that act made me angry. I marched to the door and threw it open. With a wide gesture, I pointed in the direction I wanted him to go. "Please, Pastor."

He moved out the door but turned back once he was on the step. I closed the door in his face.

"That was rude, Audrey."

"It was rude of you to call him. We do not need him, especially if all he would offer me was empty platitudes. You're all going to feel stupid when Brenda calls me back." I stormed out of the room and began putting the food away.

A few minutes later, Nora tiptoed into the room. Her eyes were red-rimmed from crying. "Oh, Nora. I hate that those police officers have deceived you. It's rather bizarre, don't you think?"

"Mom, the cops weren't lying."

"What do you mean? How do you know?"

"When you went to the bathroom, they showed Dad a picture. It was Brenda."

"No, you're lying!" I shrieked at her.

Nora stood there, tears streaming down her cheeks. She shook her head, and something in her expression sent a chill through me. I didn't want to accept it. I couldn't comprehend it. It was madness.

"No!" My knees buckled as the truth finally struck home. I collapsed to the floor, the dishes in my hand shattering around me. "Noooo!" I tried to regain my composure, but it was no longer possible. God had forsaken me. I couldn't believe it. Everything I understood about life and living burst into flames. My world shifted. I lost control, and I knew nothing would ever feel right again.

CHAPTER THREE

I don't really remember how I got off the floor. The world had lost its sound and color. I remember lying in bed that night, staring at the numbers on the clock. The orange glow blurred before I blinked to clear my vision. Those numbers anchored me as I gazed at them. Not that I was sure I wanted to be anchored, but I continued to stare all the same.

I could feel Andy's presence on the other side of the bed, but he wasn't snoring. Andy always snored, so I knew he wasn't sleeping, either. I thought about turning to him and asking him to comfort me. Maybe I could comfort him, too, but I didn't move. I didn't have the energy to try. I kept staring at the numbers on the clock.

The light in the room changed as the sun rose. Andy got out of bed, but I didn't shift from my position. I tried to imagine a world without Brenda, but I couldn't. It was inconceivable. The smell of coffee wafted up to the bedroom. I wanted a cup. I wanted to feel something. A hot cup in my hands was a good start. I threw the covers off and made my way to the kitchen.

Andy was on the phone in the living room, talking quietly, tears on his face. I walked past him into the kitchen. I poured myself a cup of coffee, wrapping my fingers around the cup. The heat burned into my fingers until it felt unbearable. I didn't remove them, needing to feel the pain. My fingers screamed to be released, but I kept them there, forcing myself to breathe.

I moved to the table and sat in my usual place. I tried to remember how the table looked last night as we sat for supper. The cloth placemats I used were still there. I usually put them away using plastic mats in the morning. We have sticky things for breakfast—jams, syrup, and honey. It seemed Andy did not know how much it took to keep the house running smoothly. I finally let go of my cup. My palms were an angry red. I looked at them before gathering the mats. I took them to the sink and shook them forcefully before putting them away. Then I reached into the cabinet and took out three plastic mats. I placed them on the table. *There, that's better.*

I drank my coffee black but added sugar before pouring in some cream. There didn't seem to be a reason for my actions. When I took a sip, I thought it was an interesting flavor—not coffee, but sweet and creamy. Taking another sip, I burned my tongue. I kept drinking, barely breaking between sips. Taking a large gulp, I felt the heat take over my body. I ignored it. I drained the cup, then poured myself another.

My stomach was hot from drinking my coffee too fast. I felt sick. Andy came in as I sat with my second cup of creamy coffee. He raised his eyebrows but didn't comment. Sitting at the head of the table, he reached over and laid one of his hands over my arm. I moved it away. A look of pain crossed his face, but he sat back without a word.

"That was Logan. He's on his way back home. A buddy will drive him to the airport in Riverton. He should be home tonight or early tomorrow, depending on flights and connections."

I nodded, tears filling my eyes. I couldn't believe that I would never see Brenda again. What kind of God allowed that to happen? I felt betrayed and abandoned by a God who should have protected me. My faith had shattered, ushering in disillusionment. I looked at Andy. "Why? Why did God allow this to happen to me?"

He shook his head. "No one knows why. There are no answers for questions like that."

I looked at him, at this face I had loved since the first time I saw it years ago. The light bulb went on. Andy never went to church and didn't believe in God. He was the reason God had taken Brenda. "It's you!"

"What's me? What are you talking about?"

"You don't believe in God. He's punishing us because you don't believe."

His face lost all color. Then Andy shook his head. "No, that's not true. It just happened because some kid lost his mind."

I couldn't let it be. I needed someone to blame. "No, I can't believe that. I can't believe that God would abandon me and take Brenda without a reason. All my life, I have served Him faithfully. I have always put Him first. He wouldn't do this to me."

"He didn't do it at all, Audrey. The world is full of sin and selfishness. That's why it happened."

"I don't believe that. I can't believe that God allowed this without a reason. Why is He punishing me?"

"I'll call Pastor Newberry. He can explain it to you."

"No!" I shouted, jumping up from the table and spilling my coffee. "No." I hurried out of the room. After running up the stairs, I threw myself on the bed. I screamed, a loud primal scream. Grabbing a pillow, I pounded my fists into the fluffy feather stuffing, feeling some satisfaction at releasing my anguish.

When I had expended every ounce of strength, I collapsed. My life was over. I didn't know how to go on from here. As I lay there, my mind swirled with thoughts and ideas that were looking for solid ground. Somewhere to roost. Fertile ground in which to germinate and grow. I was too weak, too tired to fight them off. I let them settle as my breathing became more regular.

I didn't want Pastor Newberry to come to the house so he could tell me it was the sin in my heart that caused Brenda's death. Deep down in the recesses of my soul, I knew it had to be true. Perhaps I was arrogant in my faith. Maybe I had been haughty in believing I was too good for evil to touch my life. Or maybe I was the reason, not Andy, Nora, or even Brenda herself. Was this all my fault?

A flutter of thoughts stirred up the ashes again, and I doubted the existence of God. Surely, if there were a God, the benevolent God I had worshipped for years, He would not allow this to happen? Therefore, it made sense that there really was no God at all. Andy and Brenda were right all along. I had been a fool. I had been the one who needed to be convinced of the true path, not them.

An icy breeze whipped over my heart. It settled into my chest, and peace followed. There were no more jumbled thoughts, no more contradictions. That settled it for me. God was dead. He'd been dead for a long time. Jesus wasn't coming back. He wasn't offering salvation. No one answered prayers. Answered prayers were nothing more than a coincidence.

I wasn't any happier, and these new ideas left me empty. But at least it was quiet, and I would take it. I took a huge breath. Then another. A deep sigh, and I drifted off to sleep. I didn't hear Andy come in. When I awoke, I was under the covers. The room was dark. I thought I could feel Andy beside me. I pushed my foot across the bed to be sure. He shifted. I wasn't alone. I looked at the clock. It was just after one. I had slept for sixteen hours.

I didn't want to face the world without my daughter. Snuggling deeper under the blankets, I lay there for perhaps an hour or more, thinking of happy days. When my mind went to the darkness of tomorrow, I dragged it back. I kept my eyes closed, refusing to look at the clock. Eventually, I drifted off.

CHAPTER FOUR

Andy gently rocked me awake. "Pastor Newberry is here. Do you want to come down and talk to him?"

I was confused. Why would the pastor be here? I was about to ask when I remembered Andy wanted to call him so he could tell me how fickle God was. Anger fired up the cold blood in my veins. "No," I shouted. "I don't want to see him."

Andy patted my shoulder through the covers and left without another word. I turned back, snuggling under the comforter, and drifted back to sleep.

The sun was already well above the horizon when I woke again. I felt lost and a little afraid, like the world had become a sinister place. I turned over, staring at the ceiling. My mind whirled again. Thinking about God and the Bible and all that I had based my life on, I felt as confused about God's goodness as I was about His existence. I had walked with such faith all my life—been a good and faithful servant—and spent countless hours serving Him in every capacity I knew how.

How was it possible that this was happening to me? To me, Lord? Is it because I married Andy? I was warned all those years ago not to marry him. "Do not be unevenly yoked, Audrey." I heard that sentiment so often that it made me more determined to prove them wrong. And I had.

Andy and I had an ideal marriage. We loved one another, laughed together, and were good providers. Together, we raised three happy, well-adjusted, independent children. We lived in a beautiful house, and Andy never once complained about all the work I did for the church. He accepted my service as part of who I was. The only thing was that he wouldn't come to church with me on Sunday mornings except at Christmas and Easter.

The rest of the time, he went to work. He wasn't sleeping in on weekends or drinking beer. He was a levelheaded man—a good man—the love of my life. Yet, at this moment, I wanted to batter him for his lack of faith, even while I questioned my own.

I crawled out of bed, feeling the filth of not showering yesterday. I went to the bathroom and turned on the water. When the spray reached optimum temperature, I stepped in. Standing there, I allowed the water to cascade off my back before moving farther under. I shampooed my hair twice, soaped my body, and rinsed before standing under the spray until the water turned tepid.

I stepped out, wrapped a towel around my body, and returned to the bedroom. I glanced at the family photos on the dresser: my three kids. I took down the one of Brenda, wiping away the imaginary dust. It was a recent picture taken last summer. I insisted on having studio photos taken twice a year, wanting to create pictorial records of our family as the kids transformed from babies to toddlers to youths to young adults.

My mother never took a single picture of me and my siblings, something that still irked me. We had no photographic history of our family except for a few school photos taken every other year. Sometimes, even those were missing because she never put them in frames. They often sat in a drawer before succumbing to one of her cleaning frenzies.

I looked at Brenda's pretty face. Her rich brown hair, with golden highlights, was thick and glossy, shining like a crown atop her head. She always wore her hair short, changing styles with regularity. Although she carried a few extra pounds, it never seemed to bother her or the boys who came around seeking her affections. There were plenty of suitors, but she was no fool. She didn't tolerate stupidity in the boys she dated. She was levelheaded and trustworthy.

Oh, I held no belief that she was still a virgin, though part of me hoped she was. This world was corrupt where sex was concerned. My parents had grown up in the sixties, and my mother was forever harping at us as girls to keep our knees together and our panties on. A few girls from my high school got pregnant. One left town to live with relatives, and the other walked down the aisle, but that marriage did not last. In larger cities, being pregnant out of wedlock was more normalized. In this small town, where the church still had a stronghold, being a single mother was a sin.

I jumped when a knock on the door startled me. I looked over, my eyes wide. My sister Judith stood in the doorway, tears rolling down her face. Dear Judith—never Judy. She was always so put together. Then, I chastised myself for being petty. I just wasn't in the mood for one of her lectures.

"Audrey!" she whispered. "Audrey, Audrey, Audrey." She repeated my name with each step.

I was ready to scream, *That's my name, don't wear it out!* But I stayed silent, staring at her.

I took in her clothes. As always, her attire was immaculate. I don't remember ever seeing her less than perfect. Her hair was expertly colored and styled—her makeup was flawless. She looked like she'd just stepped out of Heaven's salon because she didn't look artificial. Everything about her looked natural. She wore an exquisite black pantsuit with a cream-colored blouse that set off her brown eyes.

"You're not dressed, dear," she said. "Why aren't you dressed? It's nearly noon."

I stared at her as she sat on the bed beside me. Her perfume reached out and assailed me. I hated flowery perfumes, and even more so when liberally applied.

"I'm so sorry, Audrey. This is such a horrible thing. I just can't get my head around it. Brenda, your little girl, gunned down by a madman."

I looked away. Judith had married well. She lived well. But no amount of culture could subdue her mouth. "Thank you for that, Judith."

"Audrey! Audrey!" A loud cry came from far away.

I recognized the voice belonging to my sister Elaine. Out of all my sisters, this was the one with whom I had the most contact and the most connection. I heard her stomping up the stairs, and my heart broke open. Before she even got to my room, I was bawling. She swept in, past Judith, and wrapped her arms around me. I clung to her for dear life—she was my rock in times of trouble.

"Oh, Audrey. My poor girl." She pulled away from me as my tears slowed to hiccoughs. "You must be cold sitting here in your towel. What were you going to wear today?"

Judith sniffed, feeling neglected and left out. Elaine turned to her. "Oh, I'm sorry, Judith. How are you? I was so wrapped up in Audrey's pain that I didn't even notice you there."

I turned away so that neither would see my smile. Elaine was well aware of Judith. No one missed her when she was in the room. But she also delighted in reminding her she wasn't the star she thought she was. It was unfair of me to relish Judith's annoyance at being overlooked.

Elaine got up and went to my closet. Slamming through hangers, she searched for something appropriate. She found a dress she thought would be perfect. She held it up and called to me from across the room,

"This one, or would you prefer pants?"

"I think pants today, Elaine. Thank you." I got up and found underwear and socks in the dresser drawer. I slipped into the bathroom. If it had only been Elaine, I would have dropped my towel right there, but Judith always made me nervous.

Elaine knocked and then passed in a pair of black slacks and a patterned long-sleeved blouse. Once dressed, I brushed my thick, shiny brown locks and eased them into a clip. I never used beauty products. I cried again, thinking of how Brenda used to fuss over my lack of makeup.

It was her high school graduation. We had gone dress shopping to Crawford and Brenda had insisted that I buy a new dress for the occasion, too. The day had been chaotic. There had been so many young girls in and out of the house that I felt we should install a revolving door. The girls were giggling and fluttering around each other, warming my heart at the sight. They had all gone for pictures, and when Brenda came back before the banquet so she could arrive with us—she stepped into my room as I was getting ready.

The royal blue gown, bell skirt, and fitted bodice hugged my body. I had curled my hair and wore one side clipped up in a comb. I was teasing a few strands to hang down when she arrived. "You look beautiful, Mom. That dress is spectacular. I knew it was you the moment I saw it."

Leaning in, she hugged me loosely. Then we stood there together in the long mirror on the closet door, staring at each other. Brenda's gown was a soft pink. She had added some highlighting to her golden-brown locks, and despite all the fussing and primping that had gone on, her hair sparkled in the light.

She had her father's coloring, even the brown eyes. For her age, she had expertly applied her makeup. It looked natural, as it enhanced her beauty. "You look pretty good yourself." I squeezed her waist.

She turned to me. "Let me do your makeup, Mom. You will be

dynamite."

I shook my head. "I don't wear makeup, Brenda. You know that."

"Please! No one will even be able to tell."

I looked at her. She was so eager to please that I gave in despite my misgivings. Rushing to her room, she came back with an assortment of tiny cases and tubes. She wrapped a towel around my shoulders and began to fuss and flutter, not allowing me to look in the mirror. When she finished, she moved away and let me see what she had done.

I was stunned. My complexion was smooth and bright, and my cheekbones enhanced, but my eyes shocked me the most. She had used similar tones to her own but used blue to match my eyes and my dress. I don't think I'd ever seen my eyes look so blue before. Staring at my reflection, I tried to find myself. I had to admit I looked beautiful, but it didn't look like me. I wanted to grab a cloth and scrub it off. Instead, I smiled and hugged her, acknowledging my appreciation.

All night, I wanted to scratch my face. Whatever she had put on my skin felt prickly and uncomfortable. I wondered how so many women wore this daily. Many of my church friends complimented me. Some were even brash enough to tell me I didn't look like myself.

Andy held my hand most of the night. We danced often, celebrating this next stage of our lives. Our baby girl was growing up. Later, at home, when I came out of the bathroom in my nightgown, my face freshly scrubbed, he wrapped his arms around me and kissed me on the lips. "You looked beautiful tonight, my darling, but this is the face that I adore. The natural beauty. I won't begrudge you wearing that stuff, if you want, but honestly, with your looks, you don't need it. You are still the most beautiful girl in the world."

"Audrey, are you okay in there?" Elaine called as she knocked on the door.

I wiped my tears with the towel, tossed it into the hamper, and called back. "Yes, coming."

CHAPTER FIVE

Andy was in the kitchen, making another pot of coffee. He looked wrung out. I wanted to go to him, to remind him I loved him, but I couldn't find the words. The house was full of people. My sister's husbands were sitting in the living room, talking in muted tones to one another. "Where's Nora?" I asked. I hadn't seen her since the night we got the news.

"She's gone to Crawford with Pastor Newberry to pick up Logan."

"Why didn't you go?"

Andy shrugged, holding up a folder. "Nora wanted to go on her own. I didn't want her driving. Pastor Newberry was here, and he offered to drive her." He shrugged again. He looked miserable. My heart broke seeing him in such pain. Even if it was his fault, I could do nothing about that now. If I destroyed him, would that make me feel better?

I stepped over to him and wrapped my arms around his neck. His arms snaked around my waist, he nestled into my shoulder, and I felt him shudder as he endeavored to hold back his sorrow.

I stepped back from him, took his hand, and led him out of the kitchen. I closed the door in the laundry room to give us some privacy, then turned toward him.

With tear-filled eyes, he said, "I'm so sorry, Audrey. I never for a million years thought this would ever happen to us. I'm not an evil man, am I? I know you're a saint, but is this my fault? Was my unwillingness to go to church really the cause for all this? I feel so guilty. She had her whole life ahead of her. He should have taken me."

A loud sob echoed in the small, tidy room. I felt guilty for implying what I had when I first heard the news about Brenda. It seemed obvious now that God was punishing me. For my choice of husband, for my lack of faith, and even for my lack of belief as I struggled with the biggest question of my life. *Was there even a God?* I was so confused, scared, and ashamed that I had no answers. The only thing I knew with certainty was that I loved this man despite his lack of faith. And I needed him.

"Andy. Andy, it's not your fault. I'm sorry I said that—I was lashing out. God may be punishing me, or maybe He doesn't even exist. There is no way I can understand why this happened to us. I'm too numb to figure it out."

He pulled back from me and looked into my eyes, tears wetting his cheeks. "Why would God punish you? You're practically a saint. You've never put a foot wrong in your life."

"I must have, though I can't figure it out. It's impossible to understand it. Brenda wasn't a bad girl. She was defiant and strong—she knew right from wrong even if she didn't attend church. I am certain in her heart of hearts, she believed. So, why did God take her away from us? God saved Isaac at the last minute but didn't save Brenda because I wasn't worthy. It's my fault, darling. Not yours."

He wrapped his arms around me, and we wept. When we pulled apart, he handed me the folder. "This is from the police. It is a record of her injuries. I asked to see it. I had to know. That young man gave her a pretty good beating before he finally shot her in the head."

I looked into his face. I'd never seen him that angry in my life, and it scared me. I took the folder and opened it tentatively. Did I want to know? No, but like Andy, I had to know. I glanced through the typed report, catching words like broken ribs, bruising, lacerations, and crushed hand. My stomach lurched, and my knees buckled. Andy steadied me as he snatched the file from my hands.

"I'm sorry. I shouldn't have shown it to you. It's too much. What was I thinking?" He looked wildly around the room.

"It's okay. Really. I would have wanted to know this. I'm glad you showed me. Really, I am. It's just so brutal on an empty stomach." My mind was reeling. The words kept spinning through my mind. *Broken ribs, crushed hand.*

Andy nodded.

"But the kids mustn't see this, so we have to hide it." I urged.

It was my turn to look around the room. No, this space was too public. I knew where it would be safe. "Slide it between the mattress and the box spring of our bed. It will be safe there."

"Got it." Andy hugged me again. "Are you sure you're okay?"

I nodded against his shoulder. "I don't know if I'll ever be right again, but I'm fine." He squeezed me in understanding. Our lives had changed forever, and it would take time to understand what our new life, the new world, would look like.

A knock on the door broke us apart. I straightened my clothes. "Coming," I said in my cheeriest voice, which sounded insincere and sharp. One more quick hug, and we left the room.

The house was bustling. There was a party atmosphere for everything. My sisters, Melissa and Donna, had arrived. It was like old home week. Andy and I passed through the kitchen and then into the living room, accepting hugs and words of condolence. As I passed the window, I saw Andy's sister Lorraine coming up the sidewalk. The house felt claustrophobic.

An hour later, Nora and Logan pushed open the front door. I swept Logan into my arms for a brief hug. He let go almost immediately—he had never enjoyed being hugged by his mother in public. He moved off with his father, the two of them with their arms around each other's shoulders. I sighed. My two men are so alike and so different. I turned to Nora. Wrapping her in an embrace, I kissed each of her tear-swollen eyes. She burst into tears again. I whisked her off to her room. "It might be wise to get some sleep. It's going to be a long week."

She nodded. She was the most agreeable child. "Would you pray with me, Mom?" she asked as I pulled the bedcovers over her. I hesitated, not wanting to pray—I was no longer certain prayers worked. I was so full of doubt that I was certain she would see it and call me a *Doubting Thomas.* "Please?" she begged.

I felt like a traitor. I usually couldn't wait to pray. Prayer was my go-to response whenever I felt happy, troubled, or had questions. But prayer was the one thing I didn't want to do now. I felt betrayed, and the last thing I wanted to do was speak to the one responsible for letting this happen to me—if He existed at all. A flame of anger ignited.

"Nora, just get some sleep. You'll feel better when you wake up."

Tears filled her eyes again, and I felt guilty for causing her pain.

"I'm sorry, Nora, I haven't been myself." Brushing her hair off her face, I pulled the covers tighter over her as she turned away from me. My heart ached to change the situation, but I didn't know how. I slipped out of the room, closing the door quietly behind me.

I hurried down the hall to my room and sat on the bed. Holding a pillow to my face, I screamed into it. Some of the tension left my body, but I still felt tightly wound. Who am I? If I am not a woman of faith, then who am I to be?

What a stupid question to ask. I did not know who I was. I had lived my entire life assured that I was a devout Christian, loved by God. My entire world revolved around the church. It may have been lopsided because of Andy and Brenda's lack of faith, but I had enough of it for all of us until now. Now, I had nothing. I held nothing.

I washed my face and returned to the main floor. The living room was a jumble of bodies, brothers and brothers-in-laws, sisters and sisters-in-laws. Somewhere in there were Andy and Logan, but I didn't want to risk another round of hugs. I shifted directions and moved into the kitchen.

It was bustling, and a group of women prepared a late lunch for the sizeable crowd that had gathered. They had coordinated an assembly line that started with Judith slicing the tops off the tray buns. She slid these down the counter to my sister Carrie, who slapped on some butter. My sister Donna scooped egg salad or tuna salad on the buns that made it her way while Andy's sisters, Roberta and Lorraine, placed roast beef and ham and cheese on their share. When the buns reached my sister, Melissa, she sliced them apart and placed them on trays.

Obviously, someone had run to the grocery store. Four vegetable trays were stacked on the table. The noise was deafening. People were talking over one another. I contemplated running to the bathroom for pain medications. It was going to be a long week.

The neighbors and a few women from church had dropped off casseroles and other dishes. Judith had taken charge of everything. She decided sandwiches would suffice for lunch, and the hot meal would come in the evening when the rest of the family arrived. I was grateful that she was efficient because I wasn't up to it at the moment.

Elaine came through the basement door with several jars of pickles. She smiled at me. "I raided your root cellar."

I nodded. "Is there any coffee?" I asked.

"Sure, sure," Melissa said. "Take a seat, and I'll get you a cup." She squeezed my shoulder.

I tried to remember the last time I'd seen Melissa. It had been a few years. She lived several hours away, and since Mom had passed, she hadn't made a trek south, preferring to travel abroad during her vacations. Jason was a lawyer, and Melissa was a paralegal, although she hadn't worked in years. What did she do with her time, I wondered, looking at her broad backside move across the kitchen? She wasn't a churchgoer. Did she volunteer somewhere? How did she pass the time?

If I was going to give up church, which I was seriously considering, then I would need to fill my time with something. Maybe I should get a job? Doing what? You've never worked a day in your life outside of being a homemaker and a stay-at-home parent.

Carrie set a cup down in front of me and then took the chair beside me. "How are you holding up?" She ran a hand over my shoulders. I shrugged, taking hold of the cup. My hands were shaking. I hadn't eaten since the night we got the news. Food never entered my mind. I gulped a mouthful of coffee, burning my lips. My stomach heaved at the hot liquid, so I swallowed hard.

"When was the last time you ate?" Elaine asked as she sat on my other side.

"I can't remember."

She got up, put several sandwiches on a plate, and set them in front of me. She cracked open a vegetable tray and allowed me to select a few tomatoes, some celery, and carrots. "Do you want some dip?"

She didn't wait for my answer but scooted away in search of a spoon. When she came back, she scooped a spoonful of the dip onto my plate. I felt like a child, unable to serve myself. I was so grateful for the care that my eyes filled up again. Fat tears rolled down my cheeks as I raised a bun to my mouth.

"Oh, Audrey!" Melissa cried, tears filling her eyes.

The sandwich was forgotten as arms encircled me in a group hug. It was minutes before we broke apart. I looked across the room. Judith was moving the trays of sandwiches and vegetables to the dining room. A stack of paper plates disappeared as the stream of people moved around the table. A herd of children came up from downstairs, filing past us, the odd one stopping to say hello and hug "Auntie Audrey."

Overwhelmed by the noise and the crowd, my breathing grew shallow as the noise escalated. I put my half-eaten bun down, shoved back from the table, and escaped to my room. I sat in the chair, looking out the window, trying to catch my breath. Several minutes later, Elaine returned with my plate and a TV tray.

"Feeling better?" she asked softly.

"It's just …" My emotions closed off my throat.

"It's okay. None of us can imagine what you're going through, so you do what you must. If that means alone time, take some alone time. We will not abandon you for not being sociable and doting on us like you always have. It's our turn to take care of you."

She set the tray beside my chair before setting the plate on it. Carrie came in with a cup of steaming peppermint tea. "This is good for the nerves and for digestion." She placed the cup beside the plate and left the room.

Elaine stayed, her hand resting on my shoulder. "Come out when you're ready. We're all booked into that new hotel, and I think the kids will head back there after we've cleaned up from lunch. They have a water slide, so they can burn off some energy. I don't know when everyone is leaving, but I imagine some will head back home after the funeral tomorrow."

I looked up at her, confused. "The funeral is tomorrow?"

"Yes, at eleven o'clock."

"I didn't know."

"You didn't know?"

I shook my head. "Andy must have taken care of it. I've been a little out of it."

"Not Andy. Your pastor is taking care of everything."

My blood boiled. That pastor who liked to take over things. He had organized my daughter's funeral. Did he think to consult with me? How dare he? He didn't even know Brenda. He'd only come to our church three months ago when Pastor Joseph retired. I was going to give that man a piece of my mind.

A memory came rushing back. He had come early that morning. I forgot Andy had awakened me to ask if I wanted to talk to him. I did not know it was about the funeral. Damn it.

CHAPTER SIX

Forgetting the food again, I got up from the chair and started pacing the floor. Elaine was beside herself, unsure how to respond to this new me. I was the calm one, the one who took everything in stride and turned to God in prayer. I was never angry—I was a Christian soldier who knew blessings beyond measure because God had everything under control. Yet here I was, muttering under my breath and pacing the floor.

"Audrey, please. Calm down," she pleaded.

"I will *NOT* calm down. That man …" I paused, not sure how to word the feeling boiling inside my chest. "That man is a dictator. Everything must be his way. He has no concept of how things are done. How could Andy let this happen?"

"I'm sure Andy did what he thought was best." She attempted to placate me, but I resisted being cajoled.

"I'm going to phone that man and stop this. This isn't how it is supposed to go." The tears sprang up, and my anger turned to sorrow. "I can't believe I'm never going to see her again. How am I supposed to live when she's gone? Huh? Can you tell me that?"

Elaine stood there helplessly. I wasn't any less intimidating in tears. "Oh, Audrey."

My thoughts were racing, and my sorrow bounced back to anger. "You can't, can you? No one can. God is punishing me. If, and I mean *IF*, there is a God, that is. And this man, who doesn't know me or my family, who hasn't bothered to come to a single meal under my roof, is going to not only officiate but has chosen the hymns, the time, and the date of something highly personal to me. That takes a lot of … balls!"

"Audrey!" Elaine gasped. "I have never heard you use such language."

I turned to her as anger hardened my face. "Well, get used to it. It's the new me. I have spent my entire life being the "good girl." I have done everything in my power to please God and to live a good life, and this is my reward. My daughter is dead. And not just dead. A maniac brutally took her life. Did she deserve that? Can you imagine her last minutes? Can you?"

Elaine shook her head, tears streaming down her face.

I wanted to wrap her in my arms and ease her stress, but the larger part of me was on a rampage that I couldn't control. "Well, I have tried, God help me, to think that maybe she was unconscious when that gunshot came. But it is more likely that she was aware of it. Elaine, that man brutalized her. He crushed her hand! Crushed it!" Staring at her, I continued my rant. "Can you imagine the agony of that? I can't. I need a tranquilizer if I stub my toe. He must have stomped on her hand. It makes me sick to think what she went through."

Working off my anger, I paced the room again, back and forth, back and forth, before turning toward her. "She was trying to protect her friend from this monster. And she got the living crap beat out of her." My hands cramped. Unaware, I was clenching them into tight fists until the pain forced me to stop.

"I am so angry! I can't get over how angry I am." When I turned to stare at my sister, she looked frightened for me. "God's actions are confusing me. Why didn't He protect her? Is He punishing me? Or Andy? Or was she the target of his wrath—God's, I mean? Why is she dead, Elaine? Why?"

The anger left my body as I broke down, allowing me to move back into grief. Elaine crossed the room to where I stood, wrapping her arms around me. "Shhh." She soothed. "Shhh."

A minute passed, then two, and finally, I felt the clouds lifting from around my head. The calm after the storm. It was a roller coaster I would ride for months, this quick change of emotions. Though I barely knew how to paddle calm waters, I felt like I had to paddle in the rapids. It was exhausting.

"I'm sorry. It was unfair of me to dump those visions into your head."

She hugged me tighter. "I'm sorry it happened, truly sorry," she whispered back.

We stepped back, our hands finding each other to maintain connectivity. I sighed. "Thank you for being here. Thank you for understanding. I feel crazy, and I don't know what is up or down."

"It's okay. I can't imagine what you're going through. Please know that you are not alone."

Nodding, I said, "I know. And thanks."

As she moved to the door, our hands parted slowly. She opened it and stepped out. "Try to eat something and come downstairs when you're ready. I'll put the kettle on for more tea."

I nodded and moved back to my chair. In all my turmoil, I had not forgotten Pastor Newberry. There was an ember of anger reserved for him. It would keep for a more appropriate time. If he thought for one minute that I would let him get away with railroading his opinions over my family, he had another thing coming.

Minutes passed as I stared out the window. The sky was clear—

but it was windy. The tree in the backyard swayed back and forth, hypnotizing me. My thoughts drifted to Brenda.

Ten-year-old Brenda rushed through the back door. Her face was alight with mischief. She beamed at me as she shed her winter parka and boots. She dutifully hung them on the hook before bouncing into the kitchen.

"How was your day? As if I need to ask."

She flopped down in a kitchen chair and smiled back at me.

As Logan burst through the door, panting because he was out of breath, I set a plate of cookies and a glass of milk in front of Brenda.

"I was calling for you to wait for me," he yelled to her as he wriggled out of his winter gear.

"I know, I heard you."

"Then why didn't you wait?" His coat fell onto the floor beside his boots.

"Hang up your coat," I said.

He looked at it momentarily, uncertain how it hadn't magically hung itself up. Then he did as he was told.

He slid into the chair next to Brenda and grabbed three cookies off the plate. He shoved one into his mouth before she could protest.

"Hey, those are my cookies!" Brenda slapped Logan.

"Stop it, the both of you." I scolded. "There are plenty of cookies, but you can't have too many. Supper is a few hours away. Logan, that's more than enough."

He smiled at me. How could I stay mad at that face? I smiled back.

"I have the best news, Mama. It happened at school today." She picked up a cookie off the plate and delicately dipped it into her glass of milk. Then she sucked noisily on it before dipping it back a second time. I grimaced. Eating cookies with Brenda wasn't for the faint of heart.

After I set a glass of milk in front of Logan, I sat down. "I'm all ears," I said as she slurped again. "Just eat your cookies normally, please."

"But they are so much better this way. They are hard, they get softer, and the milk tastes sweet and spicy. You should try it." Looking at the dribble of milk running down her chin, I shook my head.

"That will not happen." I laughed.

Logan, however, mimicked her, though he exaggerated the noises. If the church ladies could see me now, they would rush me right out the door and off to the looney bin.

Cookies done—Brenda shared her news. The school had reinstated Grade Five Camp. The administration had canceled it two years before because the school didn't have enough participants. That was the problem with small schools in towns that weren't really growing.

Someone suggested that our school team up with several smaller schools or a larger one in the district to get the required numbers. Because our school had done this on its own, the discussions had been fierce, and liabilities had weighed heavily on the shoulders of administrators.

Brenda grabbed her backpack and hauled out a crumpled piece of paper. It was the permission slip for the trip and a request for parent volunteers. "Your dad would love to go. And speaking of going, it's time to pick up Nora from her piano lesson."

Brenda loved that camp. She called it "Survival Camp." There were no cabins or washhouses. The kids had to learn to make a shelter from the environment. They had to identify plants that were good to eat and those they could die from. Without a kitchen, they cooked their meals over open flames. Thankfully, the kids didn't have to hunt, though fishing with some string and a safety pin was available. If I remember correctly, no one caught any fish, but they all had fun trying.

An ache grew in my heart. That girl meant the world to me. She was full of life and sure the world was there to be conquered. She was fearless and confident. I still couldn't believe she was dead.

My uneaten sandwich looked unappetizing, so I set it aside and sipped the tepid tea. It took three healthy sips to empty the cup, and I was disappointed that it was empty, so I set it down with a thud. Reflecting on Brenda's story and her cookies drew me back to the kitchen.

I placed my tray on the counter, took three cookies from the jar, and poured myself a glass of milk. Then, sitting down next to my sisters, I dunked my first one into the cold liquid before sucking loudly at my cookie. They all looked at me like I'd lost my mind. I laughed and told them to try it. Elaine got glasses and cookies for everyone, and we sat there dunking our cookies. I told them the story I had just remembered.

CHAPTER SEVEN

The house grew quieter as the afternoon passed. Most of my family had returned to the hotel so the kids could burn some energy on the water slide. The house felt unsettled and empty as I wandered around. The television droned in the den, but I didn't open the door to see who was there.

I walked into a conversation between Judith and Elaine as they planned supper. Judith pointed to the vast array of covered baking dishes sitting on the picnic table on the back deck. "There are a lot of casseroles for supper, but Carrie and Kelly will bring pizza for the kids. I think someone is going to pick up some chicken, too." She shrugged when she saw me. "How are you doing?"

It should have been an innocuous question, but it picked at my sensitivity, and instead of saying what I wanted, I snapped, "How do you think I'm doing, Judith? I mean, really?"

My words wounded her. She turned away, but I saw her injured expression and was instantly remorseful. "I'm sorry, Judith. I don't know what's wrong with me."

Elaine jumped in, quick to make peace. "We understand you're under a lot of stress. Sit down, please." She pulled out a chair. "Would you like some tea?"

Judith turned back, tears filling her eyes. "I really didn't mean to offend you. It seems to be who I am, though—never knowing what to say, so I just always stick my foot in it."

With a ghost of a smile, I grabbed her arm. "It's not you, it's me."

"That's what people say when they are breaking up. Are you trying to tell me something?" Judith quipped.

I don't know how I could have been more astounded. Judith, the stoic older sister who was always laying down the rules and ensuring everyone followed them precisely, had actually said something funny. It caught me off guard. My mouth dropped open. I stared at her, laughter bubbling in my belly.

She smiled at me. "Close your mouth, Audrey. You're catching flies."

Elaine snorted, and the three of us burst into laughter. Clutching hands, we sat at the table, laughing like our lives depended on it. It didn't last long, but it felt nice to laugh again.

"The rest of the Taylors have arrived, by the way," Elaine said as she poured tea for the three of us. "They are over at Bea's now. I told Andy that if you were up to it, I would drive you over later."

In my grief and despair, I had forgotten Andy's parents. How were they coping with this? Beatrice and John were retired. They spent their summers in Grandville but wintered in an Arizona trailer park. They were less than a week away from departure when this happened. My own parents were deceased. Mom died five years ago, and Dad died a year ago last August.

When Andy and I married, we bought a house a few blocks from both our parents. The intention was that we would be close enough to visit regularly. The best-laid plans. With children, you have no time. They have school and church activities and sports events. I was constantly on the go in those early years. Then, as the kids grew up, I took on more responsibilities at church. My commitments kept me too busy to visit regularly.

I hated to admit it to anyone, least of all myself, but when my mother died, I panicked. I was so worried that Dad would want to come and live with us, and I would have to take on more than I already had on my plate. But he was adamant that he could take care of himself. After weeks of checking up on him, I realized he was right. He was doing fine.

I stopped going less and less. His neighbors looked after him in those last months, making sure he had food. I wasn't oblivious to it but grateful to avoid the burden. I was busy planning the church campout, preparing for a guest speaker, booking a campground, and recruiting people to cook, clean, and direct traffic.

He went into the hospital while I was at that campout. Andy drove out to tell me, but I didn't see him until the camp ended. I was ashamed to admit that I didn't stay because I might miss some important message imparted by the guest speaker—I didn't stay because I wanted to make sure that our departure from the campsite was coordinated and that we left things better than we found them—I didn't stay because, without me, the place would grind to a halt. No, I stayed because I needed to hear the accolades from the pulpit. The applause of my peers and the thank yous that would come my way for all my hard work.

These thoughts flashed through my mind, and I felt the shame of who I was creeping up and standing on my shoulder. I really wasn't a righteous person. I turned my thoughts back to Andy's parents. Andy and the kids visited them every week. Andy usually went there on Sunday mornings for breakfast. He took them out to the local coffee shop or took donuts and coffee to their house. He and Brenda made that their Sunday morning ritual for years. When Logan was old enough to decide about going to church or not, he quit church and joined them.

Nora didn't go on Sunday mornings. She always went to church with me. But she went over to their house every Tuesday after school. She had supper with them and then came home to do her homework. I was the only family member who failed to make time for them. Guilt stabbed at my conscience as Elaine and Judith prattled on about the family. Why was I always missing? What was wrong with me?

Finally, I couldn't stand it anymore. "I'm such a bad person," I whispered.

"Pardon me? I didn't catch that." Elaine leaned closer to me.

Repeating my thought, I said, "I'm a terrible person. I haven't thought about anyone but myself since this happened." Jumping to my feet, I knocked my chair onto the floor. Judith was up in a flash, righting the chair and setting it behind me.

"I need some air."

"I'll come with you," Elaine volunteered.

"Me, too," Judith echoed.

"No. I want to be alone—I need to think."

Rushing to the door, I grabbed my coat, slinging it over my shoulders as I shoved my feet into my shoes.

Elaine caught up with me. "It's cold out there. You'll need your gloves and a scarf, at least." She rifled through the closet, pulling out toques and mittens from a box. I reached for the burnt-orange toque with the gold thread running through it. It was Brenda's. The hat she wore the last year she lived at home. It clashed with my purple coat, but I didn't care. I pulled it on as Elaine handed me a pair of brown leather gloves and Brenda's matching scarf.

I headed out the door. The air was bitter, and a sharp wind wrapped itself around me. I pulled the scarf up and put on the gloves before I descended the stairs to the sidewalk. On the street, I hesitated. Left? Or right? I turned left. At the next corner, I turned left again, heading to the outskirts of my small town.

I walked down the street, passing houses I usually only drove by.

With so little free time, I didn't walk anymore. I had things to do. Walking was too slow. Ten minutes later, I was gasping, but I pushed on. I crossed another street and stopped in front of the church I attended as a child. It looked forlorn, and the weathered siding needed some paint.

Andy and I were married in this church, and we started our lives here. It's funny how I'd forgotten how much I loved those stained-glass windows. I was so wrapped up in the glitz and glamor of my new church, Faith Gospel Mission. It was new and very much alive.

I remember when Pastor Joseph first came to town. He was preaching in the Odd Fellows Hall. I had gone to see him mostly out of curiosity. His sermon was passionate. It stirred something inside me. I had a life-changing moment in that service. It was so powerful that I left our little family church and started attending services in that hall.

Andy wasn't happy I was getting involved with the snake charmers, as he referred to this church in the early years. He cautioned that if I became a "holy roller," he was leaving. I couldn't imagine rolling around on the floor, feeling it was undignified and certainly not lady-like, but I got a filling of the Holy Spirit and prayed in tongues. I wisely kept that to myself. Andy didn't need to know anything about it.

That was such a wonderful time in my life. I felt alive for the first time as the morning service rocked to the new Christian music. There were no stuffy hymns sung here. It was loud, upbeat spiritual music, worshiping God. This is living. This is how to worship the King of Kings and the Lord of Lords.

I stared at the sad façade of this old church, and I felt homesick. Tears pricked my eyes, and the building blurred. For that split second before I blinked, I thought I saw it in its glory, the white boards gleaming in the sunshine of a long-ago Sunday morning. The smell of oiled pews, paraffin wax, and old hymnals wafted over me. I stood there for another moment, the emptiness inside my belly overwhelming.

I walked past the side of the church to the small graveyard attached. Churches don't do that anymore. Graveyards are separate and set apart. These parcels of land, although consecrated ground, were no longer affiliated with one faith or any faith in some cases. The new graveyard just outside town became the burial place for both of my parents. My grandparents were here, though, somewhere on the far side. I hadn't visited their graves in a long time.

The gate to the graveyard was locked. I walked past, feeling sad that people couldn't just walk in if they wanted to. I remember reading that hooligans had knocked over a few stones a couple of years ago, so that's probably why they kept the gate locked. Sadly, a few rotten apples ruin things for the rest of us.

I made another left turn onto Maple Street. This would take me to the Taylor's house. I picked up my pace, suddenly wanting to be there. The driveway was overflowing with cars. I could see people in the window. Friends and neighbors. I saw Andy and Logan as I headed to the back door. There was no bell here, so I knocked loudly and waited.

I heard someone moving about only moments before the back door swung open. Beatrice looked surprised to see me. She leaned over and opened the screen door. I grabbed it, pulled it wide, and stepped into the warm house. Beatrice stepped back, and once I was inside, she closed the door tightly. We stood there, staring at each other, not speaking.

Tears welled in my eyes, and she joined me before embracing me in a big bear hug. She was a formidable woman, large in every sense of the word. Lost in her mass, I could not breathe, but I felt such a great deal of comfort in her arms. Another pang struck me as I realized I missed my mother. She wasn't a warm woman, but does a girl ever stop needing her mom?

Someone came up behind me, sandwiching me between

themselves and Beatrice. At first, I didn't know who it was. Then the cologne tingled my nose, and I knew it was Andy. We didn't move for another minute. The heat of my attire became too much. I had to break away.

Beatrice dragged me up the three steps to the kitchen. She smiled at my coordinated look. "Brenda's?"

I nodded. She smiled. "I made this for her birthday." Having forgotten so much, I said, "It was in the box of scarves and doesn't go with my coat, but it's warm, and it was hers." I choked on the words, so I stopped speaking. Andy squeezed my arm.

"Let me take your coat. You are staying for a while, aren't you?"

I nodded. "I should have been here before."

"It's okay. Really. Everyone understands."

I nodded. Everyone understands but me. I prided myself on being a good person, but I was seeing just how selfish I'd always been. A sense of true self-loathing was percolating in my core. I wasn't a gracious person—I was a selfish, self-centered woman who constantly needed her ego stroked. I was despicable, and I needed to change. But changing seemed insurmountable.

As someone stripped away my coat, a chill rushed over me. A cup of tea appeared in my hands before Bea escorted me to the living room. The conversations around the room ceased as I stepped forward. All eyes were on me. Roberta, bless her, broke the ice.

"Your cheeks are rosy, Audrey. Did you walk over?"

"Rosy Audrey!" Logan chimed in, getting to his feet. "Here, sit in my chair, Mom."

"We were just talking about the funeral." Derek piped up. "We think we have enough cars to carry the family from the church to the graveyard without taking the second limo. Of course, you and Andy will go in the limousine provided by the funeral home. There is room for ten, so if you want to take some other family with you …" He stopped speaking, looking from me to Andy and back again.

"That sounds fine. There is no sense in letting all that space go to waste, is there?" Andy stood behind me, his hand resting on my shoulder. He squeezed it.

I smiled, leaning back toward him. "Maybe we should do a lottery. Who's willing to pay for the privilege of riding in the limo?" Then I laughed.

The group looked at each other, unsure if they should laugh with me. "I'm just joking. Come on. It's far too heavy here. Brenda would be aghast at this doom. She was young and vibrant, and tomorrow, we will not mourn her passing. Tomorrow, we are going to celebrate her short and beautiful life."

I don't know where that came from. I had been dreading tomorrow since Elaine told me about it. But now, I wanted to celebrate my daughter. I wasn't sure what Pastor Newberry had in mind, but he was going to have to get out of my way because I would not allow her funeral to be a dirge. My daughter may not have been a churchgoer, but I have no doubts she was a believer. I refused to accept that she was going to Hell, and if the pastor suggested this tomorrow, he would regret it.

CHAPTER EIGHT

We stayed another hour before heading back home. When we arrived, the house was again bustling with family. I grabbed Andy's arm as we came up the walk to the front door. I wanted some peace and quiet—my nerves frazzled.

Inside, he helped me out of my coat. We tripped over footwear as we made our way farther into the house. Judith met us just inside the door. "We're sending the kids downstairs with the pizza. Then, we're all set up in the dining room for the buffet. Just like lunch only, not sandwiches." We followed her into the kitchen. The kids filed past, the first four carrying big cardboard boxes. The smell was tantalizing. My mouth watered.

"Smells good," I said.

"Do you want a piece?" Judith asked.

"No, that's fine. I can have pizza anytime."

"Okay."

With the kids out of the way, there was room to move. Judith pushed me toward the table. I picked up a paper plate and helped myself to some lasagna, chili, a macaroni salad, coleslaw, and fried chicken. I passed over a few dishes before taking a spoonful of hash browns smothered in cheese. My stomach growled.

I took my plate to the living room, found a TV tray, and sat in my chair. My sisters and their husbands took various seats around the room. Someone had moved the dining room chairs to fill spaces, and they used one kitchen chair. I loved that our living room was large enough to handle all these people. I hated that the reason we were all together for the first time since Dad's funeral was another death.

"Honestly," I reasoned, looking around the room, "I thought the next time we would be together like this would be a wedding. Brenda's or Judith's daughter, Danielle's."

Carrie nodded. "It is tragic that families don't get together regularly and that weddings and funerals do that." I stared at her, wondering how she knew what I was thinking. Then I realized I had spoken out loud. That had never happened to me before.

"Well, Danielle is pretty serious with this boy," Judith added. "She's been seeing Elijah for several months, and he will spend Christmas with us. I wouldn't doubt that a wedding will be on the horizon."

I felt the hair rise on the back of my neck. It was just like Judith—elevating her daughter above the others. Danielle had always been smarter than Brenda, prettier than Brenda, more accomplished than Brenda. Usually, I brushed it off, but tonight, it rankled me. For a brief second, I wished Danielle was deader than Brenda.

Tears sprang to my eyes. What kind of monster am I?

"I'm sorry," Judith offered. "I shouldn't have brought that up." She got up from her chair and left the room.

I sat for a minute. The conversations hung there, no one wanting to break the awkward silence. Getting up, I followed her to the kitchen. I could smell the coffee percolating in the large urn Angela had brought with her. I stopped and set my plate in front of it.

Judith was leaning against the sink, her shoulders shaking.

"Judith?"

She stilled herself, straightening her shoulders, but didn't turn around.

I walked over to her, placing my left hand on her back. She exhaled and turned her face to me. "I'm sorry. I'm sorry that we won't get to celebrate Brenda's wedding. That is so unfair."

"I know. And believe me, I am angry about that. I am beyond angry at that. But …" Taking her hands in mine, I looked deep into her eyes. "But that doesn't mean we can't celebrate the accomplishments of those still here. Why shouldn't we be happy that Danielle is getting married?"

"Well, he hasn't asked her yet." She smiled, but it didn't reach her eyes.

I smiled back at her. "Let's get back in there, and please don't worry about being happy for your kids. It's natural."

"Well, Shane always reminds me I brag a little too much about our kids, but I will try to curtail it."

"I don't think there's anything wrong with being happy about your children's successes. Bragging is a mother's prerogative, and I've done my share."

"You? Audrey, you are humble about your kids. I know Brenda got honors in high school, but I heard that from Danielle. If Danielle had done so well, I'd have been on the phone to everyone I knew."

I laughed. Judith may not always say the right thing, but she was consistent. "You are precious, Judith. Totally precious."

She blushed and ducked her head. "No, I'm not. I'm ordinary."

"Hardly! You have been organizing things here since you arrived. I am so thankful you are here, and I have you as a sister."

"Thank you." She hugged me.

"Hey, can I get in on some of that?" Carrie asked as she entered the kitchen. She wrapped her arms around the two of us.

We separated, the feeling in the room heavy with unspoken love and sorrow. We have all experienced loss, and when it happened, it seemed to dredge up the past more efficiently than happiness, which brought back celebrations.

CHAPTER NINE

We cleaned up, wrapped the leftovers in cellophane, or scraped them into plastic containers. Most of the dishes brought over were in foil containers we could discard. The glassware dishes needed to be returned to their owners.

Donna, Elaine, Melissa, and Angela joined in. The kitchen bustled with bodies, and the work was soon done. Someone got the kettle going, and the large coffee percolator finished burping. There were several types of desserts on the table now. Cakes, cookies, pies. The kids would make quick work of this if we didn't dish up first.

Angela asked for requests, and an assembly line was soon in place. Cakes, pies, ice cream, cookies, coffees, and teas—all distributed with efficiency. The kids arrived to annihilate the remaining sweets. Danielle and Nora took a garbage bag downstairs to clean up the debris left behind by the seventeen kids crammed into the large rumpus room. Nora said they were watching a movie. I trusted she would ensure it was suitable for Jordyn and Kenny, who were only seven.

The adults gathered again in the living room. Conversations ran the gamut. Judith's husband Shane and Donna's husband Gordon were talking shop. They were mechanics, and besides their trades—they shared a love of stock car racing.

Andy discussed woodworking with my brother Aaron and Melissa's husband, Jason. Gordon and Timothy were discussing the state of the country. Looking around the room, I made eye contact with Elaine, gesturing toward the kitchen. Soon, all the women were clearing away the dessert plates and refilling coffees, and after we wrangled the chairs back to the dining room table, we sat there.

I don't know why whenever we get together, we Armstrong girls—as we were known growing up—always find a large table where we can sit and discuss our lives. Growing up, we always included Angela, Donna's best friend. She and my brother Aaron didn't date through high school, but once they were in college, they found each other. We couldn't have been happier for them. Angela was like a sister to us.

During these times around a table, our conversations always rambled back to the *do you remember* stories of our childhood. We reminisced about breaking bones, pillow fights, and the many adventures we had experienced. We laughed about school dances and gossiped about boys we once had a crush on.

This night was no different. We laughed until our sides hurt. I forgot why we were here. For a minute, for one brief minute. I remember someone mentioning that Brenda and Danielle had encouraged the other kids to climb onto the roof of Mom and Dad's garage. Once up there, none of them could get down. They sat there like a flock of birds, some of the younger ones terrified.

Nora refused to climb up onto the roof. She stood there watching the others, and when she realized the state of things—she ran for help. We laughed at the story again until I said, "Brenda was such an incorrigible child." Then I burst into tears because she would never be incorrigible again. She was lost to us, gone forever.

I felt arms around me, but I didn't look to see who was there. They all were. We were in this together to varying degrees. This wasn't what we imagined we would deal with in our lifetime. No one imagines the what-if-your-child-dies scenario. We think about winning the lottery or daydreaming about trips abroad. We long for the day we can retire and sit on the porch, sipping iced tea and watching the world go by without worrying about tomorrow.

Someone said it was nearly nine-thirty, and I felt the group withdraw. I heard voices calling downstairs for the children and the thundering of many feet coming up the stairs. Sitting up, I wiped my face. Seeing that I wasn't the only one wiping her eyes was touching. A box of tissues went around. You could feel the heaviness of sorrow and loss hanging thick, like drapes around the room.

I don't know why everyone in the world doesn't simply love children. They are guileless and innocent. As they filed into the room, some of them, especially boys, looked on high alert. Eyes wide with fear because they were unsure how to deal with this situation. What were they expected to do? Were they supposed to ignore it—were they expected to fix it—were they expected to embrace it?

Among themselves, they could usually be more open and honest. But facing the grief of a parent or a respected adult, they were at a loss. They milled around—the girls circling their mothers, the boys eventually spilling out of the room. I didn't want this to end. I didn't want anyone to leave. If they left, tomorrow would come, and I didn't want to face tomorrow.

I followed the crowd to the door. I watched as family after family exited the front door. The stack of boots grew smaller, and soon, it was just Elaine and Tim. Their son, Philip, held his hand out for the car keys, but Tim ruffled his hair, and they headed out the door together. Philip's sisters, Madison and Cassandra, stood awkwardly until Elaine signaled them to go. They left quietly, whispering, "Good night, Auntie Audrey. Good night, Uncle Andy," as they went out the door.

Elaine stepped toward me. "I can stay if you want."

Inside my head, I was shouting for her to stay, but I slowly shook my head. "It's okay. I'll be fine. But thank you." I hugged her tightly. She hugged me back.

When we finally parted, she looked deep into my watery eyes. "Get some sleep if you can. I'll be here in the morning and as close as you need me to be tomorrow. You don't need to be strong. I'll be strong for you, okay?"

"I'll be here, too," Andy added.

I reached over and took his hand.

"Yes, and we'll support you, as well," Elaine confirmed.

Andy nodded, his eyes filling up.

She turned and went out the door.

CHAPTER TEN

As the door closed behind her, the quiet of the house settled around me. I looked at Andy. He put his arm around my shoulder and squeezed. We walked together into the kitchen. Logan and Nora were sitting at the table. This was the first time we had the chance to be alone as a family. I couldn't get over how incomplete it felt.

When Brenda went away to university two years ago, this was us. A family of four for breakfasts and suppers and family times. Brenda's absence was sharp in the beginning. Her vibrant personality and her constant chatter had always encircled us, and, like glue, it bound us together. We were so quiet in those early days and coped with that silence because it wasn't permanent. It was a temporary imbalance. She wasn't gone. She was only away.

But this was how it was going to be from here on. Her absence was now a permanent status, and it felt wrong. We would never again be a family of five. How was this possible? How could a loving God allow this to happen? Either He wasn't loving, or He didn't exist. I was still leaning toward the latter.

"What time is the service tomorrow?" Logan asked.

"The funeral is at eleven, but a private family service is at ten," Nora answered with authority. "Pastor Newberry says that we need that private service to grieve openly without the crowd of onlookers. He thinks it's going to be a big turnout, too."

I bristled at the mention of his name. Pastor Newberry. Authority on God, life, and death. I shrugged off my mean-spirited thoughts and sat at the table, taking Nora's hand in mine. "How are you doing, sweetie?"

Her eyes welled up. "I still can't believe it. It's like a bad dream, you know?"

I looked over at Logan. "You?"

"I don't know. I feel like Nora, but I'm also a little angry. I mean … why her? Why Brenda? What did she do that was so wrong?"

"Nothing." Andy took a seat at the table. "She didn't deserve this. No one here deserves this. But life isn't always fair."

"Life sucks." Logan snarled.

I knew how he felt, yet hearing it from his lips made me cry. I didn't like how jaded he sounded. He was eighteen, with a lot of life ahead of him. Cynicism was a trait of those who'd seen more hardship than this, although this was huge.

Nora reached over and touched his arm. He pulled away from her. She looked hurt as her eyes welled up with tears. "God has a plan for this. It isn't what He wanted for Brenda. Or for us. But He allows people the free will to decide, and sometimes those decisions don't turn out well."

I looked at my youngest daughter. She hadn't come up with this on her own. She was spouting crap that Pastor Newberry had filled her head with. That also annoyed me. How dare that man counsel my daughter without my permission? How dare he fill her head with this nonsense? I added another entry to my list of grievances with that man.

"But even if He didn't want this to happen, He can turn it into good. All things work together for good to those who love God,

Romans 8:28."

"How can He make this good? Brenda is dead! He will not bring her back, which is the only way He can make this right." My voice was harsh. Her face crumpled. She thought she was helping, and instead of getting a host of "Amens," she got my anger. I was immediately remorseful.

"Oh, sweetie. I'm sorry. Take no notice of me. I'm not myself."

"It's okay," she mumbled, but I could tell it wasn't. I had taken a shot at her, and no matter how hard I tried, I could never take it back and leave her the same as she was before. I vowed to try harder to watch my tongue.

"Let's get some shuteye," Andy said. "We're tired. We've all been riding a roller coaster, and there are bound to be bumps as we adjust to our new reality."

Rising together, we headed up the stairs to our bedrooms. "Good night, Logan." I hugged him before he went into his room. "I love you. Sleep well."

"Good night, Mom. Love you, too. Good night, Dad."

"Good night, son."

At Nora's door, she paused and turned to me. "I'm sorry, Mom." Her eyes welled up with tears.

"Hush." I brushed her hair off her face. "It was entirely my fault."

She turned to go into her room, looking so forlorn that my heart broke in two. I followed her, leaving Andy to carry on to our room alone.

"Are you going to be okay?" I asked.

Nora sat hard on her bed, bouncing naturally with the springs. I couldn't help but recall how she would frequently bounce on the edge of her bed.

"I guess. Are you?"

"I hope so. As a parent, you never think you'll have to deal with this. I thought I'd die an old woman, and the three of you would bury me. It isn't supposed to happen like this. I am not prepared to deal with this, and I am angry, sad, and confused. I'm also sorry that, in my confusion, I am hurting you. That's the last thing I want to do." I sat on the bed beside her. "I want us to always be truthful with one another. We need to be honest. We need to trust each other. So, please forgive me for being less than compassionate and understanding."

I looked at her. She was crying again but nodding. I put my arm around her and hugged her closely. "I love you more than life itself. You have always been a real blessing to me." Her arms snaked around my ample middle, and she sobbed like her heart was breaking. I held her tightly, letting her cry.

When she was done, I helped her into bed. I pulled the covers up, kissed her forehead, and left, switching off the light and closing the door.

"Leave it open, please?" she called softly.

Leaving the door slightly ajar, I looked to my right and walked to Logan's room. I knocked softly.

"Come in," he called.

I opened the door and stepped into his room. He was sitting at his desk, his laptop lid slightly raised.

"Oh, you're on the computer?"

"Sorry. I'm just talking to my friend at college." He smiled.

"Okay, don't be long. Get some sleep, okay."

"Good night, Mom." He turned back to the machine. I went out the door, and as I closed it, I looked back. On the screen was the beautiful face of a young blond woman. Friend indeed.

I smiled as I walked down the hall to my room.

CHAPTER ELEVEN

Andy was already under the covers when I entered the room. I closed the door and headed to the bathroom to get ready for bed. I washed my face, brushed my teeth, and stripped off my clothes. I slipped on the nightgown hanging on the back of the door and came out, expecting Andy to be asleep. He wasn't.

I climbed into the bed, feeling like a new bride. Pulling the covers up tight, I turned on my side before reaching over to turn off the bedside lamp.

"You want to talk?" Andy whispered.

"About?"

"About how you're feeling?"

"I don't know how I'm feeling."

"Do you want to talk about that?"

I thought for a second. Do I? Don't I? "What is there to say?"

"I'm sure there is lots to say. You've never been at a loss for words, Audrey."

I rolled over toward him. "No, I don't want to talk about my feelings. But if you want to talk, tell me how you are doing."

Surprised that I turned the tables on him, he seemed at a loss for words. He wasn't used to doing the talking in our relationship. I did the talking—he listened.

"Oh, okay. I guess I'm numb. That would be the best way to describe it. For example, when the dentist gives you that needle, you know your teeth are still there but can't feel them. Your tongue is thick, and you can't speak. Well, that's how my heart feels. It's numb, and my chest feels thick, and I can't breathe properly."

Expecting to see tears in his eyes, I looked over, but he wasn't crying. He was stating his feelings so matter-of-factly that it scared me. As I thought about how he was feeling, I wished I felt like that. Sitting on the volcano, I wished I felt numb instead because my insides were on fire, and nothing seemed to quench the rage that simmered on a low boil. I was terrified that one day I would not keep the lid on it, that it was going to blow and take with it more casualties than a major war.

I no longer knew who I was, and I didn't trust myself, either. I took pride in my ability to keep a cool head and see the silver lining in everything. In this situation, there wasn't one to find. My warm, safe, and cozy world had disappeared, and in its place was a barren wilderness with hissing geysers and quicksand. There was barely enough light to see what lay ahead on a path that wasn't clear. Barriers blocked it, and I would have to overcome them. The shadows hid many thoughts, ones I feared to let loose. I didn't want to be in this place. I hated being here. And I was terrified that I would be here forever because I felt incapable of moving on.

I brushed off my fears and moved over to snuggle against Andy. He pulled his arm out from under the covers, wrapping it around my shoulders and pulling me close. We lay there for a few minutes. Listening to Andy's slow breathing, I was grateful for his presence. It helped keep my thoughts from Brenda and what tomorrow would bring. I didn't want to forecast what might happen. I didn't want to plan how I would deal with the day. In some ways, I hoped that the day would simply never come. There was a knock on the door and a soft call. "Mom?"

I moved away from Andy, pulling the covers in place. "Come in."

Nora opened the door. Her tear-stained face was puffy and red. Immediately, I was out of bed, crossing the floor to wrap her in my arms. "Oh, Nora," I whispered as I rocked her in my arms.

Fresh tears ran down her face, seeping into the shoulder of my nightgown. I looked back at Andy. He nodded at me, silently permitting me to take care of things. "Let's get some tea." I grabbed my robe, and we went out the door, closing it behind us.

Down in the kitchen, I busied myself with the tea. Nora got a couple of cookies from the jar, and we sat at the table, hot steaming cups of chamomile in front of us.

"Do you want to talk about it?" I asked as I watched Nora stir a generous helping of honey into her tea.

"It's my fault." Her chin quivered—her mouth contorted, making her next words nearly impossible to make out. "I'm a bad person. God is punishing me for my sin."

My heart broke open. Nora was sixteen years old. What on earth could she have possibly done to deserve this? I slid my chair over and wrapped her in my arms, letting her cry. I whispered soothing sounds as I rubbed and patted her back. When the torrent slowed, she pushed away, wiping her face with the collar of the T-shirt she wore to bed. I went into the mudroom and brought back a fresh washcloth warmed by hot water. She wiped her face properly then.

I pulled my chair back and sat down. I watched Nora as she fiddled with her cup. Her eyes were red-rimmed and puffy, her nose as red as her cheeks. I marveled at how our two girls were so different from each other. Brenda, even carrying a bit more weight than she should have, was a beautiful girl. She was all girl, all the time.

Nora was athletic, slim, and firm, with hardly any curves. She wore her mousy brown hair long, usually pulled back in a ponytail, and used no makeup. She was a tomboy through and through.

"I just don't understand, I guess." She started again, her words mirroring my thoughts. "There must be a purpose behind this, a reason for this to have happened. Is it me? I don't get why God would let this happen to her. And then I wonder if maybe this is my fault, you know."

My heart shattered at her words. How could this innocent girl ever imagine that she was at fault? "Hush." I reached over and pushed her hair off her face. "It's not your fault."

"Well, what if it was?"

"What could you possibly have done that is so bad?"

"Aargh." She groaned, putting her head down on the table.

"What is it, Nora, please? You can tell me."

She sat up, tears streaming down her face. "I was downstairs watching movies tonight and laughing with Danielle, Michael, and Joseph, and I never even thought about Brenda once. I am a terrible sister, a bad person. Who does that? I mean, everyone is here because she's not, and yet, I'm watching some stupid movie, eating popcorn and laughing."

"There's nothing wrong with that. If you thought only of Brenda and what happened, you'd go crazy. It's perfectly natural to become distracted by people and things. These distractions allow us to see that life goes on."

She turned toward me, her eyes full of pain and sorrow. "It's more than that. I was jealous of Brenda. I wanted to be like her, but …" I knew my daughter, and I knew this was just another crumb. There was more underneath that she wasn't willing to share yet. Nora had always been a dribbler when confessing anything. She seldom blurted out the entire story in one go.

Brenda was an open book. She spoke her mind—clearly and concisely. You never had to pull something out of her, she volunteered information. You always knew where you stood with Brenda. Nora wasn't deceptive, but she also wasn't forthcoming. If you wanted to know the complete story, you tugged gently, cajoled, or waited. I didn't mind this usually, but tonight, I was struggling with her reticence. I wanted to shout, *Spit it out, for crying out loud. Just spit it out!*

I took a deep breath. "That's normal, honey. It's not jealousy. It's admiration." I placated.

"No. It's more than that." She wailed as she pulled the face cloth over her face.

"Okay. It's more than that. But it doesn't make it worthy of causing your sister's death."

"But God says a sin is a sin."

I thought about my conclusions and how I blamed myself, Andy, and even Brenda for this horrible situation. Now, here was Nora, going down the same path, making the same assumptions. Regardless of who was to blame—I doubted a sixteen-year-old could harbor enough sin to be responsible. Besides, I was her mother, and my job was to give her direction when I thought she was on the wrong path.

The foundation I built my life on had crumbled around me in the past few days. I didn't know what to stand for or stand on when this was over. I was on a journey to discover a new philosophy and direction. In the irrevocably shattered fragments, I scrambled to find something to help. "That's what He says, Nora. Sin separates us from God, but that doesn't mean we receive immediate punishment. If God were going to punish the wickedness of this world, he certainly wouldn't start with a sixteen-year-old girl who wanted to be like her sister. The only person to blame is that stupid boy who killed her."

Unsatisfied, she said, "So, then why? Why Brenda? Why us? I want to understand, but I just don't."

"Honestly, honey, I don't either. I'm struggling to find my way through this, too." My current feelings of inadequacy grow stronger because I feel I should know the answers. I didn't tell her I had lost my faith in God. She didn't need to know how lost I was. She needed to know we would get through this, even though I wasn't sure I was up to the job.

Nibbling on a cookie, her tea growing cold, she sat there quietly. Her eyes were glassy from all the tears and lack of sleep. I felt my heart swell. She was my baby, my youngest. She had a long life ahead of her, filled with babies and a husband. What she was going through was bigger than anyone should have to bear. She didn't deserve this.

I did not know how this would shape us in the future. Maybe we would have many nights of tea and cookies in the wee hours of the morning while we tried to make sense of life. Maybe this was the only time we would talk like this. I hoped not—I hoped we could always open our hearts to one another.

"Are you ready to sleep yet?" I asked as I set my cup back down and pushed away from the table.

She nodded, put her uneaten cookie on the table, and walked back up the stairs before me. She turned as she walked into her bedroom. "Thanks, Mom. Goodnight." We hugged.

"Goodnight, dear. Sleep tight." I waited until she was back in bed before I pulled her door partially closed. Andy's gentle snoring greeted me as I entered our bedroom and closed the door. I crossed to the bed, scooted under the covers, and snuggled close. The bed was so warm that I realized how chilled I was. I turned on my side, my back against the radiator of Andy's body, and sighed, hoping sleep would come quickly. It didn't. My brain rattled around my conversation with Nora, doubting myself.

This was new. I never doubted myself before. I always knew the answer, and if I didn't, I confessed my ignorance and made it my mission to find out the answer. It was God or the Bible I looked to for clarification. Since we got the horrible news, I hadn't picked up my Bible once, nor had I prayed, and as I continued to ponder things, I realized that I no longer felt a closeness to God. Was that because I had pulled away? Or had He? Or was the closeness merely manufactured by my beliefs?

I rattled those thoughts around and around, driving myself mad because there were no answers. It was an impossible situation. For the first time, I longed for assurance that God was real. I had heard of fleecing God for answers. I just didn't know if I had the courage to listen to the answer. What if He didn't answer? What if He did? I groaned. This was getting me nowhere.

Tomorrow was going to be a full day. Many people would want a piece of me, though they might think of it as helping. Every single person who held my hand or hugged me with tears in their eyes took away a piece of me as I did my best to assure them I was okay; it was okay; it would be okay. No one simply gave in situations like this. They needed comfort, too. I didn't know if I was up to the challenge, and if I didn't get some sleep, I wouldn't be.

I didn't count sheep. When my mind wouldn't settle, I played a geography game by naming all the states in the US in alphabetical order. When I made a mistake, I started again until I got to Wyoming. If I wasn't sleepy by then, I would do the state capitals. Then, I would start again. I had never gone through them twice. The game's simplicity took my mind off the cycle it was stuck on and allowed me to relax. Sleep would follow.

Alabama, Alaska, Arizona, Arkansas …

CHAPTER TWELVE

Andy let me sleep in, waking me with plenty of time to get ready. The house was already bustling with people when I finally made an appearance. Andy wore his only suit, a dark navy worsted wool with a blue-on-blue tie. He looked handsome, leaning against the pantry, holding a cup of coffee in his hand. He smiled at me as I walked into the room.

I looked for Nora, needing to check she was okay. She was sitting at the table, toying with a pancake. She looked like she hadn't slept. I approached her, caressing her shoulders as I kissed the top of her head. She grabbed my hand, hugging my arm in the crook of her neck.

Elaine handed me a cup of milky coffee. "Do you want something to eat?"

My stomach flipped over, but I knew I needed to eat. "I'll have a toasted bacon sandwich if there's any bacon left."

"Lots. Find a seat, and I'll get it for you."

"Thanks."

I found a chair and moved it to the table next to Nora. She had stopped playing with her pancake and moved her plate toward the center of the table. Elaine set my food down: two folded pieces of toast stuffed with bacon. My mouth watered. I took a big bite. Mmmm.

Nora shifted her chair back. I looked over, trying to assess where she was at. Her face showed no emotion—it was blank and pale, stressing the dark circles under her eyes. She looked truly shattered. I wondered what else she was holding on to. What other secret shame she harbored that was keeping her from sleeping? She had only given me a glimpse of her pain last night, but I knew she wasn't ready to give it up yet. I hoped she would before she cracked.

I finished both sandwiches, grateful for them and Elaine for stuffing them full of bacon. People started pulling on coats and heading out. I looked at the clock. It was nearing ten—showtime. They wanted us to be at the church no later than a quarter to. We needed to be out of the way before people started arriving. We have such strange customs, like seeing the mourners before the ceremony was sacrilegious.

It was going to be a long day. I swilled back the last of my coffee, then regretted that. The warm liquid landed on top of my breakfast with a thud. I shuddered and swallowed hard.

A stretch limo from the funeral home sat at the curb, waiting for us. It was far too much for the four of us. Logan and Nora sat facing the back window. Andy and I sat facing them. I should have insisted that others join us. The trip to the church didn't take too long. We walked into the large open foyer, where Pastor Newberry greeted us solemnly. Then, he led us down the hall to a large Sunday school room.

Someone arranged the chairs in the room in rows. No one was sitting. They stood like cattle in a pen, waiting for slaughter. Elaine stepped toward me. "I think we should put the chairs in a circle around the room. It won't feel so claustrophobic that way."

I nodded.

She pulled the chairs out of line, and soon, everyone was helping.

We ended up with two rings, and people started sitting down. Andy's family had arrived while we were sorting the chairs, and they took one side while my family took the other. We weren't exactly strangers to one another. We had all grown up in the same town, but the only common denominator was Andy and me. We had come together for one reason, and it wasn't a pleasant one.

Time ticked by slowly. I watched the clock high on the wall move gracefully to ten thirty and then to ten thirty-five. Then finally ten forty. I thought I was going to scream. No one was speaking. There were tearful outbursts here and there, but most of us sat in shocked silence, not believing this was really happening.

Ten forty-five. My stomach turned over. I swallowed hard and took a few deep breaths. I tried to concentrate on Brenda, to picture her as she was only a few days ago—full of life. Tears pricked my eyes, but I refused to give in. I would not fall apart—I would be strong for Brenda, Nora, Logan, and Andy. I would not be the one who needed to be held up.

Elaine caught my eye. She didn't smile or nod, she just stared, and I felt the tears well up again. I looked away. This was hard—much harder than I thought. How was I going to get through this? The door opened. It startled me. Pastor Newberry pushed into the room, squeezing all the air out. I panted. Andy put his arm around my shoulders as I gulped in a mouthful of air and then another. My heart was trembling.

"Let us pray." Pastor Newberry announced in his most tempered voice. He bowed his head and closed his eyes. I sat staring at him as he prayed for us and the service ahead. The prayer didn't last long. He looked up, catching my eye as he turned toward the door. He left, and all the air rushed back into the room. I caught my breath.

"We're ready for you now." I recognized the voice of Carol Newberry, the pastor's wife. She propped the door open. "Please follow me."

She led us back down the hall, then down a set of wide stairs toward the set of doors that opened near the front of the church. We would not have to walk down the long-sloped aisle past the crowd of mourners who came to say goodbye. That was a relief. Andy and I were the last to enter. As we passed by Carol, she grabbed my hand. "I'm so sorry for your loss, Audrey. If there's anything I can do …" I didn't know what to say. I pulled my hand away and walked past her.

The church band played softly, the piano and guitars setting a solemn mood. The congregation shifted in their seats as they whispered to one another. I looked up toward the back of the church. The place was brimming—there were even people standing along the back wall. It felt strange to see so many faces, lots that I didn't even know, as I scanned the crowd. Lots of young people, university classmates perhaps.

Andy and I had front-row seats. A short wooden panel was in front of us, followed by a wide expanse of blue carpet leading to the three stairs to the stage. I looked up unwillingly. The coffin sat there—a highly polished, light-colored wooden box with brass handles. A spray of red and white flowers rested on top.

This is wrong. This is all wrong, I wanted to shout. Brenda would have chosen yellow flowers, not red ones. She shouldn't be inside that ornate box. What had I done? I should have taken charge. Why had I allowed a stranger to make choices for her? It should have been my job. Andy, sensing my anxiety, grabbed my hand and squeezed it. I relaxed at his touch.

Pastor Newberry swept to the podium. He wore his black robe, which he reserved for funerals and weddings. I couldn't look at his face, so I concentrated on his robe, watching it ebb and flow around his legs. He stopped when he reached the podium. Then he just stood there. A commanding presence, waiting for the crowd to settle. He finally opened in prayer.

Even though I promised myself to interrupt the service if it didn't celebrate her life, I found myself unable to move. I knew Brenda would be angry with me. The service wasn't what she would have wanted. It was a one-man show. A man who didn't even know her, who had never met her. He read from the Bible, led us in hymns and prayers, and eulogized my daughter as if he knew her well. He did everything, all by himself. Where were her friends? Why was no one else involved? Why weren't we involved?

I stopped listening and cried. I had done my daughter a huge disservice—I would never get another chance at this. It wasn't like this was a rehearsal. Guilt and shame nestled into my heart, and I welcomed them in. I was a horrible mother. I knew people would point fingers at me and discuss my lack of involvement. It was a farce to be here. I wanted to leave and take my daughter with me.

And go where? She was dead. Where are you going to take her? I didn't know—just away from here. It was getting on top of me. I was panicking. I needed to get out. *Now!*

I stood. The congregation stood with me. I didn't understand. Then I realized Pastor Newberry was center stage, his arms raised as he prayed the benediction. It was over. Six strapping young men marched up the stairs. They stood beside the coffin, waiting. On Pastor Newberry's signal, they hoisted the casket onto their shoulders and trudged down the stairs and up the aisle to the main doors. Logan and Nora followed, side by side. Then Andy and I were in the procession.

I kept my eyes down, afraid I would see people point and whisper. My heart was still hammering wildly in my chest. I was feeling physically sick. We finally exited the sanctuary and entered the huge foyer, and I looked up. There were more people here, standing in front of folding chairs. The number of people here astonished me, and I didn't recognize anyone.

We kept walking out the doors into the waiting car. I got Elaine's attention, and she, Timothy, and their three joined us there. The trip to the cemetery was quick, and soon, we were standing around a hole in the ground. The wind whipped at my coat, and I shuddered. Andy put his arm around me, pulling me closer. I grabbed Nora and dragged her into me on the other side.

The wind stole the words spoken by Pastor Newberry. I caught the odd one here and there, and then I stopped listening to the disjointed sounds. Staring at the coffin, I tried to imagine that my daughter was in there. I didn't know that for sure. Andy had seen a photo, and he refused to let me see the body. Maybe this was a mistake. Maybe she was alive, and this was some other woman's daughter.

Even as I thought it, though, I knew I was only fooling myself. She had gone from this place. I tried to imagine her in Heaven. I tried to imagine Heaven. My mind couldn't conjure up an image. I couldn't even picture Brenda's face. It had only been a few days.

Nora quivered beside me. I hugged her tighter. She choked back a sob. I stepped around her, maneuvering her between Andy and me. It was unconscionable that she had to go through this at her age. She should be an old woman before death came for her parents. There was nothing right about this. Nothing.

I looked at the coffin angrily. Why had this happened to our family? What had we ever done to deserve this? I don't know if I would ever answer that question. I took a moment to look around the group of mourners. Most of the people had tears streaming down their faces. Danielle wasn't doing very well. Judith stood behind her daughter, her arms holding her up. She caught my eye, and we stared at each other until I had to look away. The compassion in her eyes was too much to bear.

The coffin shuddered as Pastor Newberry lowered it into the ground. He stopped the process when the lid came even to the surface. Then, in an elaborate gesture, he removed the spray of flowers and brought them to me. I stepped back. I didn't want them. They were supposed to go down with her. I shook my head. He shoved them at me again. I took another step back, bumping into someone behind me. I stumbled and lost my footing.

Landing on the ground, I cut my knee on the edge of a nearby headstone. For a second, I didn't understand what was happening. Then, the terror of the day broke over me, and I collapsed onto the ground, sobbing. Andy was beside me, kneeling to help me up. Pastor Newberry grabbed my other arm, but I shook him off. On my feet, I swiped the dirt from my jacket, noticing the blood dripping down my leg.

Taking a moment to settle myself, I took a couple of deep breaths. Then, I moved close to Pastor Newberry. Making sure that no one else would hear, I whispered. "Don't you ever try to touch me again. Don't speak to my family. Just leave us alone." I spun away and then turned back. "Oh, and throw those damn flowers into the grave where they belong."

Then I turned, took Andy's arm, grabbed Nora with my other arm, and limped out of the cemetery. I didn't care if the service was over—I was over. I was done with this farce.

CHAPTER THIRTEEN

I knew that convention dictated that we attend the reception at the church hall. Because I would not disappoint my friends and neighbors, I went. It was the longest two hours of my life. Everyone was sincere in their consoling words, and I graciously accepted them. I spotted my best friend, Tiffany Nash, several times and desperately wanted to talk with her.

She had dropped off flowers and a card at the house but thought it best to stay away with all the family in attendance. She was right. We needed our time alone, uninterrupted by other people. She would understand me. She wouldn't judge me.

Our next-door neighbors, Emil and Doreen Wilkins, stopped by the table. They were old when we moved into our house and appeared unchanged in the years since. Today, though, they looked older. Emil squeezed Andy's shoulder as Doreen took my hand in her thin, papery ones, massaging my fingers as she spoke. "This is such a shame, her whole life before her. I don't know why this happens, but I know you are strong, and you will carry on."

I nodded, and she and Emil moved on. Following them were our other next-door neighbors, Blanche and Reggie Sharpe. More consolations, more tears. Members of the church, mothers and daughters from Brownies and church camp. I lost track of the names. Finally, the throng thinned, and the flow of people coming by our table slowed to a trickle. Then Tiffany was there with her husband, Lowell.

Tiffany swept me into a hug. A sob caught in my throat. How often had we sat at our respective kitchen tables talking about our children over tea? How many concerns had we shared, cares had we unburdened, and loves had we shared throughout our friendship? A lifetime of sharing, friendship, and love flowed between us.

We were unlikely friends. She was a tall, wispy woman with hair like liquid honey. Lowell was an investment banker in Crawford. They had lived in the city until their first child was born. Then Tiffany dragged her husband to Grandville so the children could play in the playground and ride their bikes on the streets without fear. She wanted to give them the same experience she had growing up in a small town.

I became a mentor to Tiffany when she started coming to church. They called it "disciplining the new believers." For a few months, we spent an evening together every week learning the principles of faith. In the end, she had a solid foundation, and I had the best friend a woman could ask for.

Tonya Burnett was the third in our three musketeers' group. I hadn't seen her at the reception, but I was certain she was in the kitchen, ensuring the food was set out, and the coffee and tea were hot. That was what Tonya did best. She was a laborer. She was the hardest worker, and with her on your team—you didn't need anyone else. You could count on Tonya for anything. She was a large woman with a heart of gold.

She and her husband—Todd—couldn't have children of their own, so they adopted Amelia and Hayden. Ten years older than Tiffany and me, we met Tonya when our kids were in kindergarten together. Amelia, Brenda, and Tiffany's son, Eric, were friends only because we were. Even before hitting junior high, our kids didn't spend time together unless forced to.

Brenda used to say that Amelia was as dull as a dishwater. She protested loud and long whenever we had our family nights together. Eventually, both girls stayed away from these nights, and soon, they became couples' nights, and our children were no longer included.

I often wondered about Brenda and Tiffany's son, Eric. He was such a good boy and as handsome as his father. I had hoped in the early days that they would grow into a relationship, bonding Tiffany and me together as in-laws. But she showed no interest in him—nor he—in her.

Amelia wasn't as quiet and reserved as we all presumed her to be. Imagine our surprise when Amelia turned up pregnant in grade twelve. She refused to name the father and was adamant she would not be giving the child up for adoption. I remember Tonya crying with shame the day she found out. Over tea and sympathy, Tiffany and I talked her round to understand that as parents, all we can do is guide. We can't make our children walk the paths we choose for them.

Tonya was now raising her granddaughter, so she had less time for us. She was back to changing diapers and making play dates. Life had thrown her a curveball, but she handled it like she did everything else. She just did what needed to be done. Amelia left her daughter behind and moved to Calgary to attend university. Last I heard, she had dropped out, was living with some boy, and was working at the Home Depot. She had no interest in her daughter because taking care of her was cutting into her social time.

Little Grace was the light of her grandmother's eye, and I was happy that Tonya had something to make her happy. Watching the two of them together was a joyful experience.

What were our lives going to be like now? Were we still going to get together and talk about our husbands, our kids, and God? Could I talk about Brenda? Would I want to? I had no answers. Tomorrow seemed a long way off. I had lived my life by rote, and now I was floundering in the sea of uncertainty. I didn't know what anything meant.

Tiffany promised she would stop by next week and then she and Lowell were gone. A few more church friends dribbled by as the crowd thinned. Very few young people stopped by to offer condolences—that surprised me. Maybe they didn't know what to say. I pushed my cold coffee away and prepared to leave. I stood, my knee throbbing in agony. Andy was right there, taking my arm.

"I need to visit the little girl's room," I whispered. He released my arm, and I hobbled off to the washroom. As I washed my hands, I studied my face in the mirror. I looked old. How did I get this old? Trying to recall my life a week ago, I found nothing there. I felt empty, like someone had walked in and erased my history. I sighed.

Coming back into the hall, I noticed the crowd had thinned even further. It was mostly family now, sitting around at several tables. I looked toward the kitchen and then headed there, hoping to catch Tonya. She stood with her back to the door, talking into her cell phone. I waited, listening to her baby talk to her granddaughter. "Gamma will be there in a few minutes, sweetie. Listen to Lauren and be a good girl, okay? Gamma loves you."

She turned around. "Oh!"

"Hi, Tonya. How's Grace?"

"She's fine. Lauren is looking after her this afternoon." She said this as if I should know who Lauren was. Maybe I should, but it wasn't coming to me.

"I am so sorry …" Tears sprang to her eyes. I could see sorrow in her watery blue eyes, and I could see guilt there, too. She wrapped me in her arms. I thought I heard her whisper, "It should have been Amelia." But that was probably wishful thinking. I squeezed my arms around her ample girth and rested there for a moment longer.

She stepped back and began fussing with some sandwiches,

moving them from one of the church's serving trays to paper plates. She looked over her shoulder at me. "So, it was a nice service, don't you think? Paster Newberry did a good job."

"Yes, it was fine."

She heard more than my words and looked at me hard. "It wasn't, okay?"

Not wanting to get into my feelings about Pastor Newberry, not here and certainly not now, I waved it off. "I'd rather have not been here."

"Oh." She nodded.

"You holding up okay?"

"With all the people at my house, I haven't had time to *not* be okay. Next week, it'll be different when Andy goes back to work, and my sisters all go home."

"Well, I'm only a phone call away. Except Wednesdays when I take Grace to the YMCA in Crawford for swimming lessons and Thursdays when we have story time at the library."

I smiled. This was the end of the road for us. It was a long time coming. We had nothing in common anymore. My daughter was dead, and hers wasn't. She didn't know how to handle the situation and her guilt. I felt the pang of loss, and tears welled up in my eyes. "It's okay, Tonya. I'll be fine. You just take good care of that wonderful granddaughter, okay?"

A wistful smile crossed her face and then disappeared. She nodded. "I'm taking these home to Todd. He couldn't come."

Couldn't or didn't want to? People are funny that way. Some people can't handle funerals. They remind them that death is imminent. "Say hello to him for me."

"I will."

"Well, I'd better get back out there." I turned to go and then paused at the door. "Thanks, Tonya. For everything." Then I left as quickly as my wounded knee would let me, my heart heavier than it was before. I should have left it alone, but I think I knew what was going on when I hadn't heard from her all week.

Carrie and her family were standing at the table, ready to leave. She hugged me and said she'd be in touch. Melissa, Donna, and Aaron were close on their heels. Andy's family had left while I was in the kitchen. They wanted us to stop by the house later. Elaine was clearing tables, and Judith helped.

I could feel the exhaustion of the day in every fiber of my being. I wanted to climb into bed and stay there for a week. Nora came up behind me, wrapping her arms around my waist and resting her head on my shoulders. I gripped her hands with mine, thankful she wasn't ashamed to show her affection.

I spotted Logan holding court a few tables over, several young women hanging on his every word. He caught my eye and ducked his head. I shook mine, smiling. I hoped he was going to be okay. He always had a tight rein on his emotions. I promised myself that we would have a talk before he went back to school.

Judith came over to the table and tugged on my sleeve. I turned to her, and she motioned for me to walk a little away from the other. "I talked to Shane, and I've decided that I'm going to stay here with you for another week to help you get back on your feet, so to speak." She paused, wetting her lips. "If that's okay with you, of course."

Part of me was reluctant to let her stay. Judith had a way of taking over, and I wanted to get my life back to normal—well, as normal as it could be considering. On the other hand, with her here, I would be free to … to what? To figure out this *God* thing—to have it out with Pastor Newberry—to get my life in order and to understand why?

I hesitated too long. "Well, if you don't want me!" She hissed in a harsh whisper.

"Come on, Judith," I snapped back. "Give me a break, will you. I am confused, angry, and worried, and I don't need your bullshit on top of it all."

Her eyes widened at my use of profanity. "You don't swear!"

"I do now." I smiled, embarrassed at the word that came out of my mouth. She was right. I hadn't used profanity before. But I was beginning to. I felt a shift from who I was to who I would be. But who was that? I had no idea.

"Okay." Judith went on. "I'll be honest with you. Things haven't been too good for me and Shane lately. I think he's having an affair."

Her words shocked me. They had always seemed so perfect together, so in sync with one another. How was it possible that Shane would take up with someone else? "How do you know?"

"I just do. A wife knows these things."

"Oh, and you think that staying here with me will fix your marriage?"

"No, I think staying here with you will let Shane figure out if he needs me or if we should stop playing at being married."

"Okay." I nodded. "You can stay." Then, I wrapped my arms around her. She stood there stiffly, allowing me to hug her. I stepped back, noticing tears in her eyes. Not sure what to say, I just repeated words recently spoken to me. "It'll be okay, Judith. You're strong, and you'll get through this."

"I'm sorry. Today should have been all about you. I do that all the time, don't I? Make things about me, I mean. At least that's what Shane says."

"Maybe. But that's who you are, and I love you just as you are."

"Well, I don't. But I don't know how to be anything else."

I took her hand and squeezed it gently. "Well, I'm questioning who I am, too. Maybe this will be good for us. Maybe we can figure this out together."

She let go of my hand. "I'd better help Elaine get this cleaned up." She moved away, and I watched her go. Her back was ramrod straight.

I came back to the table, catching Andy's eye. He stood and went to get my coat. After he helped me slip it on, we walked out of the reception hall arm in arm, Nora and Logan following behind. As we passed by Elaine, I whispered, "See you at the house later?"

She nodded. She had already expressed an interest in staying for a few extra days. I wondered if she knew about Judith's situation.

"I hear you're going to have a house guest," she whispered, looking across the hall to where Judith was.

"I am."

"What's this?" Andy asked.

"I'll tell you later," I said, tugging his arm.

CHAPTER FOURTEEN

In the car, I told him what Judith had told me. He nodded.

"You know, don't you?"

He kept nodding. "Shane talked to me the other night. He said Judith has this idea that he's having an affair, but he swears he's not."

Nora squirmed in her seat. I looked at her. She was hiding something.

"What do you know about this?" I asked her.

She looked embarrassed. "I promised not to tell."

"Who did you promise?" I asked.

"Danielle, she made me promise."

"Okay." Andy checked the mirror. "If you know something, you can tell your mother and me. Then, if we feel Judith should know, we will be the judges of that. You will not ruin your confidence by telling us, especially if it helps us to help Judith."

Nora nodded, though she seemed reluctant to share. "Well, Danielle told me she saw her dad with a younger woman in the bar of some hotel. She said that they seemed tight."

"Wow," I said at her shocking words. "Did she tell her mother or talk to her dad about this?"

"She said she wasn't supposed to be at that place, so she just got the heck out of there. She had borrowed money to see a movie and then met friends for drinks instead. And you know how Aunt Judith feels about liquor."

I did. Judith hated liquor. Like everyone else in high school, she had experimented with it. It loosened her up, and she was a lot of fun when she'd had a few, but she couldn't stop at a few. She always went past the point and ended up doing or saying things she regretted. After an embarrassing night, she swore off the stuff and has never taken a drink since. Shane could imbibe with caution, but the kids were under her strict order to leave it alone. But kids will be kids, I suppose.

We arrived at the house. It looked dark and forlorn like it was mourning the loss of Brenda, too. We were going for supper with Andy's parents, so there was no need to hurry to get something on the stove. I changed my clothes, tossing my torn pantyhose in the garbage.

I washed and dressed the cut on my knee. It wasn't too bad, just in an awkward place. It would heal okay in time. Dressed in black slacks and an emerald silk blouse, I returned to the kitchen, wondering if I should make tea. Judith arrived carrying a large suitcase. Nora showed her to the guest room, and I grabbed clean sheets to make up the bed.

"We're going to Andy's parents for supper. Would you like to join us?" I asked.

"No. I think I'll stay here if you don't mind."

"Not at all. Elaine is staying for a few days, too. She and Tim are off to see his parents tonight, then Tim is going home, and she's staying. Just so you know."

"Sure, whatever." She sounded distracted.

Nora left, and I closed the door behind her. "Are you okay?"

"I'm as okay as I can be, given the circumstances," she snapped, then looked stricken. "Oh God, Audrey. I'm sorry. This isn't your fault. None of this is your fault. I'm supposed to be here to help you, and instead, I'm snapping at you like an old biddy."

"This can't be easy for you, but yes, it would be nice if you remembered I am not the enemy."

She smiled sadly, sinking down to the bed. "What am I going to do?"

I sat beside her, resting my arm across her shoulders. "You just need time to figure it out. It'll be okay."

She sighed. "I suppose—I'm just tired of pretending everything is okay."

I sighed, too.

"Why does life have to be so hard, Audrey? I mean, you grow up thinking of Cinderella and Sleeping Beauty and happily ever after. You find someone and think you've got it made, but it's a battle. Every single day, it's a fight over something. The kids, money, the house, everything."

I thought about my life and my marriage. Until a week ago, I'd been living a pretty good life. My wonderful, loving husband provided well for me and our kids. Brenda had a future in psychology. Logan was living his dream for the moment before he came home to work with his dad and Nora—Nora wanted to be a veterinarian.

"I can't imagine what you've been through."

She turned away, and tears ran down her cheeks when she turned back. "We haven't made love in six months." Her voice warbled. "And that last time …" She choked on her words.

I couldn't imagine what she would say, so I patted her back soothingly and waited for her to collect herself. It took a minute. "He came home that night, and I told him his behavior needed to change. We had a tremendous battle. I had enough of his …" She halted and stood.

She walked to the window and pulled back the curtain. I waited for her to speak. When she turned back, her face was blank. "Anyway,

I don't want to keep you from your supper."

Dismissed, I stood. "We can talk when I get back if you want."

"I think I will take a hot bath and have an early night. I'll see you at breakfast."

Closing the door quietly, I padded back downstairs. Andy was sitting on the couch, waiting for me. "You ready?" I nodded. "Judith coming?"

"No, she's having an early night."

He helped me with my coat, and we walked a couple of blocks to his parents' house, hand in hand. I thought about Judith and Shane and how glad I was that I married Andy. Brenda's death had rocked us, but I also knew that he would not walk away from me because of it. He was my champion for the long haul.

I was the one I was worried about. There was a pot of hot sludge in the pit of my belly. I didn't know how I was going to deal with it, but I knew it would kill me if I didn't.

CHAPTER FIFTEEN

Supper was a cacophony of sounds. So many people crammed into one tiny house. Varied stories and thoughts voiced in unison around the table made the night seem joyous and lively. There was laughter and mirth as we forgot for the moment why we were all together. I pushed Brenda from my mind several times, not wanting to dampen the mood. As the night wore on, though, I grew tired of the pretense.

I got Andy's attention and told him I was ready to go. He looked disappointed, and then he went to get our coats. I followed him into the bedroom.

"Andy?"

"Yes?" He turned to me.

"You can stay if you want. I'm tired, and I want to go to bed. But if you want to stay and talk with Derek, then stay. You guys don't see each other often, and I don't mind, really, I don't."

"Are you sure?"

"Yes, I'm sure."

He hugged me briefly, then helped me into my coat. I came back into the living room to say my goodbyes. Nora jumped up. "Are you going home, Mom? I'll come with you." She dashed out of the room and came back with her jacket.

We went out the door together and headed back home. Listening to our shoes clip along the sidewalk, I smiled. The sound of shoes tapping on a hard surface had always made me happy. I could listen to tap dancers for hours. Perhaps the rhythm was soothing in some fashion.

I remember getting my first pair of hard-heeled shoes and tapping my way down the hallway at school. I was twelve years old, but I felt grown up. Nora usually wore trainers, but today, she wore her dress shoes, so we stepped in time. Click, click, click.

"Mom?"

"Yes?"

"If I tell you something, will you promise not to get mad?"

Oh dear. Why do people do that? The moment she said those words, I knew whatever she said would make me mad. I now had to promise not to. If I didn't promise, she wouldn't tell me. It was a no-win situation.

"I don't know, Nora. Do you think it will make me angry?"

"I hope not, but …"

"Okay. Do you want to tell me now or when we get home."

She looked left and right and then back behind us. "Here, before I lose my nerve."

My stomach flipped over. I thought of the worst news I could hear. My mind went back to Tonya and how devastated she was when her daughter was pregnant in high school. The shame she felt, not to mention the judgments that flowed from all the narrow-minded people at church. "Are you pregnant?"

"Really? That's what you think?"

I shrugged. "What else is there?"

"Other things." She lowered her head.

"Okay, so spit it out then."

"I can't."

I took hold of her arm, linking us together as we walked home. "Look, you're alive. You're here with me, and whatever your news is, it can't be worse …" I didn't finish.

"You're right. But it is big."

As we neared the corner, I noticed the lights were on in the old white church. This surprised me because I thought this building was no longer in use. The glow on those stained-glass windows lifted my spirits a little. It was such a comforting sight to see. Stained-glass windows were masterpieces that had fascinated me since my childhood.

"Hey, look. There are lights on in that old church."

"Yeah, I know. Do you remember Pastor Gallagher? He was the youth minister a few years before Pastor Joseph left."

"Pastor Dan. Really?"

I was getting a clear image of a younger man who always had a group of kids hanging around him. He had dark, curly hair and deep brown eyes.

"Didn't Brenda have a crush on him?" she asked.

I nodded, remembering. She was twelve or thirteen years old and had been rebellious about attending church for months before Pastor Dan arrived. After that, she went to his youth group and to church faithfully. Then he left to take a position in another church, and Brenda refused to go to church after that. It crossed my mind to wonder if she would be alive today if Pastor Dan had stayed.

Nora was nodding. "Well, Pastor Dan came back about a month ago, and he's starting a new church in town."

"A new church, eh?"

"I was going to go on Sunday. See what it's all about, you know."

"You're going to leave the Faith Gospel?"

"Well …"

"Is this what you wanted to talk about?"

She paused for a minute. "Yes, I wanted to know if it would be okay. I know you are happy with Faith Gospel, and so am I. I was just thinking it would be nice to support Pastor Dan, you know."

"I see."

We turned the corner and headed toward the house. "Well, I am not sure I'm going to go to church, and I am definitely not going tomorrow."

"You are not going to go to church?"

"No, I'm not going to church."

"Wow, Mom. I don't think you've ever missed a day. Certainly not in my memory."

"Well, things are different now. I am different."

"How?"

"I don't know. I just am."

"Besides, your aunt Judith is here, and Auntie Elaine is coming to stay for a few days."

"Oh, right. But it's okay if I go?"

"Absolutely. Check out this new church. It's close enough to walk there. I won't even have to get up and drive you." I smiled.

We arrived at the house, and Nora let go of my arm and raced up the stairs ahead of me. The house was quiet, and the light over the stove was the only thing breaking the darkness. I never used the light, so it must be Judith's habit. Nora kissed me on the cheek and whispered good night before disappearing into her room. I debated about making a pot of tea but decided against it. I needed to sleep.

As I prepared for bed, my heart grew heavy with thoughts of Brenda. I longed to talk to her, to tell her again that I loved her. We could make a date to have lunch together or supper if her schedule was full. I wanted to hear her voice, bright with excitement, as she announced she was getting married. There was so much left to share with her, and it grieved me that she wasn't here.

I felt old and burdened as I crawled under the covers, my knee groaning in agony. My thoughts were swirling uncomfortably. I tried to remember the funeral. Had it just been today? It seemed a lifetime ago. I couldn’t remember any words spoken. The only thing I remembered was the auspicious casket. I relived the horror I felt when Pastor Newberry tried to hand me death flowers. Shuddering, I consciously brought my mind back to happier things. I would never sleep thinking about such things.

Turning my thoughts to Nora and our conversations over the past few days, I felt something other than her sister’s death was weighing on that girl. I also didn’t think her worries involved trying out a different church. She was bearing something, maybe a harsh word spoken. No. That’s not Nora. She doesn’t speak like that. Nora was a born encourager, which in a younger child was a miracle. They are usually the ones who get all the attention. Nora was different.

She possessed the most moderate temperament I’d ever known in a child. Nothing about her was wishy-washy, and she went along with others’ choices easily, never fussing about getting her own way. She loved church and was deeply involved in the youth group.

I wondered why she was checking out that new church. It hadn’t occurred to me at the time, but she wasn’t one to shirk commitments. This reinforced my hunch that there was more to Nora’s confession that wasn’t expressed.

Andy came in. “Oh, you’re still awake.” He crossed the room to the bed. “You, okay?”

“I just can’t seem to shut off my mind.”

“Give me a minute or two. I’ll wash up and be right there. Then we can talk.”

True to his word, he pulled back the covers and snuggled up next to me. As I nestled into him, my head on his chest, I poured out my sorrows. He listened and placated me as best he could. He patted and rubbed my back. When I brought up Nora, he voiced his concern, too.

"Something is going on, now that I think about it. She's been quieter than usual since she started back to school. Do you think she's being bullied?"

"I don't think so. She's popular, but then you never know. Kids can be cruel. And now she's the one whose sister got murdered. School will not be easy."

"Well, we'll just have to do what we can to ensure she's okay." He paused. "So, what about this church? Are you worried? What do we know about it."

"Nothing, except that Dan Gallagher is the minister, and he's come home to start up this church. I'm not even sure what umbrella he's under. Is it Lutheran, Baptist, Evangelical?"

"So, are you going to go with her tomorrow?"

"Honestly, Andy. I don't know if I'll ever go back to church."

Andy pulled away so he could look at me. "Really? Is this because of Brenda?"

"Partly, well … mostly, I guess." I was ashamed to admit my feelings about Pastor Newberry.

"Well, I can't believe it. You have always been a warrior about church."

"I know." Rolling onto my back so I didn't have to look at Andy, I confessed. "It's just that I don't understand why God would take Brenda away from me. I mean, I've served Him all my life, and this is my reward?" My voice broke, and fresh tears spilled from my eyes.

"Oh, Audrey. Come here." He scooted closer to me and scooped me into his arms. "Shh. You'll figure this out. I know you feel God is punishing us for some sin, but Pastor Newberry says that—"

"I don't care what Pastor Newberry thinks."

For a minute, we lay there, neither of us willing to break the tense silence that had fallen in the room.

"I'm sensing that you have issues with Pastor Newberry."

There it was. My issue. I sighed. "I guess I do. And that's part of the problem right now. I was unsettled about him before Brenda, and then he took over the entire funeral service. He didn't even know her, for crying out loud. I don't know why you let him do that."

"Why did I let him do that? You were inconsolable, and I didn't know what to do. I couldn't deal with it myself, and when I talked to him about it, he offered. It seemed the easiest choice for both of us. If I had known you had issues with him, I would have done things differently. I guess I was wrong."

There was a tremor of hurt and pain in his voice. "Oh, Andy. I'm not blaming you, really, I'm not. I think he'd have taken over anyway. He's just that kind of person."

Andy sighed, and I shuffled closer.

"Thank you," I said.

"For what?"

"For being you. I love you—you know."

"I love you, too." He kissed the top of my head.

We lay there in the dark, comforted by our love. I rolled over, and Andy curled into my back. We lay there like two spoons in a drawer until we fell asleep.

CHAPTER SIXTEEN

Sunday mornings have always been a blessed rush for me. It was my duty to prepare breakfast for my family and still be ready and out the door for Sunday School at nine. It felt strange to paddle around the kitchen in my robe, making breakfast at a leisurely Saturday pace.

Andy mentioned going to the cabinet factory for a couple of hours to check on things as he finished his pancakes. I knew he didn't like being away from his business for too long. Of course, he trusted his plant manager, Travis McMillan, wholeheartedly, but he still liked to keep his finger on the pulse. Logan was going to go with him. Then, later, we would take him to Crawford to catch his plane back to school. I wasn't ready to let him go, but he had to get back to school. In six weeks, he would be home for Christmas break.

Nora scooted out the door at ten for the ten-thirty church service down the street. They prayed for half an hour before the worship service started at eleven. Judith appeared looking haggard and pale as Nora went out the door.

"Coffee?" I asked unnecessarily.

She sat, resting her head in her hands.

"Long night?" I prodded as I set the cup in front of her. She merely nodded. "Want to talk about it?"

"Not yet."

She poured some milk into her coffee, turning it a grayish brown. "I do have cream." I offered, even though it was too late.

She shrugged. "This is fine."

I shuddered and looked away. "Do you want some breakfast? I have pancake batter ready."

"Just some toast."

I hoped I would not have to wait on her hand and foot. "Please!" I commented.

She looked at me sharply and then crumpled. "I'm sorry. Again. I'll get my toast." She got up.

"No, you sit." I pushed her back into her chair. "I don't mind getting it, but I would appreciate some gratitude."

"You're right." She wailed. "I'm just a selfish bitch."

"Whoa!" I snapped. "You stop right there. I never said you were a selfish person."

"I know, but I am. It's always about me."

"So, after a night of rumination, you've decided you are the problem?"

"I guess." She whimpered.

"Well, I don't think that's healthy."

She wiped her eyes. "I can't help it."

"Yes, you can. Try getting some perspective."

"How do I do that?"

"Well, maybe you can see a therapist."

"Get my head shrunk?"

"Honestly, Judith. That is such an archaic phrase. I'm thinking of going myself and Andy, too. I'm not too proud to admit that what happened to us is dramatic enough to require some help. When Colleen Dickerson, you remember her, don't you?"

Judith nodded.

"Well, when she had cancer, she asked me to take her to this luncheon in Crawford for people with breast cancer. A woman's rally of sorts, I guess. The guest speaker—I can't remember her name—said that getting professional help and asking for it was braver and stronger than trying to figure it out on your own. She encouraged every woman there, struggling with disappointments or questions or emotional pain because of her disease, to talk to someone."

I took a sip of my coffee, thinking back to that day. "Anyway, I don't have cancer, but I am disappointed and angry. I'm sitting on a powder keg of fury and don't want the fallout to destroy me or my family. I was whipping up the pancake batter this morning, and I accidentally got some eggshells in it. It made me so angry I nearly broke the bowl. I need help—I need to talk to someone, or this is going to eat me alive. I am so damn mad at God …"

As the rage rose, I stopped, not wanting to live in that place right now. Tamping my anger back down, I sighed.

"Oh, Audrey. I'm sorry. You have enough on your plate. Maybe I should go."

"Sure, sure. You go, and I'll feel guilty that I drove you away in your time of need."

When she looked at me, I could see the anger in her eyes. "So, what do you want me to do? I'm obviously a burden whatever I choose to do."

"That's right. You are. And I'm your sister, so it's okay to be a burden sometimes. That's what sisters are for."

"It's the worst possible timing, isn't it?"

"Yes, it is. But there is a reason for this, too. So, let's stop being maudlin and figure out how to deal with our lives."

She placed her hand over mine and nodded. We sat there for a minute, at peace with one another again. Then she pulled her hand back. "So about that toast?"

I laughed. It felt good to laugh. Then I felt guilty for laughing. How could I laugh when my daughter was lying in the cold hard ground? To cover myself, I leaped up to make Judith some toast.

CHAPTER SEVENTEEN

We were on our third cup of coffee when Elaine arrived. She came in towing a good deal of the crisp outside air with her. "Goodness, I feel winter in the air this morning." She announced. "Is there any coffee going? I sure could use some after that weak stuff at the hotel."

I got up and poured the dregs of the pot into a cup. It looked disgusting. I poured it out and began a fresh brew. My hands shook with the caffeine load, so I switched to decaf but didn't tell anyone. The flavor was the same, or at least I thought so.

I found some cookies in the freezer and brought them to the table as well. As I sat down, Elaine asked, "Why aren't you in church?"

I shrugged.

"Something's going on with you. You want to talk about it?"

Shrugging again, I said, "I don't really know all of it. I'm angry at God for letting this happen to my daughter, and I can't figure out what I've done or what any of us have done that was bad enough to warrant this. I mean, she's never coming back. This wasn't an exile to an island as punishment. This is forever! As long as I live, I will never see my beautiful girl again, and I am damn angry about that." I was shouting by the time I finished. Neither Elaine nor Judith said anything.

"Is it wrong to be mad?" I asked, not expecting an answer. "I mean, this doesn't happen to everyone, and I've been so dedicated to the church that I take up more of my time than my husband does, for crying out loud. And this is the thanks I get? What's up with that?" I burst into tears. "This isn't how it's supposed to go, you know. She's supposed to care for me in my old age. How am I going to manage without her?"

"You have two other children," Judith pointed out.

A howl rose from my lips. "I know, but it doesn't make it right that she's not here?"

"You're right," Elaine said. "You are absolutely right. God is an asshole. He took your daughter just because he could. So, what are you going to do about it?"

"How can you say that?" I yelled. "You can't call God an asshole."

"Why not? He is, isn't He? So, call a spade a spade."

"I can't say that."

"Sure, you can. You can do all things through God who strengthens you."

"Are you kidding me? How can God give me the strength to blaspheme Him?"

"I don't know. I'm just repeating what the Bible says." She took a sip of her coffee and studied me. "He already knows your heart, and if you're feeling He's an asshole for letting your daughter die, then saying it out loud will not change how He feels about you. But it might change how you feel about Him."

"Well, being mad at someone isn't the same as hating him."

"Now we're getting somewhere." She smiled.

"What do you mean?" I used the napkin to wipe my eyes.

"Well, we've established that you're angry at God. That's good.

It's healthy to be angry when someone lets you down, and God let you down. Big time. But you don't hate Him, and you don't want to hate Him. So, let's get back to motive."

"Motive for what?" Judith asked, entering the conversation.

"Her motive for not going to church."

"I just told you." I avoided eye contact.

"Look, Audrey, I was at the graveyard yesterday. I saw what happened."

"When? What happened?" Judith asked.

I looked at my sister and wondered when she had gotten so wise. She was hitting all the points, and I was feeling uncomfortable. Elaine didn't clarify what she was getting at. She sat there looking at me, waiting for me to explain.

Just then, Nora bounced into the room, and the conversation veered in another direction.

"So, how was church?" I asked, though clearly there was no need.

"Oh, Mom, it was amazing. Pastor Dan is amazing. He preached from the book of Philippians. It was exceptional. Did you know Paul wrote that letter when he was in chains? In a Roman prison waiting to be executed? I didn't. I had never heard that before. And the whole letter talks about being grateful. Can you imagine? The former persecutor of Christians being grateful for God, even though he was in prison. I am totally going back."

Laughing, I looked at my daughter. Nora had not been this enthused about the Bible since Pastor Joseph retired. It was a wonderful thing to see. Her enthusiasm was contagious, and I could feel myself getting excited along with her. "That's wonderful, Nora. I'm so glad. And not to throw a damper on things, but what about youth group?"

"That's what is so great, Mom. Pastor Dan wants to start a youth ministry. I talked with him for a few minutes, and I think we'll have a few members right from the start. Remember when Pastor Newberry mandated that anyone attending the youth group on Wednesdays had to attend Sunday mornings? Well, we lost a lot of kids who came to our youth group but attended other churches. I think they will be interested in coming to this new one if we can get it started."

"Well, that's wonderful, Nora. Sounds like this new church is perfect." Elaine added.

"Oh, it is, and Pastor Dan …" she stopped mid-sentence.

"What?"

"He said he'd like to stop by sometime to offer his condolences for Brenda. He wanted to come today, but I told him we were taking Logan to the airport. So, he's coming tomorrow." She hugged her hands to her stomach. "I'm sorry, Mom. I should have asked. It's probably not a good day." She looked at the side door. "I can run back to church and tell him not to come."

"It's fine. Monday is fine. No, no, it's okay. Did he give you a time?"

Relief flooded her face. "Oh, good. He said about ten-thirty-ish."

I nodded.

Looking bright again, Nora said, "Well, I'm going to change. What time are we leaving for Crawford?"

"Logan's plane flies at four, so we should be there by three. So, I guess no later than two-thirty in case there's traffic."

Nora bounced out of the room. I turned back to my sisters. "Well, someone's got a crush on her new pastor."

Judith and Elaine looked at one another. Obviously, they knew something I didn't.

"What?" I asked.

Neither of them seemed willing to speak. "Come on, you guys. Spill. Does Nora have a crush on another boy? What do you know?"

"It's not a boy," Judith said.

"What do you mean? It's a man? A grown man?" I asked, feeling perplexed.

"No, a girl," Judith added.

"What do you mean? A girl?" Then it hit me. A girl!

"Are you kidding me?"

"Well, I don't know for sure, but she held hands with some girl at the funeral reception. A tall, slender brunette. A pretty girl, wearing no makeup."

Her best friend, Emily Sanders. "No, they're just friends."

Elaine raised her eyebrows. "I think they are more than just friends."

I couldn't believe my sisters would talk like this. This was my daughter. My baby. Surely, if she was … I couldn't even say that word to myself. But if she was, wouldn't I know it? But you know, Audrey. Remember the other night? She came to you with a secret sin. She was trying to tell you something. What about the walk home last night? Do you think all she wanted to tell you was that she wanted to try another church? Surely, that wasn't something that was going to make you mad. You allowed yourself to be misled both times because you really didn't want to know.

I crossed my arms on the table and laid my head down. A deep sigh as Elaine rubbed my back. "It's not the end of the world, you know," she whispered.

"Isn't it?" I sat up. "I've lost one daughter, and now the other one will never be a wife and mother. What about grandkids?"

"She can have kids," Judith said. "There are so many ways to get pregnant these days."

"Judith!" I exclaimed.

"Well, there are." And then we were laughing. Nora came back wearing jeans and a T-shirt.

"What's so funny."

I looked at my daughter with renewed eyes. She was so lovely, and I thought it was a loss that she wouldn't get married and live a normal life. The path she was on was going to be hard. Many people, especially in a small town, would not understand her choice. It wouldn't be my choice for her. "Life. That's what's so funny. Life."

CHAPTER EIGHTEEN

At quarter past two, the four of us bundled into the car. Since we were going out for supper in the city, Elaine and Judith, who were staying behind, had also opted to go somewhere to eat. Thankfully, Judith had her car, so they could choose from many restaurants, not just the ones within walking distance.

We were quiet as Andy navigated the twists and turns to get to the highway. I had spent hardly any time with Logan, and I felt bad about that. Once we hit the highway, I started my interrogation.

"How are you doing, Logan?"

"Good." It was barely a grunt.

"That good, huh?"

He smiled. "That good."

"I need to know that you are going to be okay. I will not be there. I'm a long way off. If you aren't, I'd really prefer that you don't go back."

"I'm going back."

"Okay. So, you're fine, then."

"Mom, I'm as okay as anybody can be, considering. I just lost a sister. It hurts like hell, knowing that some jerk shot her for no good reason, but what can I do about it? Nothing. That's what. I could get lost in a bottle of liquor, I could do some drugs, but nothing will change the fact that she's still dead."

"You're not on drugs, are you?" I asked, shocked by his words.

"No, Mom. I'm not on drugs. Drugs are for stupid people. But what I am saying is that I can't change what's happened, so I should get on with my life, whether or not I like it."

Andy reached over and patted my arm. "He's going to be okay, Audrey."

I smiled over at him and let the conversation go. Nora had her earbuds in, and Logan spent the rest of the trip looking out the window, watching the world go by. When we got to Crawford, Andy missed the turn to the airport.

"Where are we going?" I asked.

"When Logan and I were working this morning, he mentioned he'd like one of those cinnamon buns from Jack's. I told him we'd stop there and pick one up."

"Oh. Okay."

He parked the car and handed Logan a twenty-dollar bill. "Buy all you can."

Logan got out of the car and ran across the street. He was back a few minutes later, carrying a small white box and holding a huge sticky bun in his hand. He climbed back in. "Thanks, Dad. I cleaned them out."

"Good boy." Andy started the engine as the smell of cinnamon filled the car.

"I've got change, but my hands are kind of full."

"Keep it," Andy said.

"Thanks. Anyone want one?"

I shook my head, but Nora took one from the box, ripped it in two, and put the smaller half back.

A few minutes later, we arrived at the airport. Andy parked at a meter and got out to plug in the required fee. Logan gently squeezed the box of cinnamon buns into his backpack. We traipsed across the lot and into the building. After Logan checked in, we sat in the waiting area. Logan would have to go through security, but until then, we had a little time.

"I wish you weren't going," I said as tears filled my eyes.

"Oh, Mom, I know. But I'll be back before you know it. Christmas isn't that far away."

I nodded. Andy put his arm around my shoulder.

"Do you want anything from the concession?" I asked.

"Can't take it through security. They have one on the other side, anyway. I'll be okay. The flight is not that long, and they'll feed me something."

"You've got someone meeting you on the other end?"

"Yes, Mom. It's taken care of."

"I know I sound like I'm mothering you, but I am your mother."

He laughed. "Yes, you are." Then he got serious. "I wish I weren't going back so soon, but I have commitments, you know."

"I know, dear. I know."

They announced his flight, and the security people unlocked the doors and stood beside them. I could see the scanners inside as a herd of travelers stood to get in line. People all around were hugging one another, shaking hands, and uttering wishes for a safe trip. My heart skipped a beat. It was too soon. I wasn't ready to let him go.

I burst into tears, embarrassing myself. Logan stood and crossed the small space between us. He kneeled in front of me. "It's okay, Mom. I get it."

I looked up into this face, so like his dad's. His eyes filled with tears. I reached for him, and he wrapped me in his arms. "I love you, Mom," he whispered.

"I love you, too."

And then he pulled away. He hoisted his backpack up from the floor. Andy stood, and they clapped each other in a manly hug. Nora edged in for her turn, and then he went through the door. He looked back, one last wave, and he was gone out of sight. I thought my heart would break in two.

Andy remained standing, and Nora sat on the edge of her chair across from me. I looked from one to the other, took a deep breath, and got up. "Okay," I said as tears flowed down my cheeks. "Let's go get something to eat."

Andy put his arm around me, and we walked out into the cold gray November afternoon.

The restaurant got busy fifteen minutes after we found seats. I was glad that we didn't have to wait. I was too tired and cranky to stand in a crowded foyer waiting for a table.

We ordered our food, but I merely picked at my meal. I wasn't hungry. Nora cleaned her plate, even though she had eaten half a large cinnamon bun earlier. I looked at her slim frame and wished that calories were as friendly to me as they seemed to be to her. Brenda and I were more alike that way. Easy keepers. That's what my grandfather called me.

The server boxed up my meal. I wasn't even sure why. I didn't know if I would eat it tomorrow, but maybe Andy would. We climbed back into the car, and the conversation was as lively as it had been all day. We all seemed to be lost in our own thoughts.

When we arrived, the lights in the house were burning brightly. Judith and Elaine were curled up on opposite ends of the sofa, watching a movie. It was still early, way too early to go to bed. I went into the kitchen and placed my leftovers in the fridge. Then, I put the kettle on for tea.

I wasn't one to watch a lot of television. Andy, of course, watched his sports, and the kids watched shows they had to see, but for me, television hadn't much appeal. I enjoyed the occasional movie, but these new reality shows were worse than any show they used to broadcast. There were shows, of course, with merit, but I didn't have the time or inclination to seek them out. I just turned on the radio to the Christian music station and sang along. That passed the time of day nicely. Most of the time.

Tonight, I was restless. There was nothing to look forward to. The funeral was behind me. Not that anyone looks forward to a funeral, but it was a distraction. Having all those people around had kept me from facing the dark thoughts and those questions that were crying out to be answered. Why Brenda? Why now? Could anyone have prevented this from happening? What kind of sick monster did this kind of thing? What did his parents have to say for themselves?

I knew, of course, that his parents weren't responsible for this boy's actions. He was a grown man. He did what he did, but I sure wanted to know why. Why did he shoot an innocent girl? I could only imagine that Brenda stood in the way of him getting to Andrea. She would protect someone she thought was in danger. That's who she was.

So, she stood in his way, and rather than going around her—he took her out permanently. That showed a great deal of malice. He came to her house armed with a weapon. Brenda was unarmed, which made him a coward. The fear that my girl must have felt as he brutalized her must have been intense. What did that report say about her injuries? He smashed her hand—she had bruises, contusions, and a couple of broken ribs. That showed a lot of anger. Why was he so angry? What had she ever done to him?

I flashed back to the weekend this happened. Brenda had come home for a visit, dragging Andrea along. It wasn't a planned visit, but I was quite happy to see them on my doorstep.

Looking back, I realized they were both distracted. Were they aware of the danger that lurked back in Crawford? Brenda knew something was wrong because she asked me to pray for Andrea. I should have asked questions. Instead, in my simple faith, I lifted the situation to God. God had done nothing. Why? Why didn't he protect them?

There were days when I wanted to sit down face-to-face with God and have a conversation. No guessing—no reading between the lines. No subterfuge. Just sitting down and getting straight answers. But that isn't how things worked, and that was the most frustrating part of faith. Being blind and following anyway.

I didn't have much experience with struggles. My major concern was always the lack of faith in my family. Nora was the only one I never worried about. I read and reread Bible passages, asking for clarity for my children who were walking away from God. I never got answers. It was disappointing to see them following the world, doing things I thought were demoralizing. But I loved them despite this, and I prayed for them daily.

What good did that do? Those prayers had gone unanswered, and Brenda was dead. No one had stood between her and a madman. Her last minutes on Earth were not surrounded by the people she loved holding her hands. No, she had …

I pushed back from the table—I couldn't continue. I didn't want to think about the horrors that she had endured. There was nothing I could do to change it. Stuffing my seething rage at God back down, I took several deep breaths, staring at my cup of tea that had gone cold.

I felt disconnected as I wandered back into the living room. The movie credits were rolling as I arrived. Elaine stretched and yawned. Judith was fast asleep. Nora was curled in a chair, a blanket covering her. She yawned, too. "That was a stupid movie."

Elaine chuckled softly so she wouldn't wake Judith. "Yes, it was. At least you got spared from that misery." She reached for my hand. "You, okay?"

"Yeah. I'm fine. Just thinking."

"Thinking is good. What were you thinking?"

"Oh, just stuff."

"Okay." She shrugged, not willing to push me to open up. "You want some more tea? Or how about some cheesecake? Judith and I picked up one from the bakery on our way home from supper. You want some?"

I thought about my supper sitting in a foil pan in the fridge—but I was a big girl. I could have dessert without finishing my supper. "Just a small piece."

I linked arms with Nora, and the three of us walked into the kitchen. Andy arrived home in time to join us for fresh tea and a fluffy piece of strawberry cheesecake. It was just what I needed. Or maybe it was the company? Knowing I wasn't alone while I sorted out the truths from the lies in this life I'd constructed for myself. Without these grounding forces, I think I would choose to fly to the moon and never come back. But I had a family who loved me, and though the road ahead was uncertain, I was on the path. One step at a time.

CHAPTER NINETEEN

The next morning, Nora headed back to school. I told her I would give her a note to stay out another day, but she wanted to go back. The resilience of youth, I suppose. Judith, Elaine, and I were lingering over a third cup of coffee when the doorbell rang.

I opened the door to a young police constable. My heart flipped upside down. My mouth went dry. No more, *please*. No more.

"Sorry to disturb you, ma'am. I'm Constable Tim Chase. I came to inform you that you can now enter your daughter's home. The investigation is complete."

The relief flooded back so quickly that I nearly fainted. "Thank you."

"Now, normally, they would just call, but I wanted to come by to offer my condolences in person. I knew your daughter and was quite fond of her." My expression must have been peculiar because he laughed. "I know. I met her at a party in Crawford about six months ago, and we had a couple of coffee dates. She was captivating." He blushed. "Well, to me, anyway."

I looked at this man, who was hardly more than a boy himself. He wasn't handsome, and his pale complexion showed scars from a severe case of teenage acne. His eyes were intense and gray, and I knew he wasn't Brenda's type. But for one second, I wished with all my heart that she had found him attractive and been safe in his arms instead of facing her executioner.

There was an awkward silence as my mind raced to find words. Shaking my head, I said, "I'm sorry. I don't know what to say."

He smiled at me, and I saw the goodness on his face. "Well, that's all I wanted to say." He reached for my hand and squeezed it. "I can see where your daughter got her beauty." Then, he was galloping down the stairs. I watched until he climbed behind the wheel of his cruiser before I closed the door.

"I was just about to come and see what was up," Elaine said as I entered the kitchen.

I told them what had transpired. "I think he liked her, but she wasn't interested in him. He isn't that much older than her. If only they were dating. She wouldn't be dead."

Elaine and Judith exchanged looks.

"What?" I asked.

"You can't live in a 'what if' or an 'if only' world," Judith said.

My heart fluttered wildly as my temper surged. "Well, you're doing quite fine living there yourself while your husband is off somewhere having sex with a woman young enough to be your daughter."

All the color drained from her face. Her mouth dropped open, and then she crumpled. My regret was instant. "Oh, Judith, I'm sorry. I shouldn't have said that."

She continued to sob. Elaine moved to the chair next to her. "Come on, honey. You know Audrey didn't mean that. She's hurting, too."

Judith pulled herself together while I sat there, berating myself for my insensitivity. I lashed out because I didn't like what I heard. I knew it wasn't beneficial to spin alternate realities for an outcome I wasn't happy with. It changed nothing. But being told that and knowing it are two different things.

"You know, the hardest thing about your husband being unfaithful is wondering what's wrong with you. How often have I looked at myself in the mirror and tried to see what he saw? I have spent hours thinking about our lives together and wondering if I missed the warning signs or if he was ever faithful?"

She took a tissue that Elaine passed her and blew her nose several times. "Shane was a good provider. He let me stay home with the kids when they were small. He worked long hours, but he always came home. Then, when Justin went to school, I found a part-time job, and things changed. I don't think I was aware of it at the time. It was subtle, you know." She looked at us for confirmation. We nodded.

"Anyway, he stopped … you know." She blushed. "We went weeks without touching each other. I was chasing the kids and working, and for the first time, I felt a sense of fulfillment—I had it all. A husband who loved me, three adorable kids, and a little job that brought me a sense of community, not to mention a tiny wage that let me buy things for myself without having to ask."

"Maybe that was the problem. Maybe you hurt his male pride. You didn't need him anymore."

"What kind of bullshit is that? I didn't need him because I could buy his Christmas present with my money. He was my husband!"

We sat there in silence. I didn't know what to tell her.

"Anyway," she finally continued. "When I mentioned to him, we hadn't … you know … he obliged me, but it was functional. Any intercourse we had after that was at my request, and it never felt loving or intimate."

She laughed then, a bitter laugh that oozed pain and heartache. "Well, that's not as shocking as finding lipstick on your husband's collar, smelling someone else's perfume, or laying there alone at night, knowing he was curled up with someone else."

Another silence fell over the table. I was thinking about Andy and how glad I was that he was mine, and before I could stop myself—I was lifting a silent prayer to God that he would always be faithful.

"Anyway, we have had some knockdown, drag-out fights, and I've threatened to divorce him more often than I've said 'I love you' in the past couple of years. It's insane to live like that, but I don't know what else to do. He's my husband, and I don't want to lose him, but I don't know how to get him back from the clutches of someone, like you said, young enough to be my daughter."

"Have you tried counseling?" Elaine asked.

"I wanted to go in the early days, but Shane wouldn't go. He denied anything was wrong. Now, he wants to go, and I don't know if it will change anything. I don't know what to do. I don't even know if I love him anymore. Maybe I should just get a divorce and move on."

"If he will go for counseling, then you should go," Elaine said. "Don't let pride stop you from fixing something you don't really want to throw away."

"Don't I? Even if we go for counseling, what's going to change?" She sighed. "Maybe I'm just afraid to hear the reality. I don't want to know how many bimbos he's been with. I don't want someone pointing the finger at me and telling me that because I refused fellatio, Shane needed to find someone who would give it to him."

Another shock. Although I knew what that was, I didn't want to think about Shane and my sister that way. I didn't want to think of anyone that way—I was uncomfortable with this conversation. I fidgeted in my chair, wondering how to change the conversation, yet knowing I wouldn't.

"It's okay to be afraid, Judith." Elaine placated. "You wouldn't be normal if you weren't afraid. But think of it this way: how afraid will you be on your own? Isn't it worth it for a chance at getting something back or making what you had back then better?"

Tears filled Judith's eyes and spilled down her cheeks. "How did you get to be so smart?"

My sisters threw their arms around each other, both sobbing with relief. Judith would slip away in the early afternoon, call her husband, and agree to counseling. She would go home the next morning, ready to fight for what she wanted. By Christmas, she and Shane would work hard at making a life together that mattered. It was a hard walk, full of pitfalls and traps, but together, they would weather all the storms. The next time I saw Judith, she differed from the woman who sat at my table that morning. Her confidence would no longer be phony—her strength came from within rather than from arrogance. She was happier than I'd ever seen her.

CHAPTER TWENTY

Later, as promised, Pastor Dan appeared at the back door. I was not looking forward to having a conversation with him. I was grateful that Elaine and Judith would be here to buffer things.

He was coming to offer his condolences, but he wouldn't be a pastor worth his salt if he didn't ensure that spiritually, I was doing okay—which I wasn't. I was having a major crisis of faith, but I didn't wish to talk to anyone about it—not until I figured things out, and I hardly had time for that. Maybe when my sisters were gone, there would be time to figure things out.

I took Pastor Dan's coat and showed him to the table. He accepted coffee over tea, so I poured him a cup and puttered around, putting cookies on the plate. I was just biding my time, waiting for Judith and Elaine to appear. When they hadn't, I excused myself and rushed to find them.

They were in the guest room. Judith was packing, and Elaine was sitting on the bed watching. "You guys, Pastor Dan is here!"

"We know," Elaine said. "We heard you when you announced it."

"So, why aren't you downstairs with me right now?"

"Because he isn't here to see us. He's here to see you," Judith piped in.

I shot her a dark look. "But I can't do this. I don't know what to say to him. Please don't make me do this on my own."

Elaine got off the bed and wrapped her arms around me. "I know you're scared. We won't be too far away if you need us, but you need to do this." She guided me toward the door. "Besides, you're being rude by leaving him all alone in the kitchen."

I left reluctantly. My stomach was in knots as I entered the kitchen. I poured myself a cup of coffee with shaking hands and then sat across the table from Pastor Dan. He was so young, barely ten years older than Brenda. How was he going to make it as a spiritual leader?

We sat in silence for a few minutes. Pastor Dan took a second cookie and dunked it into his coffee before he spoke. "It was distressing to hear the news about Brenda. I think it's a tragedy that domestic violence claims so many innocent victims each year. I know I don't have all the answers, but I have been praying."

"Have you now." I snapped. "Well, it seems to me that God isn't interested in answering prayers."

Embarrassed, I clapped my hands over my mouth and burst into tears.

Pastor Dan took my outburst in stride. "When Nora told me you hadn't gone to church yesterday, I wondered how you were really doing."

I wanted to shout at him, but it wasn't his fault. He was simply the emissary. How many times have we been told not to shoot the messenger?

I pulled myself together. "I'm sorry, I shouldn't have said that."

"Why not? Is it not the truth?"

"No. Yes. I mean, it's how I feel, not necessarily the truth."

He chuckled. "Well, at least you know your feelings aren't necessarily the truth. That's a good start."

I let those words sink in. If Pastor Newberry had said them, it would have offended me. They were patronizing words. But coming from this young pastor, they seemed encouraging. Perhaps it was his tone or his manner. I didn't know.

"I can tell you, Pastor Dan, that I have been a faithful follower all my life. I have never swerved from service and have been in a pew every Sunday, praising Him with my whole heart. I have prayed for everyone and everything—spent days fasting for causes dear to me, and my reward for all of this? My daughter gets murdered."

He sat quietly, not saying a word for several moments. He didn't appear shocked or seem to struggle for an answer. Quietly, he reached over and laid his hand over mine. I didn't pull away. "That was not your reward."

Tears rolled down my cheeks as he continued. "God didn't want this to happen."

"But He didn't stop it either." I wailed. The pain in my chest threatened to tear me in two.

"I know. And it makes no sense to us. It's unconscionable and, dare I say, barbaric. And I will pray that you find your way through. This is a wilderness experience for you. I imagine you feel abandoned by God and angry. Don't shut yourself down to avoid these feelings. Work through them."

I nodded, the tears flowing freely. "Is this a test, then?"

"No." He shook his head. "God doesn't need to test your faith. He knows your heart. He is with you now, whether or not you believe it. And I am not far away, and if you need to talk, please come see me." He drained his cup. "Now, before I go, can I pray for you?"

Too distressed to speak, I simply nodded. He stood and placed a hand on my head. "Lord, I thank you for your compassion and your great love. I ask for mercy, Father, for Audrey. I ask that You guide her footsteps and thoughts so she might find her way through. Keep her feet on the path, Father, and keep her from stumbling or getting lost in the myriads of beliefs and explanations that will assail her in the coming months. Help her know that sometimes there is no explanation when evil triumphs. Lord, I also ask that You help her know Brenda is with You and that one day, they will be reunited. Please wrap Your loving arms around her and keep her safe as she journeys through this troublesome situation. Help her know You in a deeper way and show her Your love and mercy. I thank You for Your loving grace. Fill her now, Father, with Your love. In Jesus name, I pray. Amen."

I can't explain how prayer works or how faith plays a part in our feelings, but I felt marginally better after his prayer. He didn't stick around long after that. He left, but not before he reassured me again that he was only a phone call away.

I walked him to the front door, gathering the mail from the mailbox before returning to the kitchen. Using a knife to slit open the envelope from Eden's Funeral Home, the sight of how much Brenda's funeral cost shocked me. It was likely less than we would have spent on her wedding, but I would have looked forward to that bill. This one hurt. I felt taken advantage of and knew it was my fault for allowing someone else to look after the details.

I tucked Pastor Dan's card in the cabinet where I put all the important papers along with the bill, and then I cleaned off the table. It was time to get ready for lunch.

CHAPTER TWENTY-ONE

Over a lunch of grilled cheese sandwiches and cream of tomato soup, Judith suggested we go shopping. She wanted to get a few new outfits before she returned home. Grandville has a small clothing shop that caters to low-budget fashions, such as cheap knitwear and denim. We opted to go to Crawford, which was only a half-hour drive.

I texted Nora to see if she wanted to join us. She declined as the drama club met that afternoon. Three plays were on the list, and she hoped she could persuade the group to do something other than the old standbys. I wished her luck, and we set off for Crawford.

Several stores in Crawford would meet our needs. I drove to the mall first and hit one of the chain stores, hoping there was a sale. Judith tried on several outfits, and I was jealous of her style. She was a good five inches taller than me and slender as a teenager. The clothes she tried on hung beautifully. I had a muffin top, which detracted from every outfit I put on. Not that I was shopping today.

At least it hadn't crossed my mind. Elaine was flicking through the clothes racks, pulling out this or that. She was in search of something. After Judith went into the dressing room, I sat on the chair outside and waited to offer my opinion. Clothes shopping and I were old enemies. We got together when we had to—we kept a wary eye on one another, and one of us usually came out as the winner. It wasn't usually me. I had gone home frequently with nothing new.

Judith found a stunning silk blouse and black pants that showed off her long legs. She draped a set of fake pearls over the dark blue material and pulled her hair up. We agreed she looked amazing. She redressed in her own clothes and made her purchase.

The next place we stopped was somewhere I'd never been before but had wanted to try. Urban Threads. It was also in the mall. Several ladies from church had been and said the quality was good and the prices were reasonable. I had thought that one day before Christmas, Brenda and I could have a girls' day out and do some shopping. Brenda was good at helping me find clothes.

Thinking of Brenda brought a shroud down over my day. I had put her out of my mind, trying to concentrate on having fun with my sisters, but she seemed unwilling to be sidelined. I touched Elaine's arm and said, "I'll meet you at the car." I left before she could say anything.

The weekday mall crowd was thinner than the weekend crowd, but I still got a few curious looks as I trotted down the long hallways toward the exit. Tears poured down my cheeks. I didn't bother to wipe them. I just kept walking.

CHAPTER TWENTY-TWO

Stepping outside, I gulped in some refreshing air. I hadn't realized how cloying the mall had been until I felt the cold snap of the winter air upon my face. I unlocked the car from a distance, climbed in, and closed the door behind me. Bending my head over the steering wheel, I let my grief free. The car grew too warm, so I turned the ignition until I could roll down the window slightly. As my sorrow lessened again, I rummaged for a tissue to wipe my eyes.

I had barely got myself settled when Elaine and Judith appeared. "Pop the trunk, will you?" Judith asked as Elaine climbed into the back seat behind me. I did as I was told. She put her purchase inside and then got in the front seat beside me.

"You, okay?" she asked.

"Yeah. I think I'll have many of these when her memory is sharp." She patted my arm, and I started the car. "You still want to try Fashion Sense."

"Absolutely," she exclaimed. "This is fun. I haven't shopped with anyone in forever. It's nice getting opinions other than the sales assistant who is intent on making a commission."

"I hear you."

A few minutes later, we were entering Fashion Sense. It was a nice store with lots of room and lots of merchandise. We each went in a different direction, searching through racks and pulling out items that appealed to us. Judith entered the dressing room, and we took items we thought would suit her tall, lanky frame.

Elaine brought a brilliant blue dress over and handed it to me. "I think this dress would look good on you."

I held it up in front and then pulled it back against me. Elaine stopped me when I turned the price tag over. "No," she said. "Don't look at how much it costs. Just try it on."

"Okay."

I slipped out of my jeans and blouse, catching a view of myself in the mirror. I sighed. My bra was ill-fitting, my panties had seen better days, and I wore knee-high socks carefully folded down to my ankles. Overwhelmed by my feelings of worthlessness, I sat on the bench, feeling fat and unattractive.

"You ready?" Elaine called as she tapped on the door.

"Almost." I removed the dress from the hanger and slipped it over my head. I couldn't get the zipper, so I opened the door and turned around so Elaine could zip it for me. Facing the mirror again, I noticed how the blue in the dress poured color into my eyes. The dress hugged me in the right places, and because there was no waistline, it was slimming.

I turned around. Elaine was smiling. "I told you. This dress looks amazing on you."

Judith popped out of the dressing room next door, wearing a mauve blouse and high-waisted black pants. "You look amazing. That is such a splendid color on you."

"Thanks," I replied, walking down the short hall to the three-way mirror.

"Those socks really make the outfit." Elaine giggled.

Her words were funny, and ordinarily, I would have laughed. But I was raw, and humor wasn't part of my being at the moment. I bristled and ignored her.

In the mirror, I looked at myself from all angles. It was a wonderful dress. The material felt nice against my skin. It had pleats that helped to give me hips. The drop waist gave me height and minimized my broad shoulders. It was a perfect fit.

"Are you going to buy it?" Judith asked. She reappeared from the stall wearing a different outfit.

"I don't know. Maybe."

"Get it—the designer created this dress for you," Elaine said.

"We'll see. Could you unzip me?" She pulled the zipper down, taking a moment to caress my shoulder. A wave of affection rushed over me. Elaine had always been supportive and encouraging. I closed the door to the dressing room, slipped off the dress, and looked at the price tag. My eyebrows shot up. Wow, that was more than I spent on clothes in a year. I couldn't afford it. As nice as it was, I couldn't justify spending that kind of money on one garment.

I left the dress hanging in the dressing room and walked out into the store. Judith was at the till with some items, and Elaine was flipping through the rack closest to the door.

"You're not getting that dress?" Judith asked.

I shook my head.

"Why not?"

Not wanting to share this information with the clerk behind the counter, I gestured by rubbing my thumb over my fingers, the universal sign for money.

"Oh," she said, turning back to the clerk.

"Let's go wait in the car," I said to Elaine. She followed me to the door. "We'll be in the car," I called back to Judith.

"Okay," she said.

"So, why didn't you get the dress?" Elaine asked when we neared the car.

"It was too expensive."

"But it looked so good on you like someone designed it for you."

"I know. I just can't justify the cost."

"Well, it's not like you and Andy can't afford it."

"We're not made of money," I snapped. How dare she say something so uncouth! "I'm done talking about it. I'm not getting the dress, and that's the end of it."

"Okay. Sorry. I guess I hit a nerve."

And that was all it took. I cried. "The funeral costs were astronomical. I couldn't believe how expensive it had been and how quickly the funeral home had submitted their bill for payment. They expected the invoice to be paid upon receipt. I can't believe that I let this happen. What kind of a person lets someone else handle funeral arrangements? I mean the things we paid for."

"Really? I did not know."

"I haven't even shown it to Andy. It came this morning. It makes me sad it costs so much for something that we all must go through. Just think about it. No one is getting out of here alive, and that greedy Grim Reaper is waiting at the end with his hand out, demanding a king's ransom to put your body in the cold, hard ground."

The conversation died there. I don't think either of us knew what to say to that. It was a wake-up call to put something in place before my kids had to pay to do this for me. A minute later, Judith came out with a couple of bags. Having finished shopping, we headed back to Grandville.

CHAPTER TWENTY-THREE

There was a definite chill in the air now. Winter wasn't far away. The forecast might even call for snow, but I hadn't checked the weather since Brenda died. It would come when it was time and could go just the same. I wasn't looking forward to it. My least favorite time of year.

When I opened the door, I could hear Nora's music blaring through the house. At least it was Christian music, I used to remind Andy. Now, it set my teeth on edge, and I wanted to stomp up the stairs, hammer on her door, and tell her to have some respect. But I didn't. I gritted my teeth and headed to the kitchen to start supper. Elaine followed. Judith said she'd just put her bags away and be right back down to help. She hadn't been gone a minute when the volume diminished on the music. My shoulders relaxed, so I rummaged through the fridge for inspiration. I put some brown rice in the cooker. I found a package of pork chops in the freezer. The pork chops popped apart with a little persuasion. I counted one for each of us, two for Andy, and an extra two, just in case.

With the pork chops defrosting in the frying pan set on low, I peeled the potatoes while Elaine took some lettuce, celery, tomatoes, and red onions to make a salad. When the potatoes were on the stove, I made the sauce for the pork chops. Real cream, fresh mushrooms, chicken stock. I loved cooking from scratch. I know many people use cream of mushroom soup on their pork chops, but my sauce is better than that. Or at least I thought so, and I got no complaints.

Supper was lively with Judith's impending departure. She was excited about reconciliation and finally getting her marriage back on track. The room buzzed with good cheer. Brenda would have loved to have been there, and when I went to get the ice cream for dessert, I shed a tear that she wasn't there. I didn't want to be the one to set a pall over tonight by being maudlin about her. But I felt her absence keenly.

As I got ready for bed, I thought about the day and all that happened. The spontaneous shopping trip had been fun and fatiguing. Shopping for clothes always exhausted me, so I seldom did it. I wasn't a fashionista. Brenda often challenged me on my lack of fashion sense. I would remind her I did not need to impress anyone, and if I bought quality clothes and took care of them, they lasted years. I remember telling her I had dresses in my closet that were fifteen years old, but she'd never know that by looking at them. She would disagree, reminding me that each season had its own colors and outdated clothes would be the wrong style and color.

I would laugh at her, and she would tell me that if I wanted to be out of date, that was my business. Did it fit me? Yes. Was it comfortable? Yes. Beyond that, I didn't care. She would sigh and agree. Then I would make us a cup of tea, we would eat cookies, and she would tell me all about the people in her life. An ache opened in my belly. Who was going to tell me I was out of fashion now? Who was going to regale me with tales of adventures and misadventures on the road of life? I would miss those conversations, that simple camaraderie she allowed us to have.

No one could fill her shoes or take up where she left off. Even if Nora was interested in fashion, which she wasn't, she wasn't Brenda. My girl was gone forever, and the anger I felt in that moment was stronger than the sorrow. I wanted to pummel the creep who had done this to us—the monster who had destroyed my life without a second thought. It was a good thing he was dead, or I would have killed him myself. How dare he take what wasn't his to take?

I paced the floor and tried to calm myself down. I looked at the empty bed and directed my thoughts to Andy. He had gone back to work after supper. He rarely went back to work, and if my sisters had not been there, I might have questioned him. Instead, he kissed me on the top of my head and left without being challenged. In the past, I might have lifted him in prayer and asked God to guide him, but tonight, I knew it didn't matter. Not that I didn't want him safe, but my prayers wouldn't make it so. Prayer needed faith, and I hadn't any.

That took me back to my conversation with Pastor Dan. He was alive with faith because he had faced no testing. Give it time. He'll soon learn that God, if He exists, is a harsh taskmaster. He requires complete and utter dedication and then chooses at random whether to answer the prayers of your heart. I felt sorry for Pastor Dan. His faith would hit the windshield someday, and it would not be pretty. God abandons all, eventually.

I climbed into bed and pulled the covers up to my chin, my heart heavy with such dark thoughts. Tears threatened to fall, but I refused to give in. I steeled myself against my emotions and shoved them away. I would not allow my emotions to take me where I didn't want to go. No, I was in charge. Instead, I switched to thoughts of Nora and what my sisters had told me about her.

A lesbian? I didn't understand that, and I wondered if it were just a phase she would outgrow. I tried to remember what it was like when I was her age, but all I could see was Andy. He had always been there, part of my life and world. I couldn't imagine him away or how my life might have turned out had it not been for him.

I wished he was home so I could curl into him. I hated sleeping alone. As if my thoughts conjured him out of thin air, the door opened, and he tiptoed into the room. I felt the bed shift as he sat on the edge. Then it shifted again as he rose and moved into the bathroom. I listened as the water splashed against the porcelain sink. When I heard the thumping of his toothbrush on the sink as he tapped the water from the bristles, I knew he wouldn't be long. I felt a blast of cool air as he pulled back the covers and slipped into bed.

Waiting for only a moment, I listened to him sigh deeply before I rolled toward him. I placed my hand on his chest. He put his hand over top and squeezed. Nestling closer, he shifted to bring me even closer. I moved my hand down his body and stirred his need. I let my hand linger. He growled and pushed me back before taking charge. I let go of all my doubts, fears, and thoughts of everything as I clung to this man.

Afterward, lying in his arms, I knew that in this one thing I wouldn't change. I had defied God and his laws by marrying Andy—we were unequally yoked. So many people cautioned me that if I married Andy, he would steal my faith, and before long, I wouldn't be walking with the Lord. I would become a heathen like my husband. I felt sure that would never happen.

For twenty-five years, we had loved and laughed together as man and wife, and never once did he ever tell me not to go to church. He never changed his mind about coming, but he never stood in my way. Therefore, my faith remained intact. Until Brenda. Until murder had paid my life a visit. Evil had destroyed my faith.

Marrying Andy was the one thing I wouldn't change, not for my parents, not for God. Andy was true, and I belonged to him in a way I didn't belong anywhere else. I couldn't imagine my life without him, especially during this time when I understood nothing else. My oldest daughter's future was gone, and my youngest daughter was making a hard choice, maybe a wrong choice. It was something I didn't understand for certain.

And Logan? He was far away, and, like every man who gets to that age, he kept his own confidence. I didn't know where he was or what he was thinking most of the time. Questions would elicit unsatisfactory answers. Well, unsatisfactory to me. I wondered if Logan talked more to his dad and if he allowed himself to be more open. Or possibly they didn't talk about life the way I wanted to. I enjoyed knowing the heart issues.

Thinking about talking over heart issues, I didn't even know how to talk to Nora about her situation. I tried to imagine how Andy would deal with this if he knew. And I knew for sure that if Brenda were here, I would talk to her about it. I would ask her for advice, too. This was unfamiliar territory, and I did not know where to start. I guess there wasn't anything I could do until she told me herself. Until then, all I could do was watch and wait. I snorted. Once upon a time, I would have added prayer to that list, but no more. Life was going to be different, that's for sure. I exhaled and pushed my thoughts aside, focusing on Andy's light snoring. As I fully relaxed, sleep came for me in time.

CHAPTER TWENTY-FOUR

Judith left the next morning. A flurry of goodbyes echoed through the house as she whirled into and out of each room. Shane's early morning call had elevated her mood. He had confirmed their appointment with a therapist for the following afternoon. It looked like he wanted to give their marriage the attention it deserved.

I was proud of her. She would face a lot of ugliness in the days ahead. The thought of saving her marriage was paramount, though there was no guarantee. She'd have to forgive much, and maybe it would be too much in the end. I couldn't imagine finding out that your husband was sleeping with a much younger woman. I shook my head to clear the images.

It was snowing. Winter was putting its stamp on the world. Never looking forward to this season, I trembled with rage as I watched the flakes float from the sky. I wanted to yell at God, to tell Him He was being a jerk by letting it snow. He needed to take it back—to bring back summer and, most of all, Brenda. Even though I knew I was being unreasonable, part of me insisted on behaving this way.

After we'd waved Judith off and Nora was off to school, Elaine and I sat with another cup of coffee. The house had settled into the quiet calmness that I used to love in the mornings. This was when I would pull out my Bible and devotional and spend a little time with God. I sometimes wrote about my feelings, but I often searched through my music to find the perfect song to complement the message.

"You're lost in thought," Elaine commented.

My smile didn't reach my eyes. "I was just thinking of how my mornings used to be and thinking that it seemed long ago."

"Morning devotions?"

I nodded.

"You'll get back there, I'm sure."

"Maybe," I said. "Maybe not. I don't know what I want anymore."

"Well, don't make any rash decisions. You have lots of time to decide."

I nodded.

We returned to our separate thoughts, sipping our coffees. "What do you want to do today?"

"Well, now that Judith is gone, getting that room back in order is a priority, and then you can get settled. After that, the usual things are laundry, vacuuming, and dusting. The trifecta of housecleaning."

"Let's get started."

It was so much nicer to strip and remake beds with a second person. In no time, we had all the beds remade and the washing machine chugging away at its first load. I pulled out the vacuum, and Elaine dusted. By the time Nora and Andy came home for lunch, we had the house shipshape. I made a batch of grilled cheese sandwiches to go with the chicken soup simmering on the stove.

I sipped my cup of soup, listening as Nora filled us in on the latest drama at school. I smiled, remembering that everything about high school had been dramatic for Brenda, too. The only difference between the two girls was Nora was outside the drama, and Brenda was always in the thick of it. I felt a constriction in my chest and winced at the memory of her face as she recounted how somebody had said or done something horrible. She wanted to help everyone and make every situation right.

Brenda became known as the fixer, the one with the solutions. She thought long and deeply about problems and shared her insights. This early taste of psychology set her feet on the path to a degree. She only struggled with answers when she was too close to the situation or the target of someone's arrows. At those times, she became blinded by her understanding, being too forceful and opinionated as she tried to stop someone from making the wrong decision.

I wondered if that was what happened between her and Andrea. As girls, they had been close, and perhaps her affection for her friend had limited her ability to see the situation clearly. She could be vocal and overbearing when she thought she was right. Something had been going on, and I regretted I hadn't asked questions. Did she know this Caleb person was dangerous? Or did she think she was out of reach? Why hadn't I been more curious?

I knew why. I had lifted the situation to God and expected He had the situation in His hand, He was in control, and He was working out all things just as He promised in His word. How could I trust Him again? How was this ever going to get better?

I mentally shook off my reverie. Time to get off that path to nowhere. He hadn't done what I thought, and there was no fixing that. It was done and over, and going back to it, revisiting my disillusionment, would change nothing.

I cleared the table after Nora and Andy had gone. Then Elaine and I had another cup of coffee. We moved into the living room so we could sit comfortably. I was thinking a little nap might be in order. I was tired, and I had been exhausted since I got the news. The things that needed to be done gave me the energy I didn't possess, but now, maybe, it was time to rest.

"You look tired," Elaine said as if reading my thoughts.

"I am. I was just thinking I might need a nap."

"So, go have a nap. I'll make sure there is something on the table for supper. You just rest. And if you need me, just call. I won't be far."

A wave of guilt washed over me. What kind of person was I to leave my guest in charge of my family? I was the same person who couldn't save her daughter. The negative energy took hold, and I was powerless to stop it. I held back my tears until I was in my bedroom. I walked over to the bed, flopped onto it, and cried.

At first, I was too hot, but then a chill washed over me, and I scrambled to pull some blankets over me. I lay there with my teeth chattering, trying to get warm. My breathing slowed, and I fell into a troubled sleep. When I awoke, my energy was low, and my mood was black. I heard some activity in the house. Nora was home. I got up, changed my clothes, washed my face, and headed downstairs.

It was mid-afternoon. Elaine and Nora were in the kitchen, talking. I did not want to eavesdrop. That wasn't my intention. It just happened that way.

"How can I tell Mom when she's got so much to deal with?" Nora said.

"Well, your mom is your mom. She knows and loves you, and this is a big secret to be carrying around on your own. She will not love you any less, you know."

I heard a cry of pain, short but sharp. "How do you know that?"

Part of me wanted to push open the swinging door, wrap my arms around her, and tell her the same thing. But the darker side I had woken with stood there, unable to move, listening.

"Because honey, she is your mother. She loves the bones of you. You are hers, and maybe you won't understand this kind of love until you're a mother, but believe me, nothing separates a mother from her children. Nothing."

"You're sure?" Nora pleaded.

"Yes, I'm positive. Lots of people struggle to understand

themselves. The more honest you are with that, the more honest you are with your life."

"Okay. But maybe I need to change? Maybe this isn't the right choice for me. I mean, I was trying to understand everything, and I thought it would be okay because Brenda could give Mom grandkids. But that's not possible anymore."

"Don't forget you have a brother. He can give your mother grandbabies. And besides, with all the medical innovations, you can have your own child with artificial insemination or in-vitro fertilization." Then she explained what those were.

Nora, sounding more secure, said, "I never knew that. I was sort of trying to figure out how I would give up being a mom. It's not that I have thought about it lots or anything, but when I babysat sometimes, I'd feel like this was important to me, being with kids and one day having my own. But I knew from health class that you need … you know."

Elaine chuckled. "Yes, I know."

There was a quiet moment, and then I heard a chair slide on the floor. "I'll set the table for supper," Nora said.

I turned around and tiptoed back to the stairs. Then I went into the living room and looked out the window at the monochrome world. The sky was darkening, the night was falling, and the world outside was white with slashes of gray where the sidewalks lay.

Someone shoveled our walk. Maybe Elaine. Maybe Andy had done it at lunch or sent someone from the shop. I didn't know, but I was grateful. Elaine came through and, seeing me in the living room, came over to stand behind me. I felt her warmth on my back and leaned into it.

"I was just coming to get you. How are you feeling?"

"A little better. Did you shovel the walks?"

"Yes, I did. It did me a world of good, too. It's not too cold out yet."

"Supper smells good." I took a huge sniff to amplify my words.

We stood like that for a few more minutes.

Nora came in, having set the table for supper. "Hi, Mom."

"How was school?" I asked.

"Same old, I guess. The teachers all said nice things about Brenda, and they send their condolences."

I nodded. Weariness settled on my shoulders. Is this how life was going to be now? I would be the recipient of condolences—hating that thought and longing for life to go back to normal. I wanted to be the carefree woman who danced around her kitchen singing praises to the Lord, who cooked and cleaned for her family, who prayed for the sick and expected healing. I wanted to have faith that this world wasn't a horrible place. I didn't want to think this was merely a holding cell where we learned to live with pain and loss.

I watched as Andy came down the street and parked in the driveway. His headlights illuminated the snow on the bushes before he turned them off, plunging the yard into darkness once more. I saw his shadow emerge from the truck and walk toward the side door. Time for supper.

We consumed Elaine's lovely meal in silence, each of us lost in our own thoughts. Elaine tried to get us talking, but no one seemed to have the desire to carry the ball. We lapsed into silence, and finally, she gave up. Andy wiped his mouth with a paper napkin and announced that he was going back to work. I felt surprised at that. Really? Again? The old me would have questioned him. But I was too tired, and though I knew something was amiss, I had no fight in me.

After the dishes were done and the kitchen tidied, Elaine and I sat in front of the television. The shows came and went, but I didn't register much. I wasn't there. I wasn't engaged.

Nora appeared at about nine, ready for bed. She had her hair pulled back into a ponytail. She looked so young, much more youthful than her age—fresh-faced and beautiful. Looking back, I think she wanted to talk, but I didn't pick up on that. I was still sitting in my bowl of self-pity, stewing in my juices. Miserable.

She must have realized it, or maybe she just couldn't find her courage. After ten minutes, Nora kissed me on the cheek and left the room. Elaine gave me a quizzical look. I ignored her. She was Nora's confidante, not me. I wanted to shoot her an angry look. I wanted to pick a fight with her. She was supposed to be helping, but she was just interfering. Why didn't she just go home where she belonged?

I was being unfair. I knew that in my heart, but something else was gaining control, and I was too tired to fight. It was an ugly, putrid little monster set on destroying me. I had somehow given it permission to live in the place of compassion and understanding. I fed it angry thoughts, and it grew uglier and more rancid. There was a part of me that delighted in misery. I had a ton of that, too.

I wanted to be alone but didn't want to go to my room. I sat there mentally trying to force Elaine to go to bed and leave me alone. Instead, she offered to make tea.

"And sympathy?" I snapped. She looked hurt, and I felt bad for a few seconds before my little monster reminded me she deserved it. I wanted to argue, but I didn't.

"Okay. I think I'll just leave you in peace." She stood and left the room. When she had gone, I pulled my feet up underneath me and wept. I didn't want to be this person, but I didn't know how not to be. I had tossed my oar into the stormy waters and was rudderless. Instinctively, I knew that if I didn't find my way, I would be swamped under by the violent waves.

CHAPTER TWENTY-FIVE

The next morning, Tiffany called, wanting to get together. I put her off—I had nothing to offer and certainly didn't want to talk. I was still stewing over my life, trying to make sense of things.

Elaine, bless her, made breakfast for everyone. I lay in bed long after Andy had left for work. I didn't want to get up—I didn't want to have to deal with my life.

When I made an appearance, the kitchen sparkled, and a fresh pot of coffee was brewing. I could hear Elaine in the laundry room. I poured myself a coffee and popped two pieces of bread into the toaster. When Elaine returned to the kitchen, she smiled at me. "How are you feeling?"

I knew in my heart that she was speaking out of concern, but I heard a patronizing tone. I bristled and didn't answer.

"That good, huh?"

"How do you want me to feel?" I snapped.

"I want you to be honest, which you are. But I also want you to remember that I am not the enemy. I am here to help."

"Really?"

"Yes, really. Now, what is bothering you?"

"My daughter is dead. That's what's bothering me."

"Well, your daughter was dead yesterday morning, too, and you didn't want to fight with me."

And just like that, my anger dissipated, and I burst into tears.

"I'm sorry. I didn't mean to make you cry." Elaine grabbed the tissue box off the fridge and brought it over. She pulled her chair next to mine, took my hand, and waited for me to calm down.

"I don't know what's wrong with me. I am so angry. It's gotten worse now that I am not focused on being the hostess, you know. Looking after everybody. It's like I have time to be angry now, and I don't enjoy feeling this way."

I blew my nose and grabbed another handful of tissues before continuing. "Yesterday, I heard you and Nora talking, and that made me mad. Why can't she talk to me? She should be able to talk to me, yet she's talking to you, and I'm angry at you for being there to hear her and grateful that you were."

Elaine nodded but didn't interrupt.

"I am angry that God didn't protect Brenda. I can't imagine how life is going to be without her. She was going to change the world, and now she's gone, and I feel let down. There's that loser—Emil Harvey—who lives on Oak Drive. He beats his wife and kids and is in and out of jail—a real prince of a man. Yet, he's allowed to live, and my girl is gone. Does God care? Is He even there? Have I been fooling myself all these years, wanting to believe some super-being is watching over us, keeping us safe? I want to scream at the world to stop—to rail against the brutality of this world even though I would willingly beat that son of a bitch who killed her to death. I am all over the place and don't know what to do anymore."

"Have you thought about talking to someone? A therapist or something?"

"I've thought about it but don't know where to go."

"Well, go to your family doctor and request a referral. I'm sure they have lists of professionals for every situation."

I nodded. "That's good. I'll talk to Andy, and maybe we can go together."

"Even if he doesn't want to go, you must. You know that, right?"

I nodded again because I knew I was out of my depth. I needed someone with insight to help me, or I would not have made it out of this quagmire intact. After I made my appointment, I buttered the two pieces of cold toast. Elaine offered to make me fresh toast, but I didn't care enough to be bothered. Cold toast would suffice.

When I had finished my breakfast, she suggested we go for a walk. It wasn't too cold, but I wasn't sure I was up to it. "Well, let's walk downtown and have lunch at that coffee shop on Main Street. It makes decent sandwiches. It'll do you good to get out of the house, and the fresh air can't hurt."

I couldn't argue with her, so after we had tidied up a bit and she had started another load of laundry, we bundled up and began our walk. We hadn't gone a block when she brought up Nora.

"She's confused," Elaine said. "She doesn't want to be different. She hates that she's going to disappoint you and Andy. Her life has also been turned upside down. She's struggling to find her way, too."

"I know, and I am glad you've been there for her. I don't know what good I am to anyone feeling this way. Logan and Nora are not getting what they need from me. Brenda is getting all my attention, and she's not even here to appreciate it."

"That will change as you heal."

"But will I though? I just keep feeling that life will never be the same, and I don't know how it will all shake out. Before this happened, I knew who I was and where I was going. I had direction—maybe not enough ambition—but my life was organized and content. I had everything I needed, and now I feel like, in one moment of madness, I lost it all."

"You haven't lost it all. The only change is your perception."

"So, what you're saying is that I can't see things clearly?"

"No. Don't put words in my mouth. I'm saying that you're seeing life differently because Brenda's death is a tremendous blow. Your world is off its axis, but it will right itself, and things will become clearer again. In the meantime, you find someone who can help shift things into perspective, and you work on being patient because it will be a long process."

Patience. How I loathed that word. It was a grand word for people who had it, but it was the thorn in the side of those who lacked it. I never needed patience before. My life ticked along like a well-oiled machine. The loose cog of Brenda's untimely death had twisted the mechanics of my world, and nothing worked the way it should. I took a deep breath. Patience. I wanted to sock Elaine in the mouth for saying it out loud.

Elaine and I walked through the residential areas, winding up and down streets to extend our walk, putting us downtown closer to noon. As we passed the old-fashioned burger joint on Main Street, I saw Pastor Newberry pull out of the parking lot. He waved to us. I didn't wave back. On the other side of the parking area, I noticed Andy's truck exiting the lot and heading through the back alley. I figured he was getting his lunch since we would not be home.

It was a delightful treat to have lunch out. I ordered a soup and sandwich combo and one for Nora, who joined us when she was out of school. She arrived at the same time our meals did. "Perfect timing."

Elaine kept the conversation light. I followed her cue, not trusting myself to start the topic on my mind. Before Nora left to return to school, I told her I would try therapy. I wondered if she wanted me to make her an appointment, too.

When I mentioned it, her eyes widened in surprise, and she looked at Elaine. I knew she thought her secret was out in the open. Then she settled as I explained that I felt the entire family could use some guidance about what had happened to Brenda—making sense of a senseless situation. She agreed to try it if that's what I thought was best.

The weekend arrived, and Elaine's stay with us was ending. She had to get back to her family and her life, and there was a renewed feeling of loss at her pending departure. The morning she was leaving, I wept about everything. The toothpaste tube was empty, the coffee was too hot, and the toast was too dark.

Andy offered to warm up her car when he hauled her suitcase out. She and I stood inside the door with tears streaming down our faces. "Now you call if you need anything, you hear," she said, her voice cracking.

I could only nod. I didn't trust my voice. Opening my arms, we hugged like it was the last time we would see each other. Maybe it would be. I didn't know. Life is unpredictable. I thought I would have Brenda long into my old age. Instead, she was gone as I hit middle age. I had no guarantees—no one did.

Andy came back in. He gave Elaine a brief hug, thanking her for all her help. Then Nora hugged her. When she stepped out the door and down the steps, I wanted to yell at her to come back. She turned when she got to the bottom and waved again. I thought my heart would burst. How was I going to manage on my own?

The weekend passed with a few calls from Logan. It was a pleasant change, as it was usual for us to call him. He seemed to do well with his schooling and away from all the drama of his sister's passing. Wanting to ensure he was doing well, I kept repeating my pointed questions. Andy finally took the phone away from me.

Afterward, Andy and I argued about that. He felt I was smothering Logan, and I insisted I wanted to establish he was doing okay and not just telling us what he thought we wanted to hear. Andy was certain that Logan would tell us if he wasn't doing well, but I knew our children weren't always truthful with us. I planned to make an appointment with the therapist for Logan when he was home for Christmas.

When I mentioned therapy, Andy seemed elated. He agreed I should go now, and if it helped, he would also go. I felt like a guinea pig. He might as well have said, "You go, Audrey, and see if it works. If it does, great—if it doesn't, then I have lost nothing." That really ticked me off. Of course, I got angry about many things that never bothered me before.

Andy and I had done so well during the first weeks following Brenda's death. Now, we seemed to drift apart, and maybe that was all my fault. I didn't sense in him any anger, but I felt a chasm opening between us that had never been there before. I didn't have the energy to bridge it and hoped that therapy would help arrest it before we were living separate lives.

CHAPTER TWENTY-SIX

December came in a flurry of flakes and cold temperatures. I dreaded thinking about Christmas. Because of the weather, I canceled my first appointment with the therapist. A storm had come in, icing the highways to glass. The police had requested that those not needing to drive stay home. I debated with myself, and then I lost my nerve. It seemed easier to cancel than to face the demons I might have to slay after driving on icy roads.

I knew I wasn't being true to myself and my needs and wondered if I had made the wrong decision by choosing a therapist in Crawford over someone in town. But I didn't want to fuel the wagging tongues of a small town. They were already busy enough picking up the bones of Brenda's murder and the faux sympathy they offered because they were grateful it wasn't their child.

Tiffany Nash had called several times since the funeral, hoping to make a date with me for coffee. It was easy to put her off when Elaine was staying with me, and I had become more inventive with my excuses since. She kept trying, though. I almost called her that snowy morning because I hadn't gone to Crawford as planned. I didn't want to be home alone, but I just couldn't bring myself to complete the call.

Instead, I walked down to the little white church on the corner. I hadn't been inside a church since Brenda's funeral. Andy had prodded me to go a few times, but I held my ground. I wasn't sure if he wanted time alone or if he was genuinely trying to help. I wavered between the two thoughts, depending on my mood.

The church door was open, and I walked inside. A flood of memories washed over me. This had been the church of my childhood. Our large family had filled a few pews. Andy and I were married here. But the sparkle of a new church, a charismatic pastor, and the new gospel music had turned my head. I got caught up in the vibrancy after my youth's staid and calm church. I felt alive as I lifted my voice in praise with two hundred other voices.

Pastor Dan was in his office behind the altar. He didn't have a secretary. He was a lone wolf trying to bring the church to life. His family had belonged to this church, too. They had also followed the rest of us to Faith Gospel Mission. When his dad retired two years ago, they had moved back east. I wondered why Dan had chosen this mission. It seemed hopeless against the giant that Pastor Newberry was head of.

"Hello, Mrs. Taylor. What a pleasant surprise." Pastor Dan stood and moved around the desk to shake my hand.

"Hello, Pastor Dan. Is this a bad time?" I looked at the flurry of paper scattered across his desk.

"No, no. It's a perfect time. I was just thinking I needed a coffee break. You will stay for coffee, won't you?"

I nodded, and he went through the door and down the hallway to the little kitchen. I followed. Taking a seat at the tiny table, I watched as he made the coffee. Setting out two mismatched mugs, some spoons, and sugar lumps onto the table, he turned and grabbed the cream from the fridge—he used real cream, not powdered or an artificial oil product. That pleased me. Opening a metal canister, he placed several homemade cookies on a plate and then moved the plate to the table.

The sound of the coffee machine burping and sputtering covered up the silence that lay between us. I was already trying to imagine why I'd come. I had nothing to say. It was hopeless to think that God cared. Life didn't come with an instruction manual. It was a minefield with no map of the hidden detonators. You took your chances, and sometimes you won, and sometimes you lost a limb.

Pastor Dan poured the coffee, leaving room for cream in both mugs. When he had replaced the pot, he sat down. He offered me the sugar and the cream before helping himself to each. The spoon tinkled against the side of his cup as he stirred the creamy mixture vigorously. After he offered me a cookie, he set the plate down in the middle of the table before choosing one for himself. He looked at it, twisting it slightly before dunking it into his coffee. The cookie was gone in two bites.

We sat there in silence for a minute. I was trying to figure out why I'd come. I took a sip of my coffee and sighed. This was excellent. "Yum." I nodded. "You make a good cup of coffee."

"Why, thank you. I learned from my mother. I always make a full pot, too. It seems to make better coffee than making, say, just a cup." He smiled at me, then cleared his throat. "But I'm sure you didn't come here to talk about coffee. What's on your mind?"

Did he know how to get to the point? The only problem was I didn't see the point. "I was supposed to start therapy today."

"I see." He nodded.

"But the weather didn't cooperate."

"It is rather brutal on the roads. Or so I've heard."

"Anyway, maybe that was a sign I'm not supposed to go."

"You think?"

"I don't know." I sighed, feeling my shoulders drop. "It seems I don't know much anymore."

"So, why would you think stormy weather and bad roads were a sign?"

"I don't know."

"Yes, you do."

We sat in silence. Under my breath, I was cussing Pastor Dan. What the hell was he getting at? Why was he being so obtuse? I felt my anger stir, and I tamped it down. Neither of us spoke. Pastor Dan took another cookie, dunking it into his coffee as he'd done the first.

"I guess, um … Maybe I'm …" I burst into tears.

Pastor Dan didn't move for a moment. When he got up, he grabbed a box of tissues off the counter. He put those beside me and then sat down again, picking up his mug and sipping his coffee as he waited.

Inside, my thoughts were swirling like dirt in a tornado. They spun around so quickly that I had difficulty making sense of anything. I longed for a moment of peace, a second of clarity. Since it wasn't coming, I ran away. I stood and grabbed my coat from the other chair where I had set it.

"Are you giving up?" Pastor Dan asked.

I stopped and looked at him, expecting him to be triumphant. He had no expression. He wasn't condemning or condescending—he wasn't even arrogant. His face was placid, but his eyes filled with compassion. I dropped my coat back onto the chair.

"I'm scared." There, I said it.

"Scared of what?"

"I'm scared that what I've spent my life believing is a lie. I'm afraid of the anger I feel—I'm frightened that I can never bridge this growing distance between Andy and me—I'm terrified for my daughter and the life choices she's making—I'm worried for my son because he's so far away and I don't know if he's okay—I'm petrified of who I am becoming, and I don't know how to stop any of it."

"That's a lot of fears."

"I know." I tried to speak confidently, but my voice cracked under the pressure. "Fear is my new companion. Fear and anger."

"Yes, those two are good friends. They seldom travel alone."

I laughed. That broke the tension in the room, and I took a deep breath.

"Well, let me ask you a question."

"Okay?"

"Do you believe?"

"Believe in God?"

"Sure."

My faith was being tested. The events of last month rocked me to my core, but did I still believe? In God? In Jesus? What was the truth in my experience?

With tears running down my face, I confessed. "I want to be honest here, Pastor Dan. Part of me wants to believe. I want to think that somewhere out there is a being who cares for me, loves me and wants me to excel. I feel ashamed that I never doubted it for one minute until my daughter was murdered. Now, I can't stop thinking I have lived a lie—that my entire life has been one long fabrication. A twisted tale I believed because it was what my parents taught me.

"Who am I? Really? I am nothing special. My entire life has been ordinary. I grew up and did what people expected of me. I got married, I had children. My life was on a trajectory set down at the beginning of time. I never wanted to be more than I was or am, and I wanted my children to grow up to be happy and healthy—to get married and have babies I could spoil. Maybe I would learn to quilt—I would knit booties and love them like the treasures they would be. I didn't want to save the world. I just wanted to be happy. And I was."

My words echoed around the room long after I had spoken them. Neither of us moved, letting the words have their way. My coffee had gone cold. I pushed the cup away.

"Then the worst thing happened, and there was no time to prepare.

There was no getting used to the idea that she might not be here tomorrow. It was like a giant hand reaching down and plucking her up, and she was gone. Her place in my world is empty. I have memories, but don't know if they are real anymore. I can't believe the cruelty of that."

I paused again, hoping Pastor Dan would add something, but glad he didn't.

"How does that line up with my belief that God is loving? How can I say to people—Jesus loves you—when I know that my experience is the opposite."

"So, let me ask you a question. Let's say that Brenda's future was a horrible one. She has a debilitating disease, and she lives her remaining days in extreme pain. What if God was sparing her from that?"

I thought for a minute. What would I want for Brenda? I would not want her to suffer. I could say that for certain. But I would want to say my goodbyes, and I wouldn't want her dying alone. I told Pastor Dan as much.

Pastor Dan pondered my words before adding. "You see, Audrey, God knows all and sees all. He has information we may never have on this side of Heaven. He didn't take Brenda to punish you or to punish her. The man who shot her used his free will, and that was the consequence. Maybe God will use this tragedy to shake you out of complacency. Maybe it has nothing to do with you. Perhaps Brenda's death will transform another person's life. It is not our place to question God but to accept that He knows more than we do."

His words hit me like stones. I felt thoroughly chastised, put down, and set in my place. Anger rose as I stood up, shoving my chair back with my legs.

"Well, thank you for your understanding, Pastor. Good day." I grabbed my coat and stormed off, half expecting him to follow me. He didn't. I ran through the church, slamming the door open with fury.

When I hit the cold air, I shuddered as I tried to slip into my coat. Not bothering to button it closed—I ran, his words still echoing in my head.

I ran down the street toward home. I couldn't wait to close the door behind me. When I had reached my sanctuary, I dropped my coat on the floor, ran up the stairs, and threw myself on the bed. I rolled up the comforter, forcing it to cocoon around me as I wept. I felt like a schoolchild who got caught cheating on a test. As I reviewed his words, though, I realized that he only spoke the truth, and his words softened in the heat of acceptance.

I needed to apologize to Pastor Dan. But I would not make a special trip to do it. It would happen when it happened.

CHAPTER TWENTY-SEVEN

Later that week, I went to Crawford to do some Christmas shopping. I didn't feel like shopping and would have preferred to cancel the holiday altogether. Then, I reminded myself that this is what we needed as a family. A time to be together and to celebrate that in some form.

Arriving at the mall, I thought I'd have coffee and a bran muffin before shopping. The food court was bustling—seniors were drinking coffee and playing cards, and young moms were chasing toddlers. I turned away and wandered back through the stores. I made purchases as I found items on my list. It was slow going because I saw so many things I would have liked to have given Brenda. How was it possible that she wouldn't be here with us? That still rankled me.

Packing all my purchases into the car's trunk, I wandered back to the food court for a bite to eat. I thought maybe I'd eat Japanese, but the lineup was long. I went for Chinese food instead. Standing at the counter waiting for my food, I felt a tap on my shoulder. I turned to see Tiffany smiling at me. My heart skipped. I felt trapped.

"Oh, hi. Are you getting some shopping done?" I asked, hoping my voice didn't betray me.

"I am. I can't believe I ran into you. If I had known you were coming, we could have come together and saved all that gas money."

"It was a last-minute decision, actually." I lied.

"Can I join you for lunch?"

"Sure." My food came, and I wandered into the maze of tables, hoping that if I went far enough, she wouldn't find me. But she did. She set her food down and sat across from me. Then she bowed her head and prayed over her food. I remembered doing that.

When she had finished, she looked up and smiled at me. "It's so good to see you." Then she reached over and took my hand. "I have missed you."

My heart melted, and I couldn't remember why I had avoided her. She was a delightful woman, open and honest. Repentance flooded through me, and tears filled my eyes.

"I have missed you, too. And I'm sorry that I have been such a lousy friend. I just haven't been in a good place since …" I cleared my throat. "I didn't want to taint your faith with my anger and frustration and this horrid situation. I wanted you to love God, as you always have, like I used to."

"Well, I'll tell you, your standoffishness hurt me, but I've also understood it, and because I love you, I forgave you. I figured one of these days I would catch up with you, and you wouldn't have a choice but to speak to me."

That's what I loved about Tiffany. She was direct. She would apologize if she hurt your feelings, but that never stopped her from sharing honestly.

Tears welled up as my throat closed, making speaking impossible. I reached over the table and took her hand, nodding like a bobblehead doll. She squeezed my hand, staring into my eyes, and I had to look away, or I would lose control of my emotions. I wasn't sure I deserved such a lavish gift.

Perhaps, sensing my fears, Tiffany pulled her hand back and picked up her plastic fork. We ate and chatted comfortably. After our meal, she took the plates to the waste station, and I got some fresh coffees. Then Tiffany got serious.

"Has your family quit going to church?" she asked.

I nearly spit my coffee out. "I don't know about me, but Nora is going to that new church down the street from us—Pastor Dan Gallagher's church."

"Oh. Pastor Dan is back. I had no idea. Is it a wonderful service?"

"Nora seems to think so. She comes home after church feeling happy. He's also started a youth group that doesn't discriminate, like the one at Faith Gospel. The kids are free to attend their own church, and it had quite a large turnout for its first meeting. Nora seems happy."

"And you?"

"Well, I haven't gone to a service yet, but I have had several conversations with Pastor Dan." I told her about them.

"Well, he's right, you know. God has the full picture. You taught me that years ago."

"Did I?"

"Don't you remember?"

"No."

"Remember when my father-in-law, Harold, woke up one morning and he was blind?"

I nodded. "Yes, now that you mention it."

"I was beside myself, unable to comprehend why God would allow that to happen. Of course, they rushed him to the hospital, where he underwent surgery to reattach his retinas. They restored his eyesight, but it took time. He still struggled a bit with his vision, but do you remember the surgeon? Harold witnessed to him, and he turned his life over to the Lord."

I remembered. "Didn't he share that story at church?"

"Yes, he did. It was the last service for Pastor Joseph. I can't imagine anyone being allowed to do that today."

She was right. Pastor Newberry was a one-man show. "You know, speaking of Pastor Newberry, he hasn't once called the house to see why I haven't been to church. He hasn't called to pray with me or anything. It's like I never existed in his world."

"Well, I hate to say it, but he is a bit of a snob. He came over for dinner once and … how did he put it?" She paused, trying to find the right words. "I can't remember his exact words, and I want you to promise you won't get upset."

Now, she had my curiosity piqued. I nodded my agreement.

"Okay. He said something along the lines that families, where not all members attended, were blemishes to the church."

Then I realized why he never came to my house for a meal. Andy wasn't a churchgoer. Andy and I were blemishes to the church in his narrow mind.

"Well, then, I don't think I will ever return. At least not to that church. How arrogant! I'd really like to give him a piece of my mind, but he isn't worth my time."

"No, he's not. So, let's go to this other church this Sunday. Let's try it out together."

"I don't know. I'm not ready."

"You'll never be ready. There will always be fear and apprehension. Break through all that and walk through the door. And I will be there, right by your side."

"You're a good friend, and I appreciate your offer. And I will go, but not yet."

"Okay, but I am not giving up on you."

We wandered the mall together for another hour before I left to go home. She was meeting Lowell for a meal later, so she stayed longer. Both of us were empty-handed at the end, and I can only speak for myself that I was happy to have her by my side as I wandered in and out of the stores in search of the ultimate gift. All the fears that I carried, the worry I had manufactured about failing her, fell away, and we were right back to being best friends. I hugged her at the door as I was leaving.

"See you next week for coffee?" she whispered.

I nodded and squeezed a little tighter. Walking to my car, I felt lighter than I had in weeks. I had a therapy appointment next week and wondered if I really needed it. Maybe all I needed was a friend.

Before I hit the highway, though, I knew I was just afraid. It wouldn't hurt to talk to this woman once or twice. I wasn't making a lifetime commitment.

I turned on the radio and listened to two velvety voices talk about the merits of some book I had never heard of. They were company for the trip, and I wondered if I would ever want to listen to music again.

CHAPTER TWENTY-EIGHT

That Saturday, I woke up early. Laying there listening to Andy snoring softly beside me, I sighed. I wanted life to go backward so I could call Brenda and have her tell me off for calling so early on a Saturday. I wanted to wake from the nightmare. But even as I lay there arguing with God, I knew that there was no going back—there was only forward.

Laying there, I promised myself that I would try harder to be kind to Andy, and I would try to get Nora to open up to me. I would reach out to Logan in his isolation away at college. Thinking about how I used to pray for everything—how in the past I would be on my knees, not trying to shore myself up—a sadness washed over me. I wanted to pray and ask God to forgive me for my anger and unbelief. My heart ached as my thoughts wandered.

There were so many emotions, unresolved and rancid with time. Ignoring them hadn't made them disappear—it caused them to fester until every thought got filtered through a toxic screen of grief and anger. Pulling myself away from everyone hadn't helped. I felt so far away from Andy and God. Who was I to my children? Neither of them confided in me.

If Brenda were here, she would be appalled. She was the first one to admit her bad mood and bad feelings. She was outspoken and opinionated. A rush of affection overwhelmed me, and tears stung my eyes. But she wasn't here, and I was on my own and failing to be who I needed to be for everyone.

Sighing, I rolled over to face the wall. At least I built one bridge with Tiffany, but honestly, she had done all the work. I had just allowed her to place her bridge on the uncultivated soil of my hardened heart. I was being a coward in my relationships and wondered if I had always been so fearful. Was I authentic with anyone? Had I ever been?

Andy stirred, and I froze, fearing he might want to talk or, worse, get close to me. He threw back the covers, and I listened as he pattered his way to the bathroom. He didn't close the door, so I heard him empty his bladder and shuddered at his lack of respect. Then he was running water, and I imagined him lathering his face to shave.

My bladder was cramped, but I lay there ignoring it. I knew I was being foolish. How many times had I peed while Andy shaved? A hundred? A thousand? Too many to count for sure. I wanted to push past this self-imposed barrier. I wanted to love my husband unconditionally. Then, I knew that if I didn't move, I might never have another chance. I couldn't imagine my life without him. What should I do?

I thought I heard Brenda's voice. She said, "Mom, get your fanny out of bed. March into that bathroom, wrap your arms around Dad, and tell him how you feel. Then drag him back to bed and show him how much you love him." I blushed. Brenda!

Her words spurred me to get out of bed, and I walked into the bathroom. Andy didn't seem surprised to see me. I emptied my bladder as he finished shaving. I washed my hands, trying to stay out of his way. Then I reached for my toothbrush, and he reached for his. Our hands met. I looked at him and smiled. He looked back. The ice shield around my heart shattered, and I touched his face.

He took my hand, kissing the palm. Then he pulled me close.

"I can't live without you," I whispered. "I'm sorry for being so …"

"Beautiful?" He completed it. "This is unchartered waters for both of us. I lost my daughter, too, and I'm angry about it. But I can't bring her back. I don't want to live my life without you either. So, let's just put this behind us for now and move forward, eh?"

I bristled, not wanting to move forward away from Brenda and her loss. I wanted to talk about her and her life and her loss. But maybe this wasn't the time. Maybe I needed to get guidance from the therapist because I didn't want there to be any shaky ground underneath us, nor did I want to cause a rift that couldn't be repaired.

He kissed me then, just a quick peck on my lips. I pulled him closer and kissed him again. He pulled back, looking deep into my eyes. "You're sure?"

We hadn't made love for weeks—from two to four times a week to nothing—which had frustrated Andy. He'd turned away angrily the first time I had rebuffed his advances. Then he stopped reaching for me. I was relieved and annoyed, longing for him but not wanting to be that close. Inside, I felt the swirl of paradoxes colliding, but I focused on Andy. Let me just try to build another bridge. I don't want to be all alone in my misery.

Andy locked the bedroom door, and we went back to bed. Like new lovers, we took our time getting to know one another, touching, tasting, and coming together. I ran my hands down his back, feeling his strength and power. My heart swelled with pride. How had I, little Audrey Armstrong, the runt of the litter, plump, not slender, ever won this man's heart? I was nothing special, but he saw me through different eyes, and I was grateful for that.

Afterward, I lay in Andy's arms, my head resting on his chest. He was rubbing my arm. "I have a confession to make," he said, and I stopped breathing.

"It's not a terrible confession, but it is a secret I don't want between us."

"Okay?"

"I've been spending time with Pastor Dan."

"How do you mean, 'spending time'?"

He laughed. "Well, after all these years of not having any faith, or maybe riding your coattails as far as God is concerned, I felt really lost when Brenda died. Do you remember saying it was my fault because I didn't go to church?"

"But I didn't mean that." I sat up, my eyes wide with fear, pulling the sheet around me.

"I know you apologized for saying it, but it got me thinking. I didn't understand why she had to die, and I felt responsible. So, I went to see Pastor Newberry. That man is something, and none of the definitions I can come up with are for delicate ears."

I nodded in agreement. "I know."

"Anyway, we met for coffee one morning when Elaine was still here, and he basically told me that same thing. He blamed my lack of faith for her death. I felt devastated and furious. Then, walking home from Mom and Dad's a few nights later, I ran into Pastor Dan. I didn't seek him out, but that night, he offered his condolences, and one thing led to another …"

I turned to look into his face. There were tears in his eyes. "Anyway, long story short, I gave my life to the Lord yesterday. I prayed for forgiveness in that little sanctuary and felt such peace come over me. I finally understand why you loved church and God. There is nothing like it in this world."

My soul split in two. The smaller part that wanted this and had prayed for this was doing handstands and flips of joy. The larger half, the part of me that lost Brenda and was angry at God, was furious. Why now? Why the hell now?

In a series of flashbacks, I saw myself begging Andy to come to church. I saw his resolute refusal, his condescension like he knew something I didn't. He was smarter than me, and following God was for weak fools and those with little stamina to face the world alone. Now, here he was, after all we'd lost, when I finally realized that he was right and I was wrong—yet here he was, turning the tables on me.

Pushing myself away, I hurled out of bed stark naked. I didn't take the time to grab a robe—I wanted nothing to diffuse my anger. If I stayed, even for as long as it took to slip into something, I was going to do harm to Andy. Physical harm. I wanted to throw myself at him, biting and kicking and screaming until he felt my wrath and understood that God couldn't save him, just like he hadn't saved Brenda.

Rushing to the bathroom, I slammed the door behind me, engaging the lock. Then I burst into tears. I lurched to the bathtub and sat on the edge, pulling the towel over my face to muffle my sobs. I wasn't sure Nora was awake, but I didn't want to upset her.

Andy knocked on the door tentatively. "Audrey, are you okay?"

"Go away, Andy," I said, my voice distorted.

"What's wrong? I don't understand—I thought this is what you wanted." I heard him jiggle the lock. "Let me in. Let's talk about this. Come on, honey."

Through my tears, I saw the door, and for one moment, I thought how easy it would be to throw open the door and let Andy know my pain and the depth of my sorrow. But how could I confess my anger? Deep down, I knew it was irrational, and I knew I wasn't capable of more. My entire world had crumbled with Brenda's death, and now the last solid piece had shattered. I didn't bother to answer.

Instead, I turned on the shower. I climbed into the spray, hoping it would wash away this mountain of anger building inside me. Ten minutes later, my hair and body were clean, but rage still consumed my heart. Damn him to hell. Damn him straight to hell.

The kitchen, smelling of bacon and toast, was empty. Andy was gone. My stomach lurched as the two parts of my soul wrestled for supremacy. Some coffee was left in the carafe, but I made some fresh. There was a note from Nora on the table. I read it while I waited for the coffee.

Gone to work with Dad. Isn't it amazing about his news! I can't wait to celebrate tomorrow at church. Can we have lasagna for supper? With garlic toast and Caesar salad? Love you!

My heart hurt. I didn't know how to respond. The last thing I wanted was to destroy her faith or make her miserable. She didn't deserve my anger. The phone rang, and I considered ignoring it.

It was Elaine calling to check up on me. We talked about the weather for the first minute, and then she asked that all important question, "How are you doing?"

Bursting into tears, I cried, "I just can't seem to get it together. My thoughts keep circling back to being unable to understand why. I am still angry at God and the world. I am a nightmare for a wife and a lousy mother."

"No, you're not. You're wounded and lashing out. That's not the same thing at all. How is the therapist? Is she helping?"

"I haven't been. The weather was nasty, and my next appointment isn't until next week."

"You poor dear, trying to manage all by yourself. Do you want me to come back?"

"No. You have your own life. I will be okay. Besides, Andy gave his life to the Lord yesterday." My tone dripped with sarcasm, but Elaine ignored it.

"All your married life, you have wanted this. You have prayed for it. So, I guess people are right when they say be careful what you wish for."

I wanted to laugh, but trying to break the tension with levity fell flat. Or maybe it was just me. "Anyway, Nora wants to celebrate at church tomorrow. I just don't know if I can go."

"I think you will feel better once you get inside that door. So put on your best dress and go. The worst that can happen is your feelings haven't changed, but you've made your family happy."

"I guess."

"Okay, so I'll call you in a couple of days, but if you need me before then, call me. Okay?"

"Thanks for calling, Elaine. I appreciate it."

"You're welcome. Oh … I almost forgot. Judith and Neil are in Hawaii on a second honeymoon. I guess their counseling sessions are working."

"Good for them," I said, though I didn't feel the elation. It was going to work out for Judith, wasn't it? It always did.

CHAPTER TWENTY-NINE

As expected, Andy was up and out of bed early on Sunday morning. After a stilted celebration last night, he was so chipper that I wanted to shove his head under a cold water tap to settle him down.

"Aren't you getting out of bed?" he asked, coming in from the shower. "You're going to make us late for church."

"I'm not going."

"What? Honey, why not? Is this about what happened yesterday?"

For one second, I debated whether to spare him, but ultimately, I felt he needed to know. I sat up. "You know, Andy, I walked with God all my life. He was my rock in times of sorrow and my ever-present joy. But He failed to protect Brenda, and I must learn how to live without my precious girl. He failed me, or maybe I failed myself because I believed He cared. I don't know. I just know I am not prepared to go to church and pretend it's all okay. It's not okay, and it may never be okay."

I got out of bed and threw my housecoat. "And I am also furious that I prayed for many years for you to come to know the Lord. I grew weary, asking God to give you faith. And He finally did it. He finally got through to you, but the cost for that answered prayer was my daughter. I don't know if it was a fair trade-off."

"I can't believe you, Audrey. You are blaming me for Brenda's death. Still."

I stopped in my tracks and turned around to face him. "I said no such thing."

With steel in his voice, he said, "In the pantry, over a month ago, you said I was to blame for her death because of my lack of faith. Now, you say that Brenda paid with her life, so I could have faith, meaning … If she hadn't died, I wouldn't have found faith, and you'd still have your daughter, though. Right?"

It wasn't what I meant at all, but I was angry. "Exactly." I threw it back in his face. Then I went into the bathroom and slammed the door. Part of me hoped he would read between the lines and understand what I was saying. But I knew it was a long shot. When I came out of the bathroom, he was gone.

He was making coffee downstairs in the kitchen. The atmosphere between us was cold enough to freeze water. I whipped up some pancake batter. By the time the first cakes came off the griddle, the coffee was ready, and Nora was scooting into her chair.

"Morning." She grabbed a glass and poured herself some orange juice. "You're not ready for church, Mom. You'll make us late." She came to stand beside me. "I can flip these if you want."

"Thank you, but I am not attending church this morning." I turned in time to see a look pass between her and Andy. That annoyed me. I hated conspiracies, and now I feel like I'm the focus of one.

I stood at the counter, flipping pancakes and setting more on the table as they were ready. When I sat down for my breakfast, Andy and Nora were finishing. Then Andy looked at his watch, and Nora took her cue. They both rose from the table as one. Nora gave me a quick peck on the cheek before dashing out with her father. Andy said nothing. The back door slammed, leaving me alone with my uneaten pancakes.

I burst into tears, shoving the stack of flapjacks away. My insides were raw. My head was thick with regret and anger. Never in my life had I felt so helpless—I didn't know what to do. I didn't want to be here—I didn't want to be there. If only I could talk to Brenda, to hear her voice—to have her laugh, to tickle my heart. She had a beautiful laugh that made others want to laugh along, even if they didn't know what they were laughing at.

I showered and dressed and then put on a roast for dinner. The simple, mundane task helped to calm my frayed nerves. I mentally noted the time to add potatoes and carrots, forty-five minutes before the roast came out of the oven. Looking in the freezer, I found some frozen strawberries. Making strawberry shortcake for dessert would make the dinner special. Andy loved anything with strawberries. All I needed was some whipping cream.

The corner store was several blocks away, but starting the car and cleaning off the three inches of snow while it warmed up so I could get there and back in under five minutes seemed like a waste of energy. Besides, I had loads of time, and walking would do me good.

The wind was bitter as I faced it on my way to the store. I pulled down my hat and scarf, exposing only my eyes. Then I ducked my head down, reminding myself that the store was not that far. I could persevere, so I walked on.

The corner store didn't have any whipped cream. They had some oil-based whip, but I didn't like its greasiness. I hesitated. It was twenty blocks to the grocery store. Twenty blocks walking into the wind. Or should I walk home and get the car? What a dilemma.

I turned toward the store and started walking. As I walked, I thought about Brenda. Walking so far in the winter wind would have appalled her. I could hear her chastising me like I was the child and she was the parent. I smiled at our conversation, longing for it to be real. It wasn't, but it helped me pass the time, and before I knew it, I could see the store.

A minute later, the hot air blasted me in the face as I stepped into the foyer. I made it. I tugged off my hat and unwrapped my scarf—wet from the moisture of my breath. After shaking it to release the moisture, I coiled it loosely around my neck. The automatic door opened, and I walked into the store. A few souls were wandering around the colorful produce section, but the place seemed more or less deserted. I walked toward the back of the store to the dairy case.

After checking the expiration dates, I chose the cream with the latest one, even though I was going to use it right away. I wandered the bakery aisle and pulled a loaf of bread from the shelf. Then, I headed to the checkout counter.

An elderly lady was in front of me. She wore a long fur coat, a red silk scarf, and lots of powder on her face. Her bony hands were shaking as she removed her items from the basket she carried. Her movements were slow as her long fingers wrapped around every item, lifting it onto the short conveyor. I wanted to jump in and help her, but that would be rude and impatient. Instead, when she looked back at me, I smiled at her.

She smiled back. "You look like you've been walking in the wind." She said as she reached for the bar to separate our items.

"I have. I was just going to go to the corner store, but they didn't have what I wanted, so here I am."

"Back in my day, a grocery store wouldn't be open on a Sunday. It was sacrilegious, to say the least. Even now, my son cringes when I go shopping instead of going to church."

I smiled, not sure where this was heading.

"My son is a pastor. He's big in this town. You might know him. Paul Newberry."

"You're Pastor Newberry's mother?" I was incredulous.

"So, you know him."

"Yes, I know him." I nodded and, in my head, I said, *Yes, I know the sanctimonious jackass.*

She chuckled as she passed the cashier a couple of twenty-dollar bills and waited for her change. She moved out of the way but didn't leave the line.

"I was the organist in my church for years. I finally had to give it up." She held out her hands so I could see how shaky they were. I handed the clerk my money and slipped my change into the deep pocket of my coat before retrieving my package.

I wanted to get away from this conversation, but I felt compelled to be polite. Of all people, Pastor Newberry's mother.

"Can I offer you a lift home?" She collected her groceries.

"Oh, I wouldn't want to put you out," I replied. Unsure she was a skillful driver, I also didn't want to be beholden to her. I set my grocery bag on an empty till and redressed for the long walk home.

She chuckled. "Don't worry, I don't drive. I have a driver."

A driver! Well, imagine that. I didn't know anyone who had a driver.

"It's a concession from my son. He didn't want me driving, and I refused to depend on him or his wife for rides. He might have forced me to enjoy his hospitality, but I wanted a bit more independence. And I refuse to go to his church, which annoys him to no end." She chuckled again until we hit the foyer, and the furnace blasted her. "Why do they have to have this damn thing on so high?" She grumbled.

We stepped out of the store together. I was still wrestling with my choice when a long black car slid to a stop in front of us. A tall young man stepped out and opened the back door before he took control of the grocery bags. He deposited those in the front seat before turning to help the old lady in the back of the car.

"I told my friend we'd give her a ride home, Kenny."

"Certainly." He stepped aside, and I had to make my decision right then. A blast of winter wind came around the corner of the building and slipped under my jacket. That was reason enough to take the ride. "Thank you. I really could walk, but this is so nice of you."

After I gave Kenny directions, we set off. "So, how do you know my son?"

And right there, I knew I had made a mistake. I should have braved the winter wind and walked home. I was trapped in a closed space with a stranger asking me questions I didn't want to answer.

I told her I had gone to her son's church but hadn't been for a few months. I didn't say why.

"Paulie is quite upset that I don't go to his church or that I don't go to any church. I used to when he preached in North Battleford, but I haven't been to a service here since he forced me to leave my home. Maybe I should be thankful that he didn't stick me in a nursing home and forget me. I just don't like all this laying on of hands and such that goes on in churches today. I like the simple churches, where they sing a few hymns and preach that we're all sinners destined to hell and we're out of there in an hour. Sitting in services for two hours or more, it just isn't right." She sighed.

We sat there in silence as the car slowed to a stop in front of my house. She grabbed my hand and leaned forward. "Do you have a job?"

"Well, I haven't worked outside the home. I've considered my job to be taking care of my family."

"Very admirable. Would you be free to come for coffee? Not today, of course. But next week, say Tuesday?" She hesitated for a moment. "I don't know many people in this town. Paulie is the only person who comes to visit, and although I love him dearly, he isn't someone I can talk to. I have a feeling about you, though. There is something about you … You remind me of me a little. Anyway, it would sure be nice to have something to look forward to."

I didn't know what to say. The conversation lulled momentarily as I tried to decide what to do. She was Pastor Newberry's mother.

Did I really want to be her friend? Then I thought about how few people I had in my world and decided that it wouldn't hurt to go for a visit. After all, I had no other church duties to keep me busy anymore. "I can't on Tuesday. I have an appointment in the city that day. But I suppose I can come on Wednesday."

"Wednesday works. I will see you then."

She grabbed my arm as I got out of the car. "I don't even know your name."

I laughed. "Um …" I hesitated. Should I tell her so she was aware of my plight? Would that scare her off or make her curious?

"If you tell me, I might get home before my lettuce wilts."

I burst out laughing. She was direct. I felt a rush of affection for that. "I'm Audrey Taylor."

"Not the Taylors who lost their daughter?"

I felt the kick to my gut. "One and the same."

"Well, I am very sorry for your loss. It must be a difficult time. I can't imagine."

"Yes, it's been very hard." I smiled at her, and she patted my arm. "Okay, Mrs. Newberry, I will see you Wednesday."

"Oh, how silly of me. My name is Elsbeth Prince. Mr. Newberry, God rest his soul has been gone a long while. I will see you on Wednesday morning at, say, nine. Kenny will pick you up."

"Okay."

"Now get out and close that door before I freeze to death.

I laughed as Kenny reached down to help me out. He closed the door before I could lean back to tell her I was looking forward to Wednesday already. Kenny tipped his hat to me before turning away. He got back into the car and pulled away from the curb. I watched until the car disappeared around the corner. Then I went into the house to finish making dinner.

CHAPTER THIRTY

Tuesday morning arrived, and my trepidation with it. I had mixed feelings about talking with someone about my feelings. I didn't want to crack open the walnut and see all the worms that had made themselves at home. I dressed carefully and paced around the kitchen until it was time to leave.

The drive gave me time to worry myself into a lather. When I got to Dr. Zelda Reisner's office, I was terrified. I sat in the waiting room alone, waiting for her to come and get me. A disheveled man raced out of her door, and ten minutes later, she came out of her office.

She looked nothing like I expected. Her wild, ginger hair framed her narrow face and hung down her back, untamed, giving her the appearance of a remnant from the sixties. I gauged her to be in her fifties. She wore no makeup—a smattering of freckles bridged her nose. Soft lines surrounded her eyes and mouth. She was rail thin, and I noticed she wasn't wearing shoes as I followed her back to her spacious office.

A large wooden desk sat in front of three wide bookcases, filled and beyond. There was a small seating area on the left—a dusty blue flowered couch and matching chair, with a large coffee table between them. Underneath, on top of the beige carpet, lay a dusty blue area rug. The set-up made this part of the neutral office seem cozier. I suspected that was her intention.

She handed me some forms and asked me to fill them out. She moved to the desk and began working on her computer, leaving me to do the paperwork on my own. I looked at the questions. It started with basic information and then asked what I hoped to get from our meetings. I wanted to throw the pages back at her. I tried to understand, but I was dutiful and completed the form with as little information as possible.

I set the clipboard on the table. A few minutes later, she looked up from her computer and noticed I was done. She moved back, picked up the clipboard, and perused the information, asking for a few clarifications as she went. The longer this went on, the angrier I got. I tried to imagine pouring out my heart to her. There seemed to be no rapport, and I certainly got no warmth from her. She was as far away from me as she could get with that large coffee table between us.

When she'd finished reviewing my form, our first session was over, and we had accomplished nothing. We set up a second appointment for the following Tuesday, and I left—my pocketbook much lighter and my heart heavier for the experience. I drove home wondering if this was a huge mistake. How was this going to help me? But I also felt obligated to go back.

Tiffany stopped by when I got home. As I made coffee and put cookies onto a plate, she was prattling on about the glorious Sunday service with Pastor Dan. Of course, Andy and Nora had already told me more than I wanted to know. At some point, I stopped listening to them and wanted to do the same thing to Tiffany. Instead, I changed the subject.

I told her about my meeting with the psychologist, including how distant I felt she was. "How am I ever supposed to open my innermost feelings up to someone who keeps so much space between us? It wasn't as if she was cold. She was pleasant enough. But distant—apart—aloof. I got the feeling that I was beneath her, somehow."

"I'm sorry. I had such high hopes." Tiffany commiserated. And that's what I loved about her. She didn't tell me she understood; she didn't tell me I was wrong. She simply agreed.

"Me too. Maybe I just need to give it more time. Maybe the first meeting is supposed to be clinical. An information-gathering process or something. I don't know. This is new to me."

"I have no experience either, but I hope so. I mean, it's a lot of money for nothing."

"I know. She didn't even do anything except read a bunch of short answers. I couldn't believe that she would charge for that. It wasn't like I got helped at all. And I wasn't truly sincere in my answers. What should I have said to the question—*What is your most pressing situation?* Or—*how do you expect me to help you?*"

"She asked you that?" Tiffany laughed. "Wow. I guess she wants to know if you need her to work."

"I know—I didn't really know how to answer. I think I put down something like … I just lost my daughter, and I'm angry … and … I expect you to help me. I wasn't forthright. I just felt angry with the entire process."

"I can't imagine." Tiffany shook her head.

"So, how are things with you?"

"Well, I got a call from Pastor Newberry yesterday. He apparently noticed we weren't in church on Sunday and wanted to know if everything was okay."

I looked at my friend, and for a moment, I wasn't sure what to do. She did not know that Pastor Newberry still hadn't called me to see why I hadn't been to church in weeks, yet he had called her after missing only one service. I felt hurt, and part of me wanted to blame Tiffany because she was right there. But part of me knew it was ridiculous to blame her. I took a deep breath, hoping to settle my warring emotions.

When I hadn't replied, Tiffany looked up from her coffee cup. She saw the conflict on my face and was immediately remorseful. "Oh, Audrey. How thoughtless. He still hasn't called you, then?"

I shook my head as tears rolled down my cheeks. "No, and the silly thing is—I'd hang up if he did. But he has not tried to reach out to me, which really bugs me."

"Oh, Audrey." Tiffany chuckled again. "You really are an enigma."

I had to laugh with her. I knew how silly I was being. "Speaking of Pastor Newberry, you'll never guess who I met?"

"You're right. I won't. Who?"

"Paulie's mother!"

"Who's Paulie?" Tiffany looked confused.

"Paulie Newberry. I met his mommy."

"Pastor Newberry?"

I nodded. Then I told her about meeting Elsbeth at the grocery store and her driving me home. "I'm going to have coffee with her tomorrow morning."

"Wow. I didn't know his mother was living in town."

"Me neither. She's an odd bird, but I liked her. She's nothing like him."

"Well, you'll have to tell me all about it."

We talked through the last part of the morning. She helped me make lunch for the three of us. Andy joined us for about half an hour. When he left, Tiffany was helping me clear away the dishes when she said, "So, what's going on with you and Andy?"

"What do you mean?"

"Don't give me that. You were stiff with one another."

"Were we?"

"Well, if you don't want to discuss it, that's fine. But you know I am a willing listener."

Did I want to share? Was I ready to share? I wasn't sure because I knew how petty I was being. I didn't want her to judge me or, worse, to take Andy's side. I needed her.

"It's complicated."

"Okay." She nodded. "Do we need tea?"

"You will not let this drop, will you?"

"Well, only if you really won't talk. But I have some time if you want to tell me now. You will eventually anyway."

She was right. I would eventually tell her once I figured out what was happening. "It seems rather petty, and it makes little sense. But I can't help my feelings. Up to now, I have always been so proud of how controlled I've been my whole life. Inside, my feelings might be roiling, yet on the outside, I would be smiling. I can't do that anymore. I am annoyed with Andy."

"What did he do?"

"Well, don't laugh. But I'm angry that he gave his life to the Lord."

To her credit, Tiffany didn't laugh, but she looked rather shocked. "But you've been praying for that since before we met."

"I know. I know. I told you it made little sense."

"So, what is it that has you so rattled?"

"Well, it's because it happened when I struggle to believe. I was looking forward to Sunday sleep-ins with my husband. Time to be together to grieve our daughter, maybe go away for the odd weekend. Then he does this, and I'm alone."

"You're not alone."

"I am." I burst into tears. "He's going to church. He's not here with me."

"You could go to church, too."

"I know, but I don't want to!" And I wailed as my emotions gathered steam. My insides hurt.

Tiffany wrapped her arms around me and let me cry on her shoulder. She didn't shush me or tell me how silly I was being. She let me cry until I couldn't cry anymore. Then she walked me to my bedroom, helped me onto the bed, and pulled a blanket over me.

With a quick kiss on my cheek, she left me, and I was asleep before she went out the door.

CHAPTER THIRTY-ONE

Wednesday morning, right on time, Kenny pulled up outside my house. As I rushed down the sidewalk to the car, he held the door open for me. I slipped inside, and he shut the door. A few minutes later, he pulled the car under the carport of a large, older home across town. The house, built in the sixties, was one of the many bungalows with a brick façade on the front, including a brick planter edging the patio at the front door.

She met me at the side door, welcoming me into her home. I stepped in, admiring how polished everything was. She really had a wonderful maid. The place was spotless.

Kenny came in and immediately went down the stairs.

"He lives down there. He gets reduced rent for driving me so he can work on his first novel. He's going to write a bestseller and make millions. Or so he tells me. Now, I wasn't sure what you wanted. Tea or coffee? I boiled the kettle and have a pot of coffee made because that's what I'll have."

I shed my coat and slipped out of my boots. "Coffee will be fine."

She nodded and ambled into the kitchen. I followed tentatively, unsure how to act, where to sit, what to do.

"Sit, sit." She pointed to the polished round table near a large window. I sat, wondering if I should get the coffee. She seemed rather frail to be performing such duties. Elsbeth set a sturdy mug in front of me and pointed to the cream, sugar, and spoons in the center of the table. Then she put a small cookie jar on the table, filled with store-packaged cookies. Last, she grabbed a second mug and sat on the chair next to mine.

"So, how are you doing, Audrey?" she asked as she stirred cream into her coffee.

"Good." I nodded.

She took the lid off the cookie jar and tipped it toward me. I took one, and she took two, setting one on her saucer as she nibbled at the other.

The silence pulsed in my ears. I waited for her to speak, but she seemed content to silently enjoy her cookies.

As she finished her first cookie, she looked at me. With her failing eyesight, I wasn't sure what she was seeing. Maybe her eyesight was just a smoke screen. Perhaps … I let my imagination run wild.

"You're not very relaxed. Am I making you nervous? I don't mean to."

"I'm sorry. It's not you, it's me." Then I laughed. "People say that all the time, don't they? But it usually is you, not me. I mean, with them, not with us. Okay … let me start again."

"Take your time, dear. We've got a pot of coffee and more if needed."

"Okay." I took a deep breath. "All my life, I've been the one getting it. I'm the one leading. I'm the one starting. It feels a little strange not to be sort of like—be in charge."

"Of our coffee?"

"Well, yes. That and my friendships. I was always the instigator, making the invitations to my house, where I oversaw the food and the coffee. I mean, my friend Tiffany, we seldom meet at her house. Not that she doesn't have a lovely house. She does. But it just seemed simpler to meet at mine."

"Simpler for who?"

"For me, I guess." I was feeling interrogated.

"Have you ever wondered how Tiffany feels about this? Have you ever asked her?"

"No, I mean, when we started, she was a new believer, and I was mentoring her. It just seemed natural to have her come to my house, and then it just stayed there."

She nodded. "Has she ever asked you to go to her house?"

"Of course, we've gone there for meals—at least once a year. She says she gets stressed out hosting parties, so we usually end up doing things at my house. It's just simpler."

"I see." She nodded. She let the matter drop, but my insides were whirling around. I felt judged and not the least bit comfortable.

Elsbeth got up and retrieved the coffeepot. She poured some into her nearly empty mug and asked if I wanted more. My stomach heaved at the thought, but I said yes, anyway.

"Now, before we go further, I must apologize." She settled herself in her chair. "Old habits die hard. I was a therapist in my past life, a psychologist—I only retired when I moved here about four months ago. I came because Paulie worried about my eyes and being alone in Saskatchewan. But I think I had the wrong hat on. I apologize if I made you uncomfortable."

I nodded. That made sense. She was pushing my buttons. "I accept your apology. No harm done."

"Well, I will not tell you it won't happen again. I am rather set in my ways and miss helping people discover what's holding them back."

That intrigued me. "I understand. What were you trying to get at?"

"I was helping you figure out why you prefer to be in charge, why you can't relax if you are not. There is a root cause, and perhaps it would provide help with what you're going through now. I mean, you couldn't control what happened to your daughter. That must have been frightening."

Tears welled up and rolled down my cheeks at the mention of Brenda's death. I was angry that I couldn't stop it. It left me feeling out of control, and that frightened me. She had hit the nail on the head. "You're right. I am angry about that. And about a lot more, too."

"Well, we can talk about those things, too, and there's no charge. We're just two people in the same room, enjoying one another's company. Now, I was wondering if you would do me a favor."

"If I can."

"Oh, you can." She smiled at me. "I like to listen to soothing music, but what I really like is to listen to a calm, steady voice with a pleasant tone. There are storytellers of old that I wish were still here. Voices with good timbre and melodic in a way."

She leaned back in her chair and closed her eyes, perhaps hearing those voices in her head. Then she opened her eyes and stared at me. "What I noticed about you the other day in the grocery store was your voice. You have a wonderful voice. You should be on the radio."

I blushed. No one had ever said that to me before.

"Usually, Kenny comes up and reads the newspaper to me, but I'd like to free him up to write his great Canadian novel or whatever he is writing. Something about elves and dwarves and the like." She rolled her eyes to signify what she thought of that type of story. "He tells me they sell like hotcakes. Besides the newspaper, I keep the odd bawdy romance novel because a gal has to stay luscious, and what better way to do that than by indulging in a romance, whether real or imagined. And, of course, we could just talk.

"What would we talk about?"

"The news, the weather. Discuss something from the newspaper.

I've got no friends here yet. Many of the people from Paulie's church have tried to befriend me, and some were okay. But I always felt like they could and would report back to Paulie. I don't want him monitoring my thoughts, actions, and discussions. He's a lovely boy, really, he is, but he gets so caught up in playing God's best helper he forgets he's not dealing with sheep. He doesn't see his 'flock' as anything more than fuzzy sheep in human clothing."

Again, I stayed silent—but nodded. Is that how I felt about Pastor Newberry? Was I irritated with him because he treated me as a sheep, not a human being? Perhaps, but there was more to him than that.

She drained her cup and set it on the table with care. "First thing, first. You are not to call me Mrs. Prince. You can call me Elsbeth. We can't be friends if you give me a title. And I will call you Audrey. Is that fine with you?"

"Yes. That's fine."

"Perfect. Now, let's retire to the great room."

The great room? What the heck was a great room? I imagined a large room with a stone fireplace and a throne on a platform. Maybe two thrones side by side. I followed her through the dining room and into what I would have called the living room. She gestured for me to choose a seat. I chose the chair, not wanting the bounty of the couch. She took the other chair, the one that faced mine.

"Today, let's just get to know one another. Kenny can read the paper to me later after he's taken you home. I'll start."

She sat back in her chair and closed her eyes. I thought for a minute that she wasn't going to speak. Then she spoke. "Paulie's father, God rest his soul, was a preacher. Paulie comes by his calling naturally, I guess you could say. We met at a prayer meeting. My boyfriend at the time knew someone or other, and so we went to this meeting, and that's where I met Matthew."

Elsbeth fiddled with her necklace before she continued. "It was all daunting to me. I knew little about these kinds of churches. Mine was rather staid in comparison. The music was reverent, the sermon was low-key, and the people were nice. But this church—well, it was lively and loud. The preacher on the stage was red-faced and sweating from speaking the word of God. He was on fire for God. He kept saying, over and over, and did we want to be on fire, too? By the end of the night, his voice was gone from shouting. The congregation was cheering "Amen" to everything he said, which seemed to rile him up even more. I was almost certain I would see him levitate, things got so frantic."

"Before I knew it, my boyfriend was down the aisle, throwing himself on the floor before the altar. Not a word to me, just gone. I stood there, wondering what to do—I felt my faith stirring but wasn't entirely comfortable. Some people in the pews around me started speaking in tongues. I had never heard that before, and every hair on my body stood at attention. I looked around, wondering where the chickens were."

"The chickens?" I asked, mesmerized by her tale.

"Yes, chickens. The ones they were going to sacrifice. I mean, speaking in tongues wasn't something I'd ever experienced. It was foreign, and I was frightened. Not to mention, the one person I knew was on the floor at the front of the church, wailing."

"What did you do?"

"Thankfully, things calmed down then, and we sat. John, who was my boyfriend, stayed on the floor. I noticed someone was leaning over him, probably praying for him. The preacher asked us to bow our heads. Then he asked the congregation to open their hearts to God, and if they had this problem or sin, they were to raise their hands in the air. He cautioned everyone to keep their eyes closed to keep this private, so people felt free to confess, in a way."

"He went through several things, asking for people to privately respond so he could pray. At one point, he asked if we had a relationship with Jesus, a good, solid, and honest one, and if we didn't, we should put up our hands so he could pray for us. I stuck my hand up, just a little, because although I attended church, we didn't talk about Jesus too much, and I was curious."

"After that, he called for all those who had raised their hands to come to the front for prayer. Now, I was terrified. He had lied, or at least that was my interpretation of it at the time—he had said this was between us and God. Now, here he was, asking us to publicly stand up and acknowledge that confession. I was worried that if I stayed seated, he would call me out—Hey you, in the yellow dress, yes—you. You had your hand up—why are you still sitting down? You can imagine my fear. So, I stood and went to the front with many other people."

Elsbeth played with her necklace for a moment, gathering her thoughts to continue. Enthralled by her story, I looked at her face. I could feel her panic and knew I would feel the same had I been in her shoes.

"We are all standing there, in rows at the front of the church. The preacher moved to the first person on my left, and there were probably ten people between us. I noticed John was no longer on the floor and wondered where he went. So, I'm not really paying attention to what was happening, but then the person this preacher is praying for falls. He moves to the next person, and they fall, and the panic inside me explodes. I cried tears of true terror now. I didn't understand what was happening. The third person went down, and I shuffled to the right, letting people move into the prayer line ahead of me. People kept falling, and some were on the floor, twitching and jerking like bacon on a hot griddle. All I could think of was—get me out of here."

"I'm nearly at the other end when I bump into someone. He's standing at the end of the row, praying for people and talking to them quietly. No one was falling. There is something gentle about him, something I couldn't put my finger on, but it drew me to him. When he finally wrapped up, he looked over at me, and when our eyes …" Elsbeth closed her eyes and drew a deep breath.

A minute passed, and when she opened her eyes again, there were tears swimming with the memories. "I miss that man," she whispered. "Every day."

"Anyway, I learned he was the youth pastor at this church. Newly hired, and this was his second week in his position. He knew no one in town, so he gave me his card and told me to get in touch if I needed anything. The rest is history. He was a good man—a decent man, and we had many happy years together. Paulie was our eldest. We also had a daughter. She was a beautiful child. She went to be with her Lord a long time ago, and her death broke Matthew. He never fully recovered."

Neither of us spoke for several minutes. It was unbelievable that she had experienced the loss of a child—a daughter. I wondered if we were both thinking about them. I also felt certain that even if Elsbeth's daughter had died peacefully in her sleep and not at the hands of a madman, she could understand the loss.

The silence lasted another few moments, and then she returned from her reverie and smiled at me. "Now it's your turn. Tell me about you, things I don't know."

I cleared my throat, uncertain what to say. After a minute, she advised me to start with my childhood. Did I grow up here, that sort of thing?

I turned back the clock, and visions of a much smaller and more intimate town came into focus. I told her about my large family and growing up in this small town, sharing the struggles of being overlooked because there were so many personalities to deal with, and being the agreeable child often meant that I got less attention than the others.

I told her about visiting our grandparents' farm one spring and falling into the large hole in the ground for the new septic tank.

"You didn't see the hole?" she asked.

"No. Judith wanted to play catch, so she had me stand near the tank. Then, she told me to step back farther because she would throw the ball far. I forgot there was a hole behind me, so I just stepped back, and then the world went black. For one second, I thought I was going to hell. It was rather remarkable that I climbed right out like a cat climbing a tree. Judith was bent over laughing—she thought her joke was so funny until Mom put a boot to her bottom. She stopped laughing then."

"You must have been terrified."

"I was, but mostly I felt humiliated. Judith wasn't a bully—she really didn't think of the consequences—like maybe I would have been seriously hurt. She just thought it would be funny. It's part of our family lore now—a story paraded out when we reminisce—a tale that doesn't seem to lose its appeal."

"And how do you feel about it?"

"I don't know. I guess it's just part of the stories we tell each other. I don't think about it unless someone brings it up, and it's usually Judith. It's really her story."

"I'd like to never hear it again because I always feel like I'm at the butt of some joke when they tell me about the stuff they did to me." I told her about the time I fainted from heat stroke because I was too stubborn to drink any water—I told her about our old dog that used to chase me when I ran, trying to stop me. That made me laugh, remembering how she grabbed hold of my jeans one day and ripped the right leg clear up to my butt. A wave of nostalgia swept over me. I hadn't thought of that dog in years.

Kenny appeared in the doorway. He moved with such stealth that I started at his sudden arrival. "It's nearly lunchtime, Mrs. Prince."

"Oh, Kenny. Thank you." Elsbeth pushed herself up. I could hear Kenny gathering our teacups and plates from the dining room table. He disappeared into the kitchen. Elsbeth turned to me. "This has been delightful. I hope you will come again."

"I would like that. Very much." I followed her into the kitchen.

"Is the car warm?" Elsbeth asked Kenny.

He nodded. "Your chariot awaits, madam." He bowed to me, and Elsbeth snorted.

"Don't mock people, young man." She sounded stern, but she was laughing.

"Never." He smiled. His affection for her was clear on his face. It made me happy to know that he was here with her, that she wasn't alone.

Kenny held my coat out, and I slipped into it with ease. Then he stepped out the back door. I looked at Elsbeth, wanting to hug her, but I wasn't sure if she was a hugger. I stepped down the two stairs to the back porch and pulled my boots on before turning back again. She stood at the top of the stairs, smiling. "Give me a hug before you go." She said gruffly.

I moved to the top step and put my arms around her. She was stiff, like hugging wasn't natural, and I pulled away quickly, feeling her discomfort.

Patting my shoulder awkwardly, she asked. "Next week?"

I nodded.

"Shall I send Kenny?"

I nodded again, and then I was gone. The rest of the week passed in a blur, but there wasn't a day that went by that I didn't think about Elsbeth and her daughter. I wondered what her name was and how she had died. The serendipity of finding someone with a history not unlike mine thrilled me. It was more than a coincidence. It was fate.

CHAPTER THIRTY-TWO

My annoyance toward Andy continued and, dare I say, deepened. I just couldn't accept that what happened to our daughter would draw someone closer to God. What irked me even more was his patience and understanding with me. It felt patronizing. I stubbornly refused to attend church, though he and Nora happily slipped out the door on Sunday morning, leaving me to stew in my own juices.

I paced the floor, muttering angrily at the unfairness of life. How many years had I wanted Andy by my side? How many times had he simply shrugged it off, happy to putter around the house or go to the office and do paperwork, leaving me to bear the spiritual burden on my own? I was working myself up into a true dither when the phone rang.

It was Logan. I shoved all my anger aside and answered the phone cheerfully. "Mom?"

His voice was strained, and my heart leaped out of my chest. "Logan, what's the matter?"

"Oh, Mom, it's such a mess." He sobbed. My heart, already fluttering at the sound of his pain, constricted painfully.

It took a few minutes before he could talk. "Sorry, I just didn't think anyone would be home. I wanted to leave a message for Dad to call me. Then I heard your voice and …" He started crying again.

"Okay, honey. It's okay. Tell me what's happened."

"But that's just it, Mom. It's not okay. I don't know what to do."

My patience was wearing thin. "Spit it out, Logan. I can't help you if I don't know the problem."

"It's Courtney—she broke up with me."

It seemed like such a minor upset to garner so many tears, and yet, with all he'd been through having just lost his sister, his reaction was right on track. My heart went out to him.

"What happened?"

"I don't even know where to start."

"The beginning is usually a good place." I wished he would just talk. Sometimes, he was so much like his father.

"She's going to have a baby … only I'm not the father."

Whoa. Now, that was harsh. "She told you this, and you're sure you're not the father."

"God, Mother. You are always so obtuse," he snapped. "We haven't had sex—ever! Is that enough proof that I'm not the father!"

"Okay, Logan. You need to settle down. I am on your side."

He was off on another crying jag. After repeatedly calling his name and whispering comforting words, he spoke again. "It's been all over campus for months. She's been seeing Clint behind my back."

"Clint, as in Clint Walker?" Clint was Logan's best friend. They had been friends for as long as I could remember.

"Yeah, that's the guy." He sighed. "My *supposed* best friend. He says he never meant for this to happen. You know the typical bullshit …"

"Logan! There is no need to swear."

"Sorry, Mom. It just gets to me, you know. I mean, what's wrong with me?" The tears were back.

I wanted to scoop him up, cuddle him, kiss away his tears, and tell him everything would be all right. But he was thousands of miles away and no longer a little boy. My heart nearly burst open, and tears flooded my eyes. Why did life have to be so hard? Hadn't he been through enough? He'd only just lost his sister, and now his two best friends had betrayed him in the worst way possible. They should be on his side. I wanted to wring their necks, but that wasn't the answer either.

"I think you need to come home. You've just lost your sister, and this is too much. I want you here where I can keep an eye on you."

"Mom, that's not the answer. I can't run away."

"It's not running away. I am worried about you."

"It is running away, and I won't give either of them the satisfaction that they have destroyed me. If anyone needs to tuck their tail between their legs and run away—it's them. Why should I make this easy for them and go away?"

"I see what you're saying, but I wish you'd come home anyway."

"Christmas is coming. I'll be home soon enough."

After assuring him I would have his father call him, we hung up. Thoughts of him nursing a broken heart weighed on me. It was times like this when I would pray, and the pull to drop to my knees was strong. I refused to yield to it, though. Let Andy pray for him if he wanted. I wasn't about to ask God for one more thing.

I heard the ice over my heart snap and pop as it thickened. For one second, I thought about relenting and letting God in, but I just couldn't bend. He didn't care about me, and I wouldn't give him the satisfaction of crawling back.

Andy and Nora came home after church, filled with light and love. I told Andy to call Logan but didn't tell him why. He made the call while Nora and I cleared the table after lunch. Nora had gone to her room, and I was in the living room with a book when he made an appearance. His face was lit from the inside, and my heart flipped over.

"So …"

Andy smiled. "He's willing to talk to Pastor Dan, praise the Lord."

I snapped. "That's your answer? Send him to Pastor Dan?"

"Well, no …"

"I thought I knew you. But you aren't the man I married."

"And you're not the woman I married. The woman I married would rejoice that her husband was going to church and that her son was leaning that way, too. But whoever you are …"

"Typical. Throw it back at me. Sure, I'm the bad guy in all this."

"I never said that."

"You didn't have to. I know what you meant."

We were at an impasse. I didn't mean what I said, but for the life of me, I couldn't back down. I knew Andy's heart. He wasn't an evil man—I was the person in the wrong. I hated myself, but I wasn't about to admit that. "I think you need to leave."

"Okay." Andy turned to go. "I'll stop over at Mom and Dad's for a visit and let you calm down. But I'll be back in time to help with supper."

"No, Andy. I mean—leave."

Shock and pain filled Andy's face. "You don't mean that."

At that moment, I knew I didn't mean it, but I couldn't bring myself to say it. "I think I do."

"I don't understand you, Audrey. You finally got what you wanted, and now you're going to throw it all away because it didn't happen soon enough or with your blessing?"

"You think I wanted my daughter dead in the ground?" I shouted, my anger rising like the waters in spring.

"I wasn't talking about that, and you know it."

"That's the problem—I don't know anything anymore. And here you are with all the answers. None of them mean anything. Don't you get it? Life isn't about God and church and being a good person. It's every man for himself, and it's about standing on your own two feet. It's hard knocks—not sunshine and lollipops. I could spit with anger most days, yet all you can do is smile and praise the Lord. Well, I can't stomach it anymore."

"What happened to you, Audrey?" Andy whispered.

"My daughter was murdered."

With tears in his eyes, he whispered back. "So was mine. So was mine." Then he turned and went up the stairs.

The moment he was out of sight, I fell onto the couch. Shoving a cushion into my mouth to muffle my sobs, I let out the anger, frustration, and pain. When Andy appeared with the suitcase, my eyes were puffy, and my nose was red, but I felt composed.

"I don't have to go, you know. I can move into the spare room while we get this sorted."

"There's no need," I replied.

"No, I think you need some space to sort out what you want. I don't even have to come home for lunch, but I don't want to leave, Audrey. If you insist, I will, but this isn't the answer, and I think deep down you know that."

I nodded. "Okay, for the kid's sake, you can stay. I don't want to fight with you, and I don't want you to "praise the Lord" in my presence. I don't want to go to church or pray. The first slip and it will be the door. I'm sorry."

"Me, too." I turned my back to him and flicked on the television. I never watched TV on a Sunday, but I wanted to show him this conversation was over.

I heard Andy leave the room, and once it was safe, tears rolled down my cheeks anew. How was I ever going to come back from this?

CHAPTER THIRTY-THREE

As I climbed the stairs to Dr. Reisner's office, my stomach was in knots. I sat in the chair outside her closed door and tried to calm myself. The drive in had only stirred things up in my mind. I didn't want to be here. I didn't want to open my heart to her. My experience with her last week hadn't given me the feeling that I was in safe and caring hands. Instead, I felt like a bug under the microscope—she only studied me for her benefit, not mine.

I was also still chewing on what happened between Andy and me. Part of me was adamant that I had done nothing wrong, yet I couldn't feel good about any of it. We were walking on eggshells with each other. Even Nora seemed to be artificial. I could kick myself for not conceding, but my back was up, and I didn't know how to extricate myself from my stupidity.

The door opened, and the same little man slipped out and down the stairs without a sideways glance. Just like last week, I waited ten minutes before the door opened, and Dr. Reisner ushered me onto the same couch. This time, she sat down opposite me right away.

She had her clipboard ready, and, without preamble, she jumped right in. "So, what are we going to talk about today?"

That set me back. Surely, she should determine our topic. "I don't know. What do you want to talk about?" I threw the question right back in her face.

"We can talk about what's bothering you."

I wanted to say she was bothering me. Instead, I chose the least worrisome issue. "Well, my son called this week to tell me he was breaking up with his girlfriend. Apparently, she's pregnant with his best friend's baby."

"And this affects you how?"

My dander was up. "He's my son and I love him," I snapped.

"Please hold your temper, Mrs. Taylor. I am not the enemy."

"Well, you could have fooled me," I whispered to myself.

"Pardon me? I didn't hear that."

"I said, he's my son, and I care about what happens to him."

"After that?"

"I just repeated it."

"Oh. Okay, well, let's go back to my question then. How does this affect you?"

I guess we were going to go in circles. I tried really hard to keep my temper in check, but she didn't make it easy. "He's my son and I care about him."

"I don't know if you are being deliberately difficult so, let me rephrase the question. How does this news about your son affect you?"

"Well, I am angry for him. He doesn't deserve this. He's a lovely young man. I would like to batter his so-called best friend. I mean, how do you do something like that to your friend?"

"Do you always want to fight your child's battles?"

"Are you serious? Do you have any children?" When she didn't answer, I repeated myself. "Well, do you?"

"Mrs. Taylor, please. Just answer the questions as honestly as you can. You might not see how this is going to help, but I have had years of practice. I am trying to help you."

"So, that would be a no?" I answered my question for her.

"Mrs. Taylor …"

"We're done here. I can't talk to you. We are on two different pages and I'm leaving."

"I don't agree—I think I could help you, if you'd let me in."

"Well, I don't feel comfortable with you. I don't like you. So, I'm never going to be open with you. Your questions aren't helping. They are infuriating. And last week? Last week, you did nothing, and yet you expected to be paid."

"Most of my analytical work is done outside our meeting, Mrs. Taylor. My fees are standard in the industry. I'm sorry you feel you were short-changed."

"Ripped off, more like. I guess I should go."

"Yes, I think you should. You have your mind made up. So, that will be …"

"You're expecting to be paid. I've been here ten minutes."

"My fees are by the hour or part thereof."

I wanted to jump up and walk out without paying, but I had done nothing like that in my life. I made out the check and threw it at her. Leaving her office, I could feel the anger burning. I could have gladly slapped her if she'd just given me a reason. What a waste of time and money. Do I always fight my children's battles? Well, I hadn't actually slapped Clint, had I? Wanting to wasn't the same thing as doing it.

As I drove out of downtown, I saw the sign for Jack's Diner. Those warm, gooey cinnamon buns leaped to mind. I quickly found a parking spot. Within minutes, I was inside the warmth of the small café, a cup of strong brewed coffee and a cinnamon bun in front of me. Mmmm. The cinnamon bun was delicious—a perfect balance of cinnamon and sugar, not to mention the cream cheese icing. I closed my eyes.

The cinnamon bun was gone before I knew it, so I ordered a second one. My stomach groaned as I shoved in the last couple of bites, but I ignored it. After finishing my second cup of coffee, I went to the counter to pay. I ordered two more cinnamon buns for Andy and Nora. Then, I hurried out to the car and headed home. Before I hit the highway, I had already taken a small ring off one bun. I ate them both because I couldn't arrive home with a bun for one and not the other. By the time I got to the outskirts of Granville, my stomach was roiling. I started crying—not because my stomach hurt, but because I didn't understand what had just happened.

I carry more weight than I should, but I wasn't a glutton. What I had done that morning was gluttony—pure and simple. Why had I abused my body in such a way? I needed to talk to someone. Tiffany …

I drove to her house, parked, and rang the doorbell. No one answered. I rang again. She wasn't home. Then I remembered she started going to a Bible study on Tuesday mornings. I got back in the car and headed home. Then I remembered Elsbeth. Could I just drop in on her? She was expecting me tomorrow. I didn't know her well enough but felt comfortable with her. She would listen …

Driving past, I noticed the car was in the driveway. I pulled a U-turn at the end of the road and pulled up outside her house. Before I could change my mind, I got out of the car and ran up the sidewalk. With a deep breath, I rang her doorbell. I heard shuffling inside, and a minute later, Elsbeth pulled open the door. I burst into tears as she pulled me into her warm house.

CHAPTER THIRTY-FOUR

"Kenny?" Elsbeth called down the stairs. "I need you up here, please."

Within moments, Kenny appeared. Elsbeth pulled him into the kitchen and spoke to him privately. I couldn't make out what she was saying. It didn't matter. My emotions were galloping all over the place, and I felt like I was going to come apart at the seams.

I shed my coat on the floor and headed to the front room. Elsbeth was not far behind me. I stood at the window, looking out into the white world. She let me stand there momentarily before gently guiding me to a nearby armchair. She dragged a chair close and sat facing me.

"Now, tell me what this is all about."

I spilled everything. I started with Andy and my folks, who did not want me to marry him, especially not right out of school. "Andy was—and is—the best thing about my life. He has been a blessing to me since we met—until this."

"Until what?"

"Until Brenda died. Now it's all wrong, and I don't know what to do?" I angrily wiped away the tears that fell on my face.

"Tell me what you mean."

Focusing on the green triangle on the carpet, I kept my tone low. "Well, when Brenda didn't escape that grisly death, I wanted to blame somebody. It was important to place my anger somewhere. I told Andy it was his fault because he wasn't a believer. As soon as those words were out of my mouth—I knew it was wrong. I knew it, but it was already out there. And maybe I meant it—you know?"

I looked up into her piercing blue eyes. She wasn't smiling or encouraging, and I found that comforting. I didn't want to be patronized for thinking horrible things, but I also didn't see any judgment or animosity. I continued, debating whether to tell her about her son's agreement.

"Pastor Newberry agreed with me, and Andy was struggling. He would harm no one, and here he was, being accused of aiding a murderer because he didn't have the faith to believe in God and go to church. I have been praying for that man my whole life—praying that he would get his life right with God—praying for guidance and patience to see him into the faith because I didn't want to go to Heaven alone. I wanted to meet him and be with him in the hereafter, and I wanted him to come to church with me …" I took a breath and sat back.

"For all my praying and all my pleading with God, Andy didn't budge until Brenda died, and it's too late. It's too late to save her. She wanted to be like her dad—she wanted to be her own person. I fear my daughter, after all she went through that night, is in Hell."

"Don't you think God would have been with her at the end? Don't you believe that He would have asked her to give her life over to Him before her last breath?"

"Should I? I served God my whole life. I can't remember not going to church. I have prayed for a multitude of people, and I have always served God first, and my reward is that my daughter gets murdered, and my husband has now become a believer. For the first time in my life, I struggle to believe."

"So, God has disappointed you?"

"Disappointed? *Disappointed?* I am beyond that—I am angry—I am furious. If He were standing here, I would pummel Him with my fists. I don't know how to get rid of this belly full of hatred. I haven't hated anyone before. But that young man, who did what he did to my girl—well, I despise him. It's a good thing he's dead because if he were alive, I would have to kill him. Part of me wants to find his parents and tell them a thing or two, and part of me knows he was old enough to make his own choices and that they are probably victims of that night, too. It doesn't help—but I try to keep that in mind."

"That's very gracious of you. You are very noble for offering them some grace."

"Am I? My entire world has turned upside down, and I simply cannot understand what to do anymore. I feel trapped and bitter and don't want to be bitter. But that's all I have."

"Your feelings are natural. It's okay to feel that way—you just can't live there. You will move on. I have faith in you."

"Faith. That has been my go-to word—faith. I had faith once upon a time. Now I have nothing."

"That is a feeling. It's not reality. You are a believer who is struggling with disappointment in her God. It's part of the journey for some. Some will never have their faith tested."

I sat there listening to her talk, and I realized that though she no longer attended church, she knew God and listened without judging. I felt free to continue.

Shifting the conversation to my other children, I spoke about Nora's potential life choice and how my son got his heart broken. Then I was back to Brenda's murder and my fall from grace to self-pity and self-sabotage. Elsbeth didn't speak as the words poured out of me.

I cried, I sobbed, I howled, and I screamed. Nothing seemed to garner more than a sympathetic pat on my back or my hand. She sat with me in the pit of despair, letting me empty my bitterness at God and the world in general.

When I could not go on any longer, Elsbeth helped me see that there was a way through. It wouldn't take a day; it might be months, but I had to be faithful to myself and allow the pain to be changed. She promised the wounds would become scars that would provide me with empathy I could use toward myself and others.

I don't know how long I was there. At some point, Kenny brought in tea and cookies. He left it on a tray, and Elsbeth served. I didn't want a cookie, not after what I had eaten. Tears rolled down my cheeks whenever I thought about how disgusted I was with myself.

"The most important thing in all of this, Audrey, is forgiveness. You don't need the burden of unforgiveness pulling you down into a dark pit every day. You need to bring light into your situation, love, and compassion to your family."

I nodded, knowing this was the answer, but I didn't know how to do that.

"You start with yourself."

I stared at her, waiting for some revelation to strike me.

"Audrey, you weren't responsible for your daughter's death."

"I know."

"Do you?"

The tears started again, but this time, there was no force behind them. They rolled down my cheeks—and dripped off my chin.

"You weren't responsible for your daughter's death." She repeated.

Not wanting the answer to be so simple, I said, "But God let it happen. He let me down."

"Did he?"

"Yes!" I shrieked more loudly than I meant to. Elsbeth didn't flinch. She didn't move. She didn't repeat her question.

CHAPTER THIRTY-FIVE

The room grew dark, and Elsbeth never left my side. I got to the place where I felt empty. There was nothing more to shout about. Kenny came in and snapped on some lamps, shedding light where there had been shadows a moment before.

Drawing a deep breath, I sat up straighter and looked at Elsbeth. Her face was calm, and her eyes radiated compassion and love. Leaning over, she hugged me and patted my back. If I had tears left, they would have spilled then, but there were none.

Releasing me, she asked, "Are you ready to go home? Or do you need a cup of tea?"

Realizing it must be late, I felt I should go home and face my family. They were probably wondering where I was. It was then that I remembered I had left my purse in the car, and my cell phone was inside. Andy must be frantic.

"I should probably go home and start making amends." I have many bridges to rebuild.

"Well, I want you to come back tomorrow, please. It is the day for reading, but I think I can forget that for another week, and we'll talk some more. You did great work today, and you're on the way, but there are still some thorns from your garden."

I smiled. I had never heard of the heart as a garden before. When Elsbeth shared her theory with me, it made sense that once the weeds of distrust and anger found root in the fertile land of a broken heart, they would sprout. I was feeding them, watering them, and nurturing those feelings rather than those of love, empathy, and compassion. No wonder I had gone off the rails into such a deep, dark jungle.

Kenny held my coat out and then handed me my keys. "You left your car running with the keys inside. I put your purse on the floor so it wasn't so visible. I hope that was okay?"

My mouth dropped open. "I left my car running?"

Kenny smiled. "I think you were in a hurry."

I shook my head in disbelief and was very grateful to Kenny. "Thank you so much for looking after me."

Elsbeth nodded. "He's a good young man. He looks after me all the time."

Kenny blushed, shuffling his feet.

Gratefulness at being here in this house overwhelmed me, and tears sprang anew. I smiled through them, promising to return tomorrow. Climbing into my car, I felt both exhausted and revitalized at the same time. It took less than five minutes to get home. The house was aglow with light. Relief flooded through me.

I was home.

CHAPTER THIRTY-SIX

Andy met me at the door. "Where have you been—I've been worried sick."

"I'm sorry. I …" I stopped, unsure what I should say. How do I explain the insanity of my morning, followed by what I'd gone through at Elsbeth's house? "It's a long story. Can we talk about this later? I really need to sit down."

Dumbfounded, Andy stood back, allowing me into the house. I could see that he was struggling to understand what I needed. "Do you want something to eat? Nora made spaghetti if you want some."

I realized I was hungry. "Yes, I could eat," I said, leading the way into the kitchen. Andy followed close behind. I could feel his anxiety radiating off his body.

Nora, having heard our conversation, was serving me a plate. "Thanks, love." I smiled at her.

Twisting some noodles onto my fork, a weariness settled on my shoulders. Andy sat across from me, watching me intently. I forced the food into my mouth—the sauce bursting onto my tongue, causing me to groan. "This is delicious," I said to Nora. "But, I guess I wasn't as hungry as I thought." Pushing the plate away, I lowered my head into my hands.

"Did something happen at therapy this morning?" Andy asked.

I nodded. "What happened today was …" Tears rolled down my cheeks. "I owe you all so much." My throat closed as more tears poured out. I didn't think I could cry anymore after this afternoon, but my body seemed intent on proving me wrong.

Andy shoved some tissues into my hand, and I wiped my eyes. "I'm sorry, I can't seem to get control of myself. I think I just need to go to bed."

Looking up, I saw fear in Nora's eyes. I took her hand in mine. "Listen," I said, "I am okay. I've had an emotional day, and I'm exhausted. But it's all good. I know I seem a mess, but I am far better than I was this morning. I promise."

She smiled, tears brimming in her eyes. I stood then and took her into my arms. Rocking back and forth, I cooed into her ear that I loved her, that she was lovely, and that everything would be okay.

When we broke apart, I noticed Andy cleaning the kitchen. I stepped up beside him and placed my right hand over his left. He looked over at me, and we locked eyes. I smiled—a quivering smile. My eyes filled with tears of gratefulness for this man's love and patience. I knew then that I owed him so much—I could never repay it. I squeezed his hand.

"I need to sleep," I said as I let go of his hand. "When I get some rest, I promise I will tell you what happened today. I still haven't got my mind around it, but it is a turning point." I headed to the stairs. Each step took energy I wasn't sure I had.

Andy came up behind me, wrapped his arm around my waist, and guided me up the stairs to our room. He handed me my nightgown and walked me to the bathroom. Leaning on the sink, I watched him place some toothpaste on my toothbrush, and I dutifully brushed my teeth as he went out into the room and turned down the bed.

With him outside the room, I pulled off my clothes, leaving them on the bathroom floor. I slipped the nightgown over my head and then finished brushing my teeth. Andy came in then, rinsing the sink and running the water until it was warm. He moistened a washcloth and handed it to me. I washed my face.

When I was done, he took my arm and guided me to bed. Pulling up the covers, Andy leaned down and planted a kiss on my forehead. "Sweet dreams, sweetheart." He left the room, turning off the overhead lamp and closing the door behind him.

After he'd gone, I turned onto my side and fell into a deep sleep.

CHAPTER THIRTY-SEVEN

The morning dawned, and I slept right through it. When I finally crawled out of bed, the house was quiet. Nora had gone to school, and Andy had gone to work. My body ached from not drinking enough fluids. After showering, I called Elsbeth to find out when she wanted me there.

Arriving at her house at one p.m., Kenny ushered me into the living space where coffee and cookies were waiting. As we sipped our coffees, we chatted about the process for the future. "I think we should meet for an hour every week to discuss how you are doing emotionally," Elsbeth explained. "We need to build you up again, and maybe we can regenerate your faith—although that is secondary to getting rid of all that anger."

I agreed, and for the next hour, we talked about the weeds in my garden—those thoughts that I had allowed entry once my heart broke open.

After an hour, I was all cried out. Elsbeth walked me to the door, assuring me we had made good progress. I went home to make supper for my family, feeling much brighter about the future, though I knew

I had more ground to cover.

Nora came home from school at the usual time. She had her youth meeting that night and wanted to get together with some kids early to sort out leadership. She ate a sandwich and headed out the door with a piece of fruit as Andy pulled into the driveway. This would be the first time we'd been alone since our separation.

Andy washed up and then came into the kitchen. He looked fearful, and I couldn't blame him. I had been vicious to this precious man. He was a saint to even be in the same room as me.

We sat at the table, and Andy bowed his head to pray. After a second, he started speaking out loud.

"Father, you are our light …"

"Please, Andy, could you pray silently? I am just not prepared to hear about God's goodness yet."

Andy looked at me, his expression revealing a depth of sadness. Then he bowed his head and prayed again, this time silently. I sat waiting for him to finish before I started eating.

I looked across the table at Andy as he glanced up from his prayer. I was desperate to mend the fence between us, but I obviously had a long way to go.

As Andy consumed his meal, he asked, "Do you want to talk about yesterday and what happened?"

Since Nora was not home, I felt I could at least give him some basics. I started with the horrific meeting with Dr. Reisner and my frantic trip to Elsbeth's house. I did not mention the cinnamon buns.

"Wait, hold up. Who is Elsbeth?"

I realized then that I had shared little of what was happening in my life with Andy since Brenda died. I told him about walking to the grocery store, meeting her at the checkout, and driving home. "She's actually—and you're going to find this funny—she's actually Pastor Newberry's mother. Her name is Elsbeth Prince."

"His mother? Are you sure you should talk to her? Is what you say going to get back to him? You know he thinks I am a heathen bent for Hell and you too for marrying me."

I nodded. "I know. But she does not go to his church, and she used to be a professional counselor—maybe a psychologist? I don't think she was a psychiatrist—but someone like that, so she has professional ethics. She knows I used to go to his church and that I am not going now. I think she would enjoy the atmosphere at a smaller—less flamboyant church—but we haven't discussed that much. We are working on my disappointment with God and trying to rebuild my faith—although she says that my faith is secondary to getting my anger under control."

"So you think she is helping?"

"Well, I am here talking to you—so yes. I think she's been where I am. She also had a daughter who died, so she knows about grief. She intimated her husband took the death hard, so maybe her experience isn't with her own feelings, but those of her pastor husband."

"God works in mysterious ways, doesn't he?"

I bristled a bit at his words. "How so?"

"Can you imagine that for the sake of some whipping cream—the convenience store was out of it, forcing you to go to the grocery store, where you meet this woman who offers you a lift home, invites you to her house to be a friend and a helper to her and she has the credentials to do what Dr. Reisner could not do. Can you see God's hand in that?"

"I never thought of it that way—but you may be right. I am going to have to ponder that some more."

Andy got up and cleared the table. I put on the kettle for tea and placed some cookies on the table for dessert.

"Changing the subject, I got a call from the crime scene cleaners, and we can now get into Brenda's place to clear out her stuff. Do you want to go with me?"

"These crime scene guys cleaned up all the blood and stuff. We won't be seeing any of that when we go?"

"No, it should all be sterilized. The police said they were the best in the business, so I assume it will be fine. I asked them to clean out the fridge, too. There should be no rotting food either." He took a bite of his cookie before he continued. "I can go on my own. I don't want you to feel you have to be there—unless you want to be."

"No, I should go." A shiver went up my spine at the thought of being in the same place where Brenda had died. It might not be a pleasant trip, but it was important to honor her. "But if there is no rush, can we go after Christmas?"

"Sure. The property is ours, so we can go anytime. I was also wondering if we should put the place on the market."

"What about Nora?"

"Well, we should talk to her first, but I thought she might not want to stay there, knowing what happened. She might want something different. So we can sell and buy something else for Nora."

"That's probably a good idea. We can talk to her this weekend."

"Sounds like a plan."

Finishing his tea and a second cookie, Andy stood and put his cup in the dishwasher. I handed him my cup as well. It had been such a pleasant change to talk to Andy again—like the old days before Brenda died.

"I'm going to catch the last half of the hockey game. Do you want to join me?"

"Thanks, but no. Elsbeth has asked me to journal, so I should get some thoughts on paper before Nora gets home." Andy nodded and moved into the living room. The crowd's cheers in the stands echoed into the kitchen as I pulled out the new journal I bought on the way home and a special purple pen I had picked up at the same store. It was time to get my jumbled thoughts in order.

CHAPTER THIRTY-EIGHT

Not knowing where to start with my journal, I sat thinking about my life. Within minutes, I felt overwhelmed, and I set the journal aside. I remember journaling before Brenda died, but that was all joyous and happy, even when it included a few prayers. Maybe I was reticent to put all my negative feelings on the page, somewhere others could see them. I preferred talking about this to ensure no record would ever exist. I wanted to expel them but didn't want proof they existed.

My mom was a great believer in the "Don't Rock the Boat" philosophy of life. That meant she discouraged the negative feelings about life and did not allow us to be angry at our siblings. You could not be sad. She would warn you that if you cried, she would give you something to cry about. We learned to put on cheerful faces and never rock the boat by telling someone they disappointed us or hurt our feelings. Sticks and stones …

I didn't consider myself a people-pleaser, but looking back, I saw how I shaped my life around the accolades of others. I wanted to do well, be accepted, and be part of the "in" crowd. There was little success at that in high school, as the dynamic of being a teenager is far different from being a wife and mother, a member of a church in good standing. Here, I excelled at being reliable and sought after for committees.

My organizational skills helped me to get things done. I knew who to ask and who to avoid getting involved in projects that required dedication and commitment. There were people who so clearly wanted to help, but they simply didn't possess the ability to follow through. They meant well, but their skills were better kept to duties on the day of the activity.

I knew my people. I trusted my instincts, and it served me well. Until Brenda died. Then, my world collapsed, and I was no longer serene. I was a powder keg, with all the years of swallowing my pride and my feelings as an underlying catalyst for ultimate damage. I hurt so many people as this energy exploded against the status quo. Judith, Elaine, Nora, Andy. Each of them had been on the receiving end of my sharp tongue. I couldn't take back what I had said. The vile comments were like nails in a fence post. Being sorry, removing the nails didn't return any of them to the same pristine condition they were in before I let my temper fly. I had done irreparable damage even if they extended forgiveness to me.

I didn't want to go down the road of feeling sorry for myself for allowing these things to happen. I couldn't change the past, but I needed to work on my anger for the future to hold my tongue instead of lashing out at everyone. I was doing better since I started seeing Elsbeth, but I wanted so badly to go back to being me.

CHAPTER THIRTY-NINE

I was still lamenting Christmas and wanted to escape the day entirely. One attempt to buy presents had failed, and I hadn't been in the mood to go since my breakdown and subsequent therapy with Elsbeth. Celebrating was the last thing on my mind.

Andy came home one night and called a family meeting. We hadn't had one of these since Logan went off to college.

The dishes were done and put away, and we sat at the kitchen table. Using her laptop, Nora called Logan, and when he was virtually in the room, Andy made his announcement.

"Stan Halvorson has asked me if I want his space at Emerald Lake for Christmas. He and Norma understand Christmas can be a hard time after a loss, and they aren't able to use it this year because of Norma's cancer treatments. It's for Christmas Eve through to the new year. They have a main chalet with a large Christmas tree, and our rooms would be upstairs. I understand through Stan that we don't have to take part in the opening of gifts on Christmas morning, but they put on a lovely meal that afternoon, and there is skiing and sledding and even ice skating. They also have well-marked walking trails. I think we should do this, but I wanted to see where everyone is at."

Nora was the first to respond. "This is super, Dad. I can hardly wait. Skiing, skating. It's totally awesome."

Logan was also on board, so the family turned to me. With tears in my eyes, I answered in the affirmative. I was so glad not to be in this house on Christmas day, and this sounded like the perfect holiday. We hadn't had a family vacation since Brenda was a teenager.

On Christmas Eve morning, the four of us climbed into Andy's work truck and headed to Emerald Lake. It was perhaps a two-hour drive, and the roads were clear of ice and snow, so we made good time. I hadn't been to Emerald Lake since I was young, so I wasn't sure what to expect.

As we entered the town, we passed towers of snow accumulating where plows had removed it from the streets. Being in the mountains meant they got a lot of snow—more snow than we got two hours to the east. I was in awe of the raw beauty around me: Fir trees covered in snow, snow-covered streets and yards, and even a few deer walking around the neighborhood. It was like a winter wonderland.

The chalet was gorgeous. It was three stories, log-framed, with broad balconies, a gently sloping roof, wide eaves, decorative wood details, and massive windows. Andy parked in the lot, and we made our way inside.

The openness of the high beamed ceilings and the natural light pouring in through the windows made this place seem massive. I was awestruck at the peace that fell on me and at how small I felt. In my mind, I compared it to God's throne room. It took me several minutes to realize that I had referred to my faith without negating the thought the moment it entered my mind.

The bellhop showed us to our suite on the second floor. There were two bedrooms off a central living area. The couch pulled out to make the fourth bed. Nora volunteered to take it, saying she wanted to look out the large windows first thing in the morning.

Settled in, we went for a walk through the little town. Christmas decorations adorned every store, and cafés displayed signs advertising eggnog. Not being a fan, I opted not to have one but stood in line with the rest of my family as they took some to go. I accepted a gingerbread cookie offered by someone in a reindeer outfit. It was all very festive, and I felt my mood rising along with the gaiety surrounding me.

The town tour didn't take long, but we passed the skating rink and found out the times they opened on Christmas day. The ski run was a little out of town, but the bus shelter just off Main Street posted when the bus came and went. Back at the chalet, we took a path that led into the woods. Groomed for walkers, we had no trouble navigating it. As the sun sank lower in the sky, the temperature in the trees dropped considerably, so we turned around and headed back to the chalet.

As we entered the hotel, the servers were setting the table for the Christmas Eve meal. The desk clerk advised that we had twenty minutes before they called dinner. We changed our clothes and got ready in the room. Andy and I were a little awkward with each other as we were sharing a room for the first time since that huge fight when I asked him to leave. We managed, though, neither of us commenting on the strangeness that we felt.

"I am feeling quite peaceful," I remarked as we gathered in the main living area. "This place really sets a mood, doesn't it?"

Andy nodded but said nothing.

Nora piped in, "I love this place. We need to come here every Christmas."

Our reason for being there pierced my heart, and my feeling of peace melted away. I choked back tears. "Are we ready to eat?"

With that, we headed out of the room. Andy caught my hand as I closed the door. "Are you okay?"

I nodded, unable to speak for fear that I would start crying.

The long dining table groaned under the weight of the feast laid upon it. The other diners were all in a festive mood. My heart started racing with the noise level, and I almost turned and ran back to the room. Andy caught my hand and smiled at me, pleading with his eyes for me to stay calm. I stood still as he pulled out a chair near the end of the table for me. Then he sat between me and the other diners. Nora and Logan sat across. The woman host was at our end of the table. She smiled at me, too, making me feel like I could manage this.

The host said grace before the bowls and platters of food made their way around the table. It was like being in a large family, something I experienced all the time as a child. I took a deep breath and relaxed. The conversations I could hear were all about plans for tomorrow. Those with children were eager for the gift opening that would take place at ten in the morning. Those without were talking about the ski hill or the skating rink. I stayed silent, just listening to the joy in the voices and wishing with all my heart that I could feel that again.

A staff of three cleared the table of empty plates and platters and then brought out small side plates, clean forks, and cups for tea or coffee. Several pies appeared, along with pudding cups and a selection of cakes and squares. If nothing else, this feast was a gift for the palette.

I accepted a cup of tea from a handsome young man who couldn't take his eyes off Nora. She blushed when she saw him looking and dropped her eyes shyly. I smiled at her coyness. In comparison, Brenda would have had that boy kneeling by her feet before the night was through. A single tear ran down my cheek as I thought of my daughter. I wiped it quickly, but not before the hostess noticed. She touched my hand and squeezed it. I met her eyes and smiled back, though the sadness didn't dissipate.

I was ready for bed. The kids stayed up to play board games with the other young people. Andy, too restless to sit any longer, asked if I wanted to go for a walk. I hesitated. "A walk sounds nice, but I think I'd rather just go up, get into my pajamas, and try to journal a bit. I

… been able to write anything since I started this."

"Would you like me to stay?" he asked.

"No. You go. Get some fresh air. I'll be fine on my own."

Assured, he pulled on his jacket, hat, scarf, and gloves and headed out into the night. The paths close to the hotel were all well-lit, and without me slowing him down, he could wear off some of that amazing supper.

I climbed the stairs to the room, glancing at my children happily playing some game I'd never heard of. In the room, I opened the bedroom door, slid inside, and closed the door behind me. Leaning on it for a few moments, I gulped in mouthfuls of air, trying to keep my resolve. When that failed, I flung myself on the bed and cried for what was gone.

CHAPTER FORTY

I was pretending to sleep when Andy came in. He tiptoed around, preparing for bed. I listened to the rustling of his clothes as he undressed and pulled on his pajamas. He slipped out of the room, presumably to wait for the kids to come to bed. I fell asleep before he came back.

I awoke with a start. Glancing at the clock, I wondered what had awoken me. It was just after two in the morning. Then I heard it again. It was Brenda. She was calling for me. "Mom!"

I slipped out of bed and quickly dressed. Andy lay on his side on the bed, facing away from me. A gentle rumble reached my ears, and I smiled. I had always loved listening to him snore.

The voice called again. "Mom!"

I closed the bedroom door and tiptoed across the room, making sure not to disturb Nora, who was sleeping on the pull-away under the window. In the dim light of the moon shining through the bare window, I noticed she was lying on her tummy, her head tucked between the pillows on the bed. The voice called again. "Mom!"

"I'm coming, I'm coming," I whispered. I opened the door and

...ut into the hallway, closing the door quietly behind me. I hurried down the stairs in my stocking feet toward the main door.

After pulling on my jacket, I found my boots and slipped them on. Before I wound a scarf around my neck or pulled on a hat, I was out the door, racing as quickly as I dared across the wooden veranda. Down the steps, I turned the corner and accessed the well-groomed path that led into the woods. The lights still burned as I rushed toward where I thought the voice was coming from.

Halfway to the trees, I stopped dead in my tracks. There was Brenda. She had come out of the woods and was walking toward me. I called her. "Brenda, I am here."

Looking up, she smiled—her lovely big smile—and started running. I also ran toward her. We both stopped inches from each other. I stared at her, her eyes swimming with tears, as mine were. I pulled her into a bear hug, crying. "Oh, Brenda, I have missed you so much. I love you. I am glad you are here."

She was also uttering words into my ear of affection, love, and loss. I don't know how long we stood there, locked in that embrace. I never wanted it to end. I felt her pull away and let go, keeping hold of her arms as I stepped back. She looked exactly as I remembered her. Her hair shone in the light, and I felt so lucky to have such a beautiful child. I told her.

Taking my arm, she walked us back to the veranda and across it to the other side, where there were benches and chairs. She sat, pulling me down next to her. We sat side by side, touching. Our arms and legs were so close that there was no room for a bookmark.

When I talked, she shushed me. "Let's just enjoy this moment of being together. I know how you feel. I know your thoughts. I want to be here with you to remember how much you mean to me."

We sat quietly for a while—I kept touching her to make sure she was real and still beside me. If this was a dream, I didn't want to wake up.

I don't know how long we sat there, but eventually, she talked. "Oh, Mom, I have missed you so much. I have missed hearing your voice and listening to you sing your silly gospel songs. I am worried about you. I am worried that you stopped attending church when it meant so much to you. I am worried that you and Dad are having issues because of me. I don't want this for you."

"But this isn't your fault. Everything is going to be okay now that you are here."

"That's the thing, Mom. I am not here. Well, I am here, but I can't stay. I have to go back soon. I just wanted you to know that I am okay and with God. He loves you so much and wants to see you get through this catastrophe feeling stronger in your faith and love for Him. He knows you blame Him, and He's okay with that. But He doesn't want you to live there and lose precious time lost in anger and hate."

"But how can I not blame Him? He's God, the Almighty."

Brenda looked at me, her eyes sparkling with joy. "Yes, He is. But He doesn't step in front of bullets to save humans from themselves. That's not His job. His job is to give His people faith that no matter what happens, He will turn it into good. Evil is present in the world, and we have choices. Sometimes people make bad ones."

I burst into tears. "I saw the autopsy report. I know what that boy did to you. How can that ever be okay?"

"Because I am okay. Look at me. Do I not look okay to you?"

I looked at her. "You are beautiful. Just as I remember you."

"That moment was horrible in so many ways. I knew I was going to die; Caleb had gone insane. Terror ran through me, and then there was this amazing sense of peace. Jesus was there with me. I didn't feel the pain of my injuries. Instead, He took my hand and held me until I released my last breath, and then I was no longer there. I could no longer hear the ravings of that maniac. I wanted to save Andrea, but I knew I couldn't. It wasn't my job.

"The other thing I remember about that night is hearing you pray was your prayers of protection that brought Jesus to my side. He answered your prayer. Maybe not in the way you wanted or hoped. But He came because of you."

My heart took in those words, and I physically felt it thaw. A warmth I didn't know existed poured into my chest. God had heard my prayers. It was surreal. I snuggled closer to Brenda, not wanting what was happening to me to interfere with our time together.

"I love you, Mom, and whenever you need me, I will always be here." She touched my heart. "Right here, tucked inside and as close as your next memory." She patted her hand for emphasis.

I wept then, letting her words sink in. When I reined in my emotions, I asked, "Do you want a cup of cocoa or something to eat? They have many good things inside." I looked at her expectantly.

"Sure, Mom. I'll have a cup of cocoa but nothing to eat. That sounds great."

"Do you want to come in?"

"No, thanks. I'll wait here. It's a pleasant night, and I love the view."

I moved toward the door as she called, "Merry Christmas, Mom." I smiled and repeated her words back to her before I slipped inside the chalet. The kettle boiled quickly, and I made us both a cup. I opened the door without burning myself, but when I stepped around the bow window, the chairs were empty. Brenda was gone. I set the cups down on the table and wept.

CHAPTER FORTY-ONE

Andy gently rocked my shoulder to wake me. "Merry Christmas, Audrey," he whispered.

I'm not sure why I was in bed and not out on the front veranda, but it took me a moment to respond. "Merry Christmas, Andy."

Thoughts about the nighttime visit with Brenda filled my head. Had I only dreamed about her visiting? It seemed so real to me. But I remembered nothing past the cocoa and finding her gone. How did I get back to bed and back into my pajamas? I didn't know what happened, and a pall fell over me. My heart contracted, and I wanted to cry, but not in front of Andy.

"The kids have been awake for a while. Logan just knocked a minute ago to see if we wanted to get up and get some breakfast. I think he lives for his stomach."

"Right, okay." I swept the covers back.

It didn't take us long to get ready. We came into the common room where Nora and Logan were waiting. "Surprise!" Nora called as she handed out small, wrapped packages to the three of us. I took it from her, hugging her. Inside were tiny, handcrafted ornaments she had made with her friends. She designed each ornament specifically for the person receiving it. Andy's was a wooden Christmas tree decorated with a hammer, nails, saw, and a level. It was really intricate and beautiful.

Logan's ornament was a bucking bronco, with the winning belt buckle emblazoned across the horse. Again, the detail was exquisite.

My ornament was a snowflake. It had five points. Inside these were pictures of my children. One side—a current photo—the other, a photo of each one at about six years old. Andy and I graced the other two points at our high school prom, at our wedding, and at a family barbecue several years ago. The most recent photo was taken this past summer.

Seeing the picture of Andy and me together through the years made me realize what I had so stubbornly tried to destroy. The photos of my babies and all the years of togetherness were overwhelming. Love, a deep river of it, splashed through my soul, crashing into the barriers I had erected to protect myself after Brenda's death. The tears washed away those obstructions as they flooded my eyes.

These gifts revealed how delicate and purposeful her craftsmanship was. Nora had done a great job creating pieces that spoke to each of us. I pulled her into another hug as I cried, my tender heart tugging itself back together. I was ready to start the healing process. I was ready to talk to God.

Andy sat patiently beside me. He also had done a little shopping at the stores in Emerald Lake. His gifts were also thoughtful. He got Nora a couple of books by her favorite author; he got Logan a framed photograph of some mustangs from the wild horse sanctuary near the national park. Logan had always been interested in them and had worked at the sanctuary the summer before college.

For me, Andy had bought a new angel for the tree. This one had the same hair color as Brenda. Usually, the angels you get in the store are blond. I don't know why, but I've never seen an angel with auburn hair before. Looking at her face, I imagined it was my girl who would forever guard our tree from her place up above.

I had no gifts to offer, and neither did Logan, who always waited until the last minute to buy his. Considering his state of mind over his girlfriend and his best friend, he didn't get around to doing any shopping. I didn't apologize for not having anything to offer. I simply stood and suggested we go to breakfast.

Trooping down the stairs, the smell of fresh brewed coffee, bacon, pancakes, and other tempting refreshments swirled through the air. My mouth watered as I imagined devouring fluffy pancakes and eggs and bacon. The same breakfast I would have made at home had we been there.

We were dishing up from a buffet table laden with all the festive delicacies when a server came in from outside carrying two cups. They looked like the ones I had filled last night. Nearing the other girl working the table that morning, she said, "Can you imagine this? I found these cups outside. It looks like frozen hot chocolate. I can't think of any reason for them to be there."

The other girl shrugged. "Someone must have forgotten them. They couldn't have been there long. I cleaned up last night before I clocked off at about ten."

I nearly dropped my plate. It was real. Brenda was here last night—it wasn't a dream. I stood, frozen in place, a scoop of hash browns halfway to my plate, staring at those two mugs as the girl moved past and into the kitchen.

Andy nudged me, and my thoughts came back to the buffet line. I wanted to run upstairs to the room and throw myself on the bed, and cry with joy. It was a hard debate, but I wanted to share this with the family, too. They needed to know that Brenda was okay and that she may, someday in the future, come to visit again. I hoped so.

Having finished dishing up, I joined Logan and Nora at the table. Andy was right behind me. The young male server came by with coffee and tea, his eyes seeking Nora. They smiled shyly at each other. Oh, my goodness. Had my sisters been wrong? Nora was flirting with this boy.

Small jugs of orange and apple juice sat on the table. Andy stirred cream and sugar into his coffee, and once he had set his spoon down, I asked to pray.

Andy smiled and nodded, and Nora had tears in her eyes as we bowed our heads. I prayed a blessing over the food, a benediction for the rest of our holiday in this magical place, and a devotion to the Lord. When I finished, everyone added an amen.

As we dug into our food, I told the family about my nighttime visitor. Everyone looked at me wide-eyed and skeptical. To prove that I was telling the truth, I asked Andy if he noticed the server carrying the two cups to the kitchen. He said the food had held his attention, and he hadn't noticed her.

When I reminded him, he had to nudge me. His eyes lit up. "Yes, I remember seeing her now. She was wearing a white Christmas sweater, with her dark hair pulled back into a ponytail."

"Yes, that's the one." I then told them about the hot chocolate and Brenda being gone and how I remembered nothing else except that I woke up in bed without recollection of getting there from the front veranda.

"The one thing that was impressed upon me last night, is that Brenda is okay. She is with God, and she is safe. She told me that God knows how angry I have been and wants me to let that go. I think that's why she came. God knew I needed to be assured, and even though I will never be the same, having lost a piece of our family, I will learn to trust God again and move on. This is truly a gift. I have a long way to go, but I am willing now to take those steps."

Andy reached over and took my hand. Logan reached over for my other, and Nora grabbed their hands to complete the circle. We were all going to get through this mess. We were all going to heal and learn to trust again. It was a Christmas miracle.

CHAPTER FORTY-TWO

We spent the rest of our week at the chalet outdoors. We went skating together and walked the trails side by side. I stayed in with a jigsaw puzzle on the afternoon the rest of the family went skiing. I had never learned to ski and didn't think I wanted to speed down an icy slope for fun. What I felt most was a sense of peace, though I went to bed each night, hoping to hear Brenda calling me again. It never happened.

Nora and I had some girl time. We went downtown and had a manicure while the men went cross-country skiing. I asked her about the young server.

"His name is Liam. He's from Crawford. His grandparents own this place, and he loves to help whenever possible. His folks came for Christmas Day, but he's been here on his break. He's a year older than me."

"Does he go to church?" I prodded.

Nora looked over at me and rolled her eyes. "Of course he does. It was one of the first things I asked him. His youth group sounds very active in the community. They volunteer at a soup kitchen, they visit kids in the hospital, and they also have volunteers who read to the seniors. Not everyone is involved in all the activities, but everyone does something. They sound really focused on serving."

I smiled and nodded. I knew my girl was level-headed. But I needed to understand why she had told Elaine a different story. "I don't mean to pry, but I need to know something. I overheard you tell Auntie Elaine that …"

Nora cut me off. "Oh no. Mom, I was confused. For a long time, I have wondered why I wasn't interested in the boys at church or school. I've known most of them all my life. None of them made me feel a spark. I am fond of most of them, but the thought of dating one of them was preposterous. Listening to the girls in my class gush about this guy or that one, I couldn't relate. I know you and Daddy fell in love in school, but I have no interest in the hometown boys. They don't challenge me to be better.

"Emily said maybe I was gay. I love spending time with her, and she is a lot of fun. I wondered if I might be interested in her beyond being her friend. But again, I felt no spark, just pure love for her friendship. That confused me even more. When I talked to Auntie Elaine, I was trying to figure out if my faith prevented me from being who I was—confused about what the gospel says and my desires.

"Liam is different. He's really on fire for God. He loves helping, and he's so involved. His excitement has already challenged me to do more. I have always wanted to do more with my life and want someone who wants that, too."

With that, I let the conversation about boys drop, and we finished our manicure and returned to the chalet for a hot chocolate. We sat on the veranda, bundled in our jackets, sipping our cocoa when Andy and Logan skied up. They removed their skis and stacked them on the racks in the shed.

Rosy-cheeked and warm from the exertion, they opted to enjoy their cocoa inside. Nora and I followed suit. It was a comfortable way to finish what had been a very enjoyable afternoon. That night, we celebrated the new year with the rest of the families in the chalet before returning to our suite for a few solemn minutes together to pray for and bless the new year. I felt closer to Andy, and although we slept in the same bed, neither of us had started a reconnection. I wanted us to get back on the same page, but I also knew my actions had deeply wounded him.

On our last night at the chalet, when Andy and I were alone in bed, I asked him if he would come to see Elsbeth with me when we got back. He looked thoughtful for several moments before he asked if I would talk to Pastor Dan. We were at an impasse. I wanted to go to church again, but I wasn't sure I wanted to discuss my raw feelings with Pastor Dan—at least not then.

"Andy, I am sorry. I want to go back to church. But I think that speaking to Pastor Dan about what has been going on in my head will make me feel too exposed while I try to recover what I have lost. Perhaps in time, I can sit down with him, but honestly, I don't want to do that right now. Elsbeth and I have already broken through many of my barriers, and I will continue to speak with her whether or not you come."

"Okay. I understand you have a rapport with this woman, but I don't. I don't want to feel blindsided by anything you have told her when I wasn't there."

"Oh, Andy. Elsbeth wouldn't do that. She's a professional, and she isn't on my side exclusively. She mentioned that bringing you into a few sessions would help us get a better footing going forward. If that's what we are doing. It's what I want, too. I want to repair all the damage I have done if I can. I know I can't take away the scars I gave you, but maybe together we can close some wounds and allow them to heal."

"Can I sleep on it?" Andy asked.

"Of course. Take all the time you need." Disappointed that I didn't get a resounding *yes* made my stomach hurt. Had I done so much irreparable damage that we would never go back to living as a family? I rolled over, turning away from Andy before my tears fell. I didn't want him to know how scared I was that we would never get back what we had.

I fell into a troubled sleep. When the sun rose over the horizon the next morning, I was more tired than I was when I went to bed. Andy was already up. I could hear him talking to the kids in the other room. I joined them fifteen minutes later, my hair still damp from the shower.

"I was just telling the kids that we would check out after breakfast. I think everyone has packed …?" He looked at Nora and Logan, and they both nodded. "So, if you are ready, let's eat."

It was a quick breakfast. No one had much to say. The reality of going back home was on everyone's mind. We had been in a bubble for the last ten days. Going home would take us back to what we had lost. That gap wasn't part of this.

It didn't take long to pack my belongings. Andy and Logan took everything down to the vehicle. Nora wanted to say goodbye to Liam. Alone in the suite, I did a final walkthrough to ensure we had forgotten nothing.

I pulled back the covers on everyone's bed. That was where socks went to die in our house. Logan's bed had one lone sock hidden in the sheets. I laughed because it was so typical. There was a bookmark in Nora's bed, which she had complained about losing the day before.

"How could a bookmark go missing?" she had pondered as she searched for it. Not finding the lost item, she took a brochure and tore the front page off to use as a bookmark until she could get another one. I tucked both items into my purse.

I threw the pillows off the bed and found what I thought was a business card. When I pulled it out, I saw it was a Bible verse. Romans 8:28 "And we know that in all things God works for the good of those who love Him, who have been called according to His purpose."

Guessing it was Andy's, I scooped it up and walked into the other room.

He showed up at the door moments later. "You ready to go?"

"Yes, all clear. I found Nora's bookmark and one of Logan's socks. And this …" I handed Andy the card, "… is yours."

"I've never seen this before in my life." He handed it back to me.

"I found it under your pillow."

Andy shrugged. I tucked the card into my purse. Taking one last look around the room, I turned toward the door. Andy stood still for a moment. "If Stan and Norma want to sell their shares in this place, do you think we should buy it so we can always have our Christmases here?"

The thought of being back here again was so enchanting that I immediately agreed. "Do you think we can afford it?"

"I don't know, but I will ask Stan. It will depend on Norma, of course. Cancer is a fierce enemy, but it's not always a death sentence. I hope, for their sake, that Norma pulls through, but I don't want to approach him when she just passed to ask. I think I will just plant a seed when I stop by with a thank you card and a gift certificate. That way, he can think about it but won't have to decide when decisions won't be easy."

"Good plan."

"Oh, and I have decided to see Elsbeth with you. You are important to me, and I want us to walk forward together. If this woman is helping you, then I am willing to talk to her as well."

"Oh, Andy, thank you. I know you'll like her. She is a spunky old girl."

He smiled, and we walked out the door.

We found Nora standing outside the chalet with a silly grin on her face. Logan was sitting on the bench where Brenda and I had sat, trying to tease her, but she wasn't rising to the bait. We walked to the truck as a family, and for the first time since I learned of Brenda's death, I felt an overwhelming rush of pure love flood over my body. I was so lucky to have these people in my life. I was fortunate to have Nora and Logan as my children and Andy as my husband. His willingness to walk with me through the shadows of death proved his love for me. I grabbed his hand.

He looked over at me and smiled, squeezing my hand. "It's good to have you back, Audrey, my love." I leaned closer as we neared the truck. Inside, I said a quick prayer for a safe trip home, and my lovely, beautiful family called back with Amen.

CHAPTER FORTY-THREE

I cannot say that life went smoothly from this point forward. There were days when I missed Brenda so much it hurt. This made it hard for me to function, and Andy, bless his soul, simply took my moods in stride. I knew he was hurting in his own way, but he managed his grief better. He had not moved back into our bedroom when we returned from Emerald Lake. We made strides toward reconciliation, and Elsbeth helped get us on the same page with our marriage.

During our third weekly session with Elsbeth, Andy confessed his anger and disappointment at how I managed my grief in the beginning. He addressed Elsbeth as if I wasn't in the room.

"Knowing that my daughter was dead was hard for me. I could not imagine how afraid she must have been in those moments before death. It made me angry that I couldn't find this man and beat him to a pulp just to make him understand what he did to our daughter. I was struggling with this when Audrey insinuated that her death was my fault because I wasn't a God-fearing churchgoer."

My heart constricted so hard that the pain in my chest forced me to bend over. I reached down and hugged my knees. I knew what he was going to say. He had shared this with me a long time ago. In my confusion and anger, I had caused him pain and suffering. I wished for one second that I didn't have to hear this, but I knew deep down that hearing it would help him heal his hurt.

"Audrey retracted her statement immediately, apologizing, but the damage was done. I added guilt to my already insurmountable grief and moved forward, trying to be everything for everyone. I nearly walked away. It would have been easy to get in my truck and never come back, but somehow, I knew that running wasn't the answer. I went to see your son."

Andy looked up and smiled at Elsbeth.

"He wasn't helpful. He told me much the same thing—that Audrey and I were not equally yoked, and the Lord couldn't bless us for that reason. Although he didn't say I was at fault directly, he didn't give me any assurances that I was guiltless either."

Elsbeth didn't respond. She said nothing to exonerate or convict her son. She smiled at Andy to encourage him to go on.

"I met Pastor Dan walking home from my folk's house one night, and we talked a bit about what had happened to our family. We made plans for me to see him the next day and the next. Expressing my guilt and my grief was therapeutic until, one day, it seemed so natural to repent and accept Jesus. I felt a peace like I'd never known, and I wanted to shout it from the rooftops. God is alive and well and living in my heart. The reception I got at home was not what I expected.

"Instead of celebrating this joyous occasion, my news was not welcome. Audrey no longer believed in God, and she was rather vocal about not being willing to surrender that position. For years, we had stood on opposite sides, and I never felt as much animosity for my choices as when I turned to God in my time of need."

Tears rolled down my face. This story was not my finest moment. It was my worst moment. There is no redeeming quality in how I treated my family and my husband during this time. I had already confessed this to Elsbeth but hearing it from Andy's lips again broke me anew. I wanted to throw myself at his feet and beg his forgiveness, but when I looked at Elsbeth, she silently signaled for me to stay put.

Andy was also crying at this point. His pain, caused by me, was engraved on his handsome face. He looked like a lost and vulnerable little boy. "I was happy in my faith, even though I couldn't share it with the one person I really wanted to. I looked forward to going to church and singing praises—the songs I heard Audrey singing for years. But she wasn't beside me, singing loudly in my ear. She was silent. So, I prayed for her.

"Then came the night that she asked me to leave. My heart staggered under that request. The woman I loved and still love asked me to leave the home we'd built together. I was persona non grata. My grieving heart was ripped in two. My knees wobbled, and at one point, I even wondered if I was having a heart attack. Weakness saturated my soul, and it took weeks of one-on-one prayer with Pastor Dan to feel something.

"Joy was gone, grief was gone, love was gone, and what sat in my chest was a pit of black slime that boiled up and burned my hopes. Maybe I should have left the house and not stayed in the guest room. But our kids had suffered much with the loss of Brenda, and I couldn't imagine adding to their pain and confusion by walking away. I'm sure they knew things had changed, but being there kept some of their fear at bay."

Andy looked at me for the first time. "I got to the place where I could forgive you, but I am not sure I can go back to the way we were until I know there is no chance of me being annihilated for not being perfect."

If you ever want to be humbled—let someone open the ugliness hidden in the recesses of your soul—let them hold up a mirror and show you just how wretched you are; you know how I felt in that moment. Shame, humiliation, regret, horror. Andy revealed what I had done from another perspective, and seeing how cruel my behavior was—destroyed me. Instead of showing love and grace or offering mercy, I ripped him open for speaking from the heart. His words had assaulted my pain, and instead of looking at my shortcomings, I turned my bitterness on him. Unfortunately, he wasn't the only victim.

Now, Elsbeth and Andy were both looking at me. Here was my chance to offer assurances and ask for forgiveness. My heart fluttered, and tears sprang to my eyes. "I can't believe I was such a horrible person. All my life, I tried to be kind and accepting, but when Brenda died … I guess I let that anger infiltrate every part of my soul. I hurt so bad. It was a physical ache, and I wanted everyone around me to hurt, too. I was unfair and ruthless, taking no prisoners. I lashed out at everyone and everything. My anger knew no bounds.

"I am so sorry I hurt you. You have always been the love of my life. I never want to live without you. That's why asking you to leave was such a shock to me. I couldn't believe I allowed my pain, fear, and disappointment to separate you from my life. That was never what I wanted, and if you had left, it would have killed me. Thank you for not leaving. Thank you for offering me forgiveness when I don't feel I deserve it.

"Through these sessions with Elsbeth, she has helped me to see how far I had fallen, not just from grace but from humanity. I wasn't capable of being a rational human being in the state I allowed myself to get to. I had warnings, but I ignored them. Your willingness to stay saved me from myself. There would not be an us. This family would have imploded, and the responsibility for that would have been mine and mine alone.

"Please know that I have always loved you and cherished you as my husband, and whoever I was during that time is not who I am. It is not who I want to be ever again. I promise to work with you to strengthen our relationship and become the wife you deserve. If you will have me."

Andy dropped to his knees before my chair, and I also dropped to my knees. He reached for me with an embrace that was a long time coming. I allowed myself to let go of every insecurity and every worry and anxiety I held and allowed his love to pour over me. I hoped he was doing the same.

Elsbeth offered a little more when we finally broke apart and resumed our seats. Her only words of wisdom were, "Remember that life is hard, but love is tough. You have each other to lean on and to walk with. Hold that going forward. Come together in honesty and allow each other a safe place to vent fears and frustrations, and you can't go wrong. Now, let's have some tea."

CHAPTER FORTY-FOUR

The next week, we finally went to Brenda's house to pack her belongings. It was difficult to see her things languishing in this empty home. Going through her closet, I found a few items that I wanted to keep for myself. Things that would remind me of her.

We packed most of her items into boxes for the charity shops. Nora could not wear her clothes, but I set aside Brenda's jewelry box as perhaps a treasure that Nora could keep and use. Family photos and other photographs went into boxes to keep.

Thumbing through her books, I saw many on psychology. I shook them to make sure nothing personal was left inside before I placed them into crates for charity as well. A folded piece of paper fell out of one. I picked it up and read it.

Brenda,

I need you to keep your nose out of my business. Andrea is my girlfriend. We are happy together until you decide to stick your beak into our lives. Stay out—or else.

The blood drained from my face, and my knees buckled. The letter was unsigned, but I knew its author. Andy came over, concerned I was about to faint. I showed him the letter.

"Do you think we should give this to the police?" I asked.

"No. It's not important. He's dead, and they know he murdered her. This would be of no use to anyone at this point. I think Brenda must have kept it to prove his intent should it come down to getting a restraining order. No one needs it, so we should destroy it."

I nodded, and Andy took the paper to the kitchen sink and set it on fire. The blaze consumed the paper, and as it turned to ashes, Andy turned on the water and washed it down the drain. An itchiness had crept under my skin, and I wanted to leave this house and never look back.

Andy moved all the boxes for charity to the truck, and when the house was empty, he asked me if I wanted to go with him or stay at the house. A realtor was coming over to assess the property and put it on the market. It was approaching the time he was to arrive, so I stayed, though my stomach quivered with anxiety at being left alone.

I stood on the step, watching Andy drive away, wanting desperately to call him back. I waited a few minutes in the cold before I went back inside. The hallway was right ahead of me. I walked down toward the kitchen, wondering where exactly Brenda had died. The crime scene cleaners had done a wonderful job, and no telltale signs gave that information away. I didn't see the crime scene photos either. The autopsy report was enough.

When I reached the corner leading to the bedrooms, I felt a chill wash over me, and although there was nothing to tell me otherwise, I knew this was where she had died, here in this hallway. The doorbell rang, and I screamed. The realtor was here.

Jim Southey had sold us this half-duplex when Brenda came to Crawford for university. When I opened the door, he smiled and offered his hand. We shook briefly, and he stepped into the house.

"Andy has taken some things to the charity shop. He'll be back momentarily," I said.

"No worries, I can get started without him. I pulled the sheet on this property when I sold it to you three years ago. Prices have gone up. I also pulled a few listings for you and Andy to see when you're ready to buy a new place. Some nice new duplexes not too far from here that would suit your other daughter. Quiet neighborhood across the street from a church."

"That sounds good. Our son, Logan, has also transferred to Crawford but will go to college, not university. We might need to look at options midway between the two."

"Okay. I can get you some of those, too. It's a good time to buy as school is only half finished, so people not going back in September are looking to sell with a possession date toward the end of April, middle of May, or beyond."

Jim moved around the house, looking at the property with an eye to sell. He seemed pleased with the cleanliness of the rooms. When Andy returned, I let them discuss terms and prices as I wasn't interested. I spent that time thinking about Brenda and all her unrealized potential. The note, although gone, circled through my brain as well. I wish I could speak to Caleb about what he did. I wanted him to know how much he had taken from us—from her.

I'd never have that chance.

CHAPTER FORTY-FIVE

Priced to sell, the condo was gone by the end of February, and Andy and I had purchased another place midway between the two schools. It had three floors, so Logan could have his own private area downstairs. Both put their stamp of approval on it before we made the offer.

By April, Elsbeth and I moved our meetings to once a month. A few months later, I didn't feel the need to go as often, but I went over to read to her instead. Our friendship blossomed. She was such a kind and thoughtful person.

Tiffany and I moved our weekly coffee meetings to Elsbeth's as well. It seemed important to me to expand her circle, and she had many stories and opinions that kept us chatting for hours. We had to set a timer to get home in time to make supper for our families. Elsbeth's enthusiasm to learn and to teach kept our conversations sparking with enthusiasm.

During our fifth meeting, Tiffany brought up Pastor Dan's sermon from the previous Sunday. She found his energy captivating. "Pastor Dan has so much skill in bringing the Bible to life, don't you think,

Audrey?"

"Yes. Sunday was so engaging. I didn't want to go home."

"I'm so glad you came back," Tiffany replied. "Church hasn't been the same without you."

Elsbeth leaned forward. "Do you think I would enjoy this pastor's sermons?"

Tiffany and I looked at each other, nodding furiously. "Of course. He is young and inspired. He really knows how to get us thinking about being better—doing better." Tiffany took a sip of her coffee. "My husband's attitude toward church has been rather relaxed since my conversion, but he connects with these messages, and he and Andy have coffee to discuss them. He's a new man."

Fearing what her son would say, I asked, "What about Pastor Newberry? Shouldn't you go there? I don't want to be the reason you don't attend his church."

"Leave him to me. I am and have always been my own person. I told him when I moved here that I would not be attending his church. He is a dutiful son but not someone I would follow through the shadows in the valley of death. If you know what I mean?"

"Of course. The church is just around the corner from us, but I can have Andy come and collect you."

"It's not around the corner from me," Tiffany interjected, "so my husband and I can collect you on our way. If that works for everyone?"

The matter was settled. Elsbeth would come to church with us, and hopefully, she would enjoy the music and the sermon. There was still a little niggling of anxiety at being at the rough end of Pastor Newberry's tongue when he found out where she was going on Sunday morning.

Sunday came, and Elsbeth sat between Tiffany and me. She seemed to enjoy the music, but when Pastor Dan preached, she came alive like I'd never seen her before. Her eyes sparkled, and her face beamed. Under her breath, I heard her say amen more than once. After church, we went to my house for lunch.

Nora entertained Tiffany's kids as the adults sat around the table discussing the sermon. With tears running down her face, Elsbeth said, "It was like Matthew had come back to life. The words and the inflection in his sentences made it seem like I was fifty years younger, listening to my husband preach. Thank you for bringing me such joy."

I was so happy for Elsbeth. I jumped up and hugged her from behind, kissing her papery cheek. "I am so glad for you. You brought me back to my first love, and I am over the moon that I could return the favor."

Not long after this exchange, Elsbeth asked to be taken home. She was tired and ready for a nap. Andy escorted her to the van, and Tiffany and Doug took her home. It was a wonderful Sunday, the first one in a long time that I wanted to remember forever.

CHAPTER FORTY-SIX

Wednesday appeared with the promise of spring in the air. April's arrival seemed to signal that winter was finally moving out. It made me feel like opening all the windows and letting the fresh air clean out all the cobwebs. At ten o'clock, Kenny called me.

"Hi, Audrey. Sorry to call you so early, but I have some sad news."

My heart flipped over in my chest, strangling my voice. He continued, not waiting for me to respond.

"Elsbeth passed away in her sleep last night. She was so excited after going to church with you folks on Sunday that she talked about nothing else on Monday. On Tuesday, she talked about her husband a lot, and I was concerned, but she told me she was simply reminiscing about him. Nothing seemed unusual until this morning when she didn't get up. I made coffee, which usually draws her out of bed if she's having a lie-in, but she never appeared. I finally checked on her, knocking several times and not getting an answer. When I opened the door, she was still in bed but cold to the touch. She must have passed during the night. I am so sorry." He sobbed into the phone.

I didn't know what to say. Tiffany and I were meeting there this afternoon and now we would never meet with her again. I didn't know how to respond.

"There's a letter for you over here. Do you want to come and get it, or do you want me to bring it over to you?"

Even that question caused me to pause. "Is she still there?" I wanted to see her if I could.

"No, the funeral home has collected her already. They just left. Pastor Newberry was my first call, and he efficiently made things happen."

Disappointed that I would not get a private moment to talk to Elsbeth, I asked Kenny to bring me the letter when he had time. Ten minutes later, he showed up at my door, his eyes red-rimmed, his shoulders drooping in sorrow.

"Oh, Kenny," I said when I opened the door to him. "I am so sorry for your loss."

He nodded and handed me the letter. I took it, and he turned to go. "Wait, do you want a coffee?"

He stopped but didn't turn around right away. His shoulders dropped even further as a sob erupted. He turned—his mouth twisted as he tried to restrain his grief. I moved down the steps and took his arm, ushering him into the kitchen.

He sobbed at the table, his head in his arms as I put on a fresh pot of coffee. When he gained some control, he sat up and removed his coat, setting it on the chair beside him. "She was like a grandmother to me, you know. I don't know what I am going to do now."

I had no words of wisdom. All I could do was commiserate with his loss, as I also wasn't sure what I was going to do without Elsbeth to keep me on the straight and narrow.

"I only knew her for a few months, but she impacted my life. No one can replace her. I am going to miss her wisdom and her strength." Kenny took a sip of his coffee. We sat in companionable silence for another minute before either spoke again.

"She gave me a chance to do something I always dreamed of. I could finish my first draft and have started a second book in the same series. I would not have had time working in construction to get this done. It would have taken me years. She put few demands on my time and was interested in me. In me. I don't know what I did to deserve her kindness, but I am grateful."

"Where will you go now that she's gone? Do you have a plan?"

"Pastor Newberry told me he wouldn't expect me to move out right away, but he intimated I wasn't to get too comfortable."

"I'm sorry. Does that mean you'll have to go back to work?"

"I suppose. When I found your letter, I looked for one to me, but there wasn't one. I would have liked to hear her sentiments one last time."

I nodded. I didn't know why Elsbeth left me a letter and not him. She must have had her reasons.

Kenny stayed to finish his coffee, but the conversation had run its course. I didn't know what to say to him, and he didn't seem to have any words for me either. I gave him a quick hug at the door and watched him go down the steps and walk toward the car—the car that belonged to Elsbeth, I presumed. He'd have to give that up as well.

CHAPTER FORTY-SEVEN

After Kenny left, I called Tiffany, and she came over for coffee. I took out some cookies and muffins, and we sat, as we always did, around the table, talking.

"I can't believe she's gone," Tiffany said. "It seems so sudden."

"Kenny said she was talking a lot about her husband since Sunday. Maybe she found him in her dreams and took a walk. I don't seem to know how this whole death thing works."

"Me neither. Is there a bright light? Is there a family member there to walk you into the here-after? Maybe we should ask Pastor Dan."

"I don't know if anyone alive knows what happens." I countered. "Religion believes that we all go to Heaven, and there has always been talk of the bright light. People have come back from the dead or close to death and said they walked toward a light, but where it leads …"

"I heard someone say that they were outside their body looking down. This person said nothing about a light, but just that she watched as the doctors and nurses went about resuscitating her. Maybe we don't go anywhere right away. Maybe we have a chance to visit loved ones."

"I think that may be wishful thinking. It never occurred to me to ask Brenda that night she came to me. I was just so glad to see her, and her physical form was touchable. To me, she was real at that moment, and maybe that's all we can expect. She said she was with God. She said she was safe and happy, so whether that was a walk to a bright light or my parents came to get her is the mystery that surrounds death."

"True. Maybe that's what it should be—a beautiful mystery."

After Tiffany had gone home, I took the letter from Elsbeth up to my room. I sat in the chair and slit the envelope, pulling out one thin page. I opened it and read.

My darling Audrey,

There are many things that I would love to say to you. I had hoped we would have many years together, getting to know and learning from each other, but that wasn't to be. I learned just before I met you that my cancer was back, and I refused treatment. I went through that several years ago, and the cure is worse than the disease. At least, that's how I saw it.

I prayed that I could give one more person a chance to turn their world around in my last days. God honored my request and sent you to me. The moment I saw you in that grocery store line, I knew you were the one. I am so glad you followed your heart and visited with me—to be my friend and the last person I could help before He came for me. I was so blessed. You were so angry and lost, but deep down, I saw you had faith; it just couldn't see the light through everything you were holding on to.

I was amazed by the depth of your love for your family and God when you opened up to me. I knew that if I could reach into your heart, I could help you, and you willingly granted me that ability. I know you. You see, I have been where you have been. I, too, lost my daughter. Not to murder but to the pull of drugs. My poor girl. I could not help her.

She knew God, of course, but when she got involved with a dangerous crowd in high school, she turned her back on all that was right and holy and danced with the devil instead. It was fun, I am sure, dancing, drinking, and getting "wasted." But the aftermath should have helped her see what she was doing to herself. Her brother tried to help, but his attitude drove her further into her world and further from ours. Matthew and I tried to help, but every time we paid for rehab, she would leave clean and walk right back into that world. It broke our hearts. She died of an overdose two days after leaving rehab. Matthew never recovered. He had his faith, but he was a broken man. He had tried so hard to save her, and, in the end, it wasn't to be. I admit I lost my way, too, for a while.

A good friend saw me at my lowest and helped me turn around and face my fears, quench my anger, and find solid ground again. She was a godsend.

I hope that I have helped you find your way. I know we didn't have as long as I would have liked. I feel I am leaving you in excellent hands. Andy is a good man who shares so much of your love for God. I am glad you have each other and can walk forward into tomorrow hand in hand. You may still have issues to deal with, and I hope you manage to work things out because you belong together—just as Matthew and I did.

I feel Matthew is close these days. I know he is here to walk me into the hereafter. I don't know exactly when I will go, but I don't have long. I am going to leave this letter with Kenny. He can deliver it to you upon my passing.

Goodbye, dear friend. Please know that you are loved and special. Keep singing His praises, keep dancing around your kitchen as you make supper for your family, keep the faith that has sustained you all these years, and know that you are a child of Almighty God. He loves you so much.

I will see you again when we meet in Heaven. I am a patient woman and will wait as long as it takes to share in His grace. God bless always,

Elsbeth.

CHAPTER FORTY-EIGHT

Andy and I could not attend Elsbeth's memorial service. Pastor Newberry took her back to North Battleford to be buried next to her Matthew. However, he agreed to let a few people visit the funeral home the day before they shipped her coffin. I was grateful.

Andy and I walked into the quiet space together. Pastor Newberry sat in the front row, his head in his hands. The lid to the coffin was open for viewing, and we headed directly there.

Looking down, I noticed for the first time how small Elsbeth was. Although she was small in stature, her personality made her seem larger than life. Now, she did not look like herself. The spirit that livened her face was no longer there. Her countenance was flat and dull.

Tears sprang to my eyes. She was really gone, just like Brenda.

Andy, understanding my thoughts, squeezed my hand. I took his strength, pulled my emotions back under control, and smiled at him. I stared at the coffin and said, "Thank you, Elsbeth, for your love and wisdom. I am so glad we spent these last several months together. You were a big help to me and my family. We will never forget you.

Godspeed. I know you will watch over us."

Andy added an amen but said nothing else. We turned to go.

Pastor Newberry caught my eye as we walked out of the room. He meandered toward us. "I owe you both an apology. My mom always told me how pompous and arrogant I was when it came to my church. I refused to believe her. But she was right. God does not look down on his flock, but I always wanted to have the best church. I just forgot we are all sinners, and none of us deserve God's grace. I am so sorry that I made you both feel you were not good enough to be part of my congregation. I would like to invite you back, but I will understand if you have found another church to attend. Please forgive me."

It took me a minute to grasp what Pastor Newberry had said. Andy responded before I did. "Thank you for your honesty. We appreciate it and forgive you wholeheartedly. For now, we are quite happy in our little church, but if that changes, I appreciate that the invitation will be there." He looked down at me, and I nodded, agreeing with his words.

Pastor Newberry smiled though his eyes filled with sorrow and regret.

"Andy speaks for both of us. We have been through so much this past year and hold no grudges. Life is too short. Thank you for allowing us to say goodbye to your mother. She was such a precious soul, and I will miss her." Tears sprang to my eyes again as I thought of my loss. "She told me many times about how proud she was of you. And she loved you."

Tears swam in his eyes, and he nodded, reaching out to shake my hand. I bypassed his gesture and moved in to hug him. He stiffened at first, and then I felt him soften.

"Thank you," he whispered in my ear. God bless." He pulled away, wiping his eyes, his face a little lighter than when we arrived.

Andy shook his hand, and we left, walking out into the spring morning, hand in hand.

CHAPTER FORTY-NINE

The empty spot where Brenda had lived constantly reminded me of what I had lost. We managed to purchase the timeshare at Emerald Lake, which made Christmas bearable. I longed for another visit from Brenda while we were there, but she never called for me. I got used to feeling that emptiness; it became part of me. I never wanted it to go away. Brenda's memory lived there, and over the years, it hurt less.

Andy and I were in a good place again. After Nora and Logan went to school in Crawford, it was just him and me. We found new ways to express ourselves. He took an art class, and I took up carving. Initially, I nicked and sliced my hands, but I eventually mastered the craft. I carved landscapes mostly, but one year, I tried to carve Brenda's face.

"What are you carving?" Andy came up behind me one Saturday afternoon. He had been in the garage painting a new masterpiece, his hands covered in paint splatter.

I tried to shield my work, but I wasn't fast enough. "Is that a person?" He tried to pull the wood from my hands.

"It's Brenda," I admitted, embarrassed at how poorly it resembled anyone.

"I see. It's … it's … interesting."

His remark pierced my heart, and tears welled up. Then I took the carving back and looked at it, seriously looked at it. "It's awful, isn't it?" My chin quivered, and my voice rose.

"No, it's … interesting," Andy confirmed, his voice strong and authoritative. "I know art when I see it."

I looked up in time to see a small smirk disappear from his face. I looked back at my project, and I had to agree. It was interesting. It was far from being Brenda or any other person. I think I would call it unusual.

"I think I need to stick to what I know." My voice was breezy. I laughed, and Andy joined in.

We left my studio and walked down to the kitchen. Andy made coffee, and I pulled out some muffins and cookies.

There was an envelope on the table. It arrived in the mail yesterday, and I have yet to open it. It was from Joan Bradshaw, the mother of the monster who had killed my girl. I had no interest in hearing what she had to say. It had been two years since we lost Brenda, and even though it was easier, it wasn't easy at all.

"Are you going to open this?" Andy sat at the table, placing two cups in front of him.

I shrugged. "What is she going to say? That she's sorry? Or will she offer excuses for why we should forgive them for our loss?"

"But we have forgiven them, haven't we?" Andy frowned, picking up the envelope and looking at it closely. "She didn't give us her address, but the postmark says Crawford."

"They lived in Freyden. It's close to Crawford. She probably just popped it into the mail while shopping in town."

"I suppose. But I am curious."

"Well, it's not addressed to you, so keep your mitts off." I pulled the coffeepot from the machine and poured us each a cup. Then, I placed the pot back before seating myself across the table from him. He handed me the envelope.

"Open it. I dare you."

Rolling my eyes, I took the envelope and set it far to my right. Then I took a sip of my coffee, staring at Andy as he stared back at me.

"Open the envelope. Open it, open it, open it."

"Andy, for crying out loud." I reached for the envelope and banged the end on the table before tearing a tiny strip from it. Tipping it, one piece of paper slipped out onto the table. I set the envelope aside and stared at the paper. Andy stared at me.

When I looked at him, he mouthed, *Read it.*

"Oh, come on. I opened it, didn't I?"

We sat across from one another, him silently willing me to read the letter while I took deep breaths to calm my nerves. What's the worst it could say?

"I'm scared." There. I admitted it. "I am afraid this letter will open old wounds that took forever to heal. I don't know if I am strong enough to go through it all again."

"I can do all this through Him who gives me strength," Andy quoted.

Closing my eyes, I took a deep breath. "God is my strength," I repeated. Then I picked up the letter.

Dear Audrey,

Please forgive me for being presumptuous in sending this letter. I cannot imagine the pain and suffering you endured at the hands of my son.

I hope that you and I, along with Barbara O'Shea, can get together at Jack's Diner. I know you owe me nothing, but I would like to meet with both of you in person. I hope our meeting will bring each of us some healing and perhaps a little closure for the trauma Caleb inflicted on us.

I will be there waiting.

The information included the date and time written below. She did not provide a phone number or ask for a response. I guess she would wait for us to arrive, and if we didn't, that would be her answer.

Barbara and I were not bosom buddies, but we saw each other occasionally because our husbands were friendly. She was married to Kevin again and was now Barbara Pritchard. That obviously wasn't well known. Only a few of us attended the wedding. Barbara had given birth to a lovely baby girl. They called her Sophia Anne. The Anne was for Andrea and Brenda Ann, our daughter. It felt right. I got to hold her during the ceremony. I couldn't wait for my own grandchildren to arrive, though I knew it was a long way off.

I handed the letter to Andy. He read it. When he finished, he set it down. "Are you going to go?"

"I don't know. This has come out of left field. Life is ticking along pretty good mostly. What if meeting up with her shakes it all loose again."

"You already know how I feel. You can do whatever you set your mind to. Think about it, at least. I won't push it one way or the other."

I snorted. He already had.

CHAPTER FIFTY

Before deciding to attend this little soiree, I called Barbara to see if she planned to go. There is safety in numbers, after all.

Barbara, like me, felt unsure what would be gained. "In the beginning," she said, "I wanted to call them. In fact, I did call, but no one answered the phone. I wanted to yell at them and scream my anger and grief at the whole family. Even back then, I am not sure it would have made me feel better. Then, a year ago, one of Andrea's journals showed up in the mailbox with a note from her, and she gave me her telephone number. I think it's still tucked away. I never called her."

"Do you think this is what the invitation is all about? To make her feel better?"

"I don't know. I can't imagine what she thinks she'll gain by meeting us. But I confess that I am curious."

"Curious?"

"Yes. A part of me is curious to know what she's up to. That's the part that is prodding me to go."

"What does Kevin think?"

"Kevin thinks I should do what I think is best. Whatever I decide, he will support.”

“Andy thinks I should go. Not for her, but for me. And yet, I’m still not sure it will be good for me to have those old wounds opened.”

“Do you think she’s going to profess innocence?”

“No. I didn’t get that feeling. I think she’s going to explain why Caleb did what he did. As if anyone, especially one’s parents, ever know what’s happening inside their kids’ heads.”

“True. So, you’re considering going despite your misgivings?”

“I am. But I’ll only go if you go.”

We were silent for a moment, pondering the situation. “Yes, Audrey. Let’s go. We can always leave, and if you’re there, I’ll feel I have a friend.”

“Okay. Despite my misgivings, I will go with you. I will come by your house and pick you up so we can arrive together.”

“Sounds good.”

We finished our plans, and I hung up, my stomach tight. I had a week to prepare, though I didn’t know what to prepare for. War? Peace? Hope? I wouldn’t have long to wait.

CHAPTER FIFTY-ONE

My stomach churned as I pulled up to Barbara's house. I could not believe that I was meeting with the mother of the man who murdered my daughter. It seemed insane to me. I had prayed about it. I had talked to Pastor Dan about it, but nothing seemed to give me the peace I thought I needed to walk through that door.

Barbara came out, dressed to the nines, as usual. She was such a beautiful woman, and I felt like the country mouse next to her.

Once she climbed into the car, she smiled and asked, "Are you ready for this?"

"Not in the least," I replied, putting the car in gear and backing out of the driveway. "You?"

"I am at peace with it. Kevin reminded me we can leave any time. We are not to stay if she makes us uncomfortable. Besides, Jack's has the best cinnamon buns."

I hadn't had one since that fateful afternoon years ago when I ate four in one sitting. My stomach turned over at the thought of having one now.

We drove to the restaurant silently, and I parked at the curb, a few doors down. We sat for one moment after I had killed the engine. Then I sighed and opened my door. "Well, let's get this over with." Barbara climbed out after me.

We walked the distance to the restaurant together, and Barbara stepped forward to open the door for me. I entered first, wondering if that's why Barbara got the door, so I would have to walk in first. I chastised myself for trying to find fault or to have a reason to leave.

The restaurant was nearly empty. A couple of ladies were having tea near the front window, and an older man was reading the paper as he drank his coffee. Further back, a striking woman with short brown hair sat at a table for four. She stood as we entered. We walked toward her.

"I am so glad you came. I didn't know if you would. Please sit down. Can I get you anything?"

It seemed odd that she offered to get us something, like she worked there. A tall blond walked out from the back. She stopped at the table as Barbara and I sat down.

"Good afternoon, ladies. What can I bring you?"

Barbara asked for tea and a cinnamon bun. I asked for tea and then debated. Did I want some carrot cake? The tall blond waited.

"Just the tea for now, I guess."

Joan smiled and asked for tea as well. "Thanks, Beckie," she said as the server left to get our drinks.

"You must come here often to be on a first-name basis with the server," Barbara said.

"Well, I spend a lot of time here," Joan admitted.

We sat silently until our orders arrived. Barbara dug into the cinnamon bun, moaning as she took her first bite. "These are so good."

Joan shifted in her seat. Then she spoke. "I know this seems strange, to meet the mother of someone you must both despise, but I have a reason for wanting to meet you both."

I braced myself, and Barbara put the bun on her plate. She wiped her fingers on a napkin before dropping her hands into her lap, focusing only on Joan.

"I know that what happened to your families was beyond horrific. Caleb had never shown me signs of violence, so what he did shocked me. His warped thinking became clear to me as I read his journals. He seemed to need to control his world."

I interrupted her, my voice rising. "So, you're saying Caleb was a good boy who just went crazy one night and killed my daughter and her best friend? Get real. You raised a monster. Take ownership."

Barbara placed her hand on my arm as the server moved toward us.

"Is everything okay here?" she asked.

Joan responded. "Yes. Thank you, Beckie. Mrs. Taylor is just telling me her thoughts. It's all good."

"I'm sorry," I said. "I got a little ahead of myself. I just don't want to hear how innocent your son was in all of this. That there might be a reason he isn't culpable."

"Oh no," Joan replied. "Caleb is guilty. He made a terrible decision, and then he took the coward's way out and took his own life. I have no illusions."

"That's good to hear," Barbara said. "I came here to tell you what I thought of your parenting. You raised an animal. What was your reason for meeting with us?"

"Because I know how terrible it is to lose a daughter, and I wanted both of you to know that the pain I feel for you is real. I would not have wanted this to happen to anyone, ever. When I lost my daughter …" Joan's voice broke, and she bowed her head.

Barbara and I waited for her to control her emotions. We didn't reach out to her but sat on the opposite side of the table, watching. When she looked up, tears were in her eyes, but none ran down her cheeks.

"I'm sorry if you think it was insane for me to invite you here. We have only one thing in common: We have lost someone too young."

CHAPTER FIFTY-TWO

A voice in my head told me to have some compassion. Here was a woman who had lost a daughter and a son. Though the son might have deserved his fate, no mother deserved to lose her children. Her pain was real. I reached across the table and took her hand. She flinched but didn't pull away. "I am so sorry you have lost two children. No mother should suffer the loss of her babies, and I am really sorry. You have my sympathy. Brenda was my firstborn, and she and I were a lot alike, yet we were miles apart in our philosophies on life. I miss her every single day."

"And I miss Andrea. My story isn't as straightforward as Audrey's. Andrea was my only child, but I had walked away from my family when Andrea was three. I had demons and could not seem to get control of them. My thinking was she would be better off without me. I always assumed that when she reached maturity, we could talk about things and become friends. I lost that chance because of your son. It devastated me." Barbara burst into tears. "I think we could have been friends. Now, I'll never know. She died, not knowing she was the most important person in the world to me. She never knew that what I did was to protect her from my insanity." Her words lost their shape as her throat closed and her mouth contorted in pain.

The old man behind us harrumphed, snapped his paper into manageable shape, and stomped out of the restaurant. Joan watched him go, and then she reached for Barbara's hand.

"I am so sorry. I met Andrea several times. She was such a lovely girl. If I had known what was happening, I would have stepped in, but Caleb wasn't reachable. He wouldn't pick up my calls and never returned them. I was frantic to speak to him after he failed to come home for Thanksgiving. I was going to … Oh, it doesn't matter. By the time I got my act together, it was too late. The police were on my doorstep."

CHAPTER FIFTY-THREE

It took Barbara some time to get herself together. She excused herself and went down the hall to the washroom. She came back looking less put together than she had when I picked her up, which made me see her as more human and less like a professional model.

"I am so sorry for my outburst." Barb settled back into her chair. "I had not meant to get emotional, but it's so hard knowing that the chance I wanted was so close at hand. I will probably always live with that burden."

The three of us sat in silence for a few minutes. The tension that had been sitting over us since we sat down dissipated. It no longer seemed abnormal to be sitting here with the mother of the man who killed my girl. I think Barbara felt that, too. The server came over and asked if we wanted more hot water. We all agreed, and I asked for a piece of carrot cake.

After she had delivered our order, I took a bite of my dessert and moaned. I love carrot cake, and this one was moist and spicy. The icing was a perfect pairing for the sweetness of the cake. "This is so good." I pointed to the cake with my fork.

"So is the cinnamon bun." Barbara licked the sticky toffee off her fingers. "I am so glad you chose this place to meet."

"Well, I must confess that my boss made me have the meeting here. She wanted to keep her eye on the situation to ensure I didn't get bombarded with hateful accusations."

"Your boss?" I asked, looking around to see if I could see her.

"Yes," Joan replied. "The server is my boss. Her name is Beckie. I work here. I am the person who made the cinnamon buns and the carrot cake."

"You're the baker?" Barbara exclaimed. "You're very good at what you do. How long have you been here?"

"I started the Monday after Caleb's funeral. I left my husband, got a job, and … here I am."

We talked about the changes in our lives. How the loss of a child had shaped our view of the world and how, in some ways, what happened had made each of us stronger in her own way.

Barbara and I stayed another hour. When we left, I knew I would never see Joan again. She had said her piece, and I knew she regretted her son's actions. That didn't change the outcome, and I think I might have known all along that a mother never imagined her child would ever do something so brutal.

Our lives intersected at a moment in time, and it had devastating results for all of us. We survived, and we learned to live without the person who was lost. Joan was like us, and she wasn't. Her loss was greater because her son caused it, and even though she wasn't responsible, a mother was always ready to carry the burdens of her child on her shoulders.

None of us would ever be free of our pain, but learning to bear it was how we coped. The future was still ahead, and although all three of us would have preferred not to be on this road together, the crossroads allowed us each to take our own path forward into tomorrow.

I think Brenda and Elsbeth would be proud of me for meeting with Joan and for facing the truth that none of us can change what happened; none of us is responsible, yet we all hold the gift of loss that provides motive and stimuli to live better lives in the future.

The end.

AFTERWORD

Dear Reader,

People don't talk about whether they believe in God or not. Religion, like politics, is a topic with great divisions. Even those who believe don't agree across the board. Hence, the many denominations.

In grade five, the Gideons came to our school, and everyone got a tiny little New Testament Bible of their own. I still have mine. It provided suggested daily readings, which I did my best to follow. It was the King James version, so it was not exactly easy to read. Toward the back, there was a prayer to accept that I am a sinner and that Jesus died for my sins. I wrote the date in my juvenile scrawl and then signed that page, probably not really understanding what I was doing. I was nine years old.

It didn't matter. My siblings called me *The Religious One*. I believed in God. I loved the nativity story; even the crucifixion story gave me hope. God was real and alive to me, though living thirty miles from town, I couldn't attend church.

Living in the town of Lacombe in my early twenties, I started going to church. I like to sing, so I joined the choir. The choirmaster gave me a gown, and for two weeks, I sat in the choir loft with the other choir members and was quite content that I had found a place where I could be part of this world.

In the third week, a lady came into the choir room and whirled around like someone had pinched her bottom. She marched over to me, grabbed the back of my gown, and twisted it out to see the tag. Then she told me I was wearing her gown and demanded I remove it immediately. Several choir members tried to intervene, but it was no use. I offended her by wearing *her* gown, though the choir leader gave it to me. I removed the gown, and someone gave me another. It was too large, but it was all they had.

In the choir loft, she sat beside me, and I could feel her bristles. She immediately disliked me, making me uncomfortable. The moment church was over, I removed the choir gown, and I never went back. No one called to see why. I just disappeared from their world.

Several years later, I was working in a bank in a small town south of Lacombe, and Reverend Peter Walker from the United Church came in every single day. He withdrew money one day, and the next, he put it back. He did this over and over as an excuse to be in the bank so he could preach to me. I listened and asked questions and eventually went to his church.

For fifteen years, I immersed myself in my beliefs. I joined committees. I sang in the choir. When I moved on to a more evangelical church, I became part of a worship team and eventually led one. There were prayer services to attend, and I believed with all my heart that I was exactly where I was supposed to be.

As the years passed, I felt less accepted. I was a late thirty-something single lady, and no one knew what to do with me. Where did I fit? Not with single parents, not with college and careers, and not with married couples. I was adrift even among the worship team. Most weeks, I would overhear congregation members gushing over some cookout or party they had attended together, but no one included me.

The end came when I was sitting in my usual chair, feeling vulnerable and alone, and a lady approached me and told me I couldn't sit there. I looked at her, and that experience I had so many years before slammed into me. *Take off that gown.* This time, though, I did something I am not proud of. I said two rather unpleasant words to her, picked up my Bible and purse, and walked out.

That very afternoon, the pastor called me, demanding an apology or threatening my expulsion from the church. Obediently, I apologized the next week, sat through the long sermon, and left, never entering the door of any church again.

A year later, I met the pastor in the parking lot of a home improvement store. He told me they missed me at church, even though no one from that church had called me during that time. I smiled, thanked him, and said I didn't miss them. Then I walked away.

That year, on my own, was my moment of disappointment with God. Why hadn't He seen fit to provide me with a partner so I would be acceptable to the other congregation members? Why was I always alone in my battles? Why did I always have to be the one to apologize? Why didn't she have to apologize to me for making me feel so unwanted? Why were my feelings always negated? Why?

I grappled with my anger, and I was angrier than I had ever been. God had let me down, so I railed at Him almost every time I drove home from work that year. I fleeced Him, and when I didn't get the response I wanted, I fleeced him again.

Nothing worked. I promised Him I would stop praising Him if He didn't fix my situation. He did nothing, and I stopped singing. I stopped listening to music. I switched off the car radio, and at home, I chose the refrigerator's hum over listening to heartfelt songs of any kind.

My world became quiet. Until I finally found talk radio. I never looked back. Nearly thirty years on, I still listen to talk radio. I remember traveling with my mom, and she was singing along to an Anne Murray song, and she asked me why I wasn't singing, too. "You have such a lovely voice." Tears filled my eyes, and I shook my head but didn't explain. I couldn't explain. My silence was self-imposed. How could I explain it to her? I regret that I never sang for her.

Since my mom's passing, I have tried to sing, but my voice no longer has that lilting quality. I lost that while I lived in anger and silence. I don't know how to get that back.

Whenever I think about going to church, an immense fear rises in my heart. I trembled, and I knew I could not go through the door. Church no longer suits me, even though I have made my peace with God. He knows where I am, and I pray sometimes, but not like I used to. I banished my demons, but I no longer want to risk being attacked by someone who hasn't done the same.

I feel close to God when I am in nature. Walking in the mountains or along a lakeshore, listening to the lapping water, I know this is God's handiwork. I see Him in His creation and know I am one of those. I trust I am exactly where I need to be.

Eventually, I found and read *Disappointment with God* by Phillip Yancey. He answers three questions: Why does God seem so distant if he is so hungry for a relationship with us? If God cares for us, why do bad things happen? If God's promises are true, why do they feel so far from personal experience?

Audrey's disappointment in God is valid. She believed in a merciful and loving God. She didn't understand that walking with God does not protect us against the world. He allows free will for all people. Had Caleb been listening, he might have heard God tell him that what he was doing was wrong. But he wanted to exact his revenge, to make Brenda pay for interfering in his relationship with Andrea. His actions were deliberate and valid in his warped thinking.

God is not a magic pill. Walking with God is hard because it doesn't make us special. What it gives us, though, is peace in knowing that whatever happens, however ugly and brutal it may be, He will turn it into good for those who believe.

I hope you have enjoyed Audrey's journey. If you haven't read the previous two books, you will find Joan and Barbara, who go through their own journey to make sense of a senseless situation. *AFTER …* is a series that has been with me for a long time, and I hope it brings you some joy or peace knowing that people can heal and change—if they want to. It often takes a catalyst to shift us, but once we are uncomfortable, we have faith that we are on our way to something more beautiful.

God bless you all. Stay safe.

Leslie Johnson

leslie.johnson2014@gmail.com

ABOUT THE AUTHOR

Leslie Johnson grew up in the shadow of Chief Mountain near the Alberta / Montana border. She loves to read, spending countless hours inside a good book. Many nights, her mother would find her under her covers with a flashlight reading her latest library find, long after she was supposed to be asleep. She still lives in windy southern Alberta where she moderates a writing group. If she's not writing, reading, or gardening, she's working on a jigsaw puzzle, playing with her cat, Milo or taking a walk in one of the many parks in the area.

Manufactured by Amazon.ca
Bolton, ON

45464364R00157